# The Last Watchman Still Rides

By: Jonathan Watkins

Other Books by Jonathan Watkins

*Motor City Shakedown*

*Dying in Detroit*

*Isolated Judgment*

*A Devil's Bargain*

*for my Mother and Father*

*The coward believes he will live forever*
*If he holds back in the battle,*
*But in old age he shall have no peace*
*Though spears have spared his limbs*
--The Hávamál

# O N E

The bloody face wedged inside the envelope led me to Buster Long.

Perrien Park was like the majority of Detroit. Rectangular lots of scorched, untended grass. Pitted, convulsing avenues. Sagging and weather-blasted mounds of debris where houses used to stand. Here and there, long-vacant buildings that hadn't been knocked down yet obstinately lingered. The city was so flat-busted it couldn't afford to demolish its thousands of rotting derelicts. Thirteen arsons a night was not unusual. New wounds were the priority.

Detroit is a permanent emergency.

I chose to make the trek from my home in midtown to Perrien Park on foot, taking it at a brisk jog. I'd skipped my morning workout because of Buster. When I came to a stop in the gravel parking lot of Simonson's Gym, I felt properly loosened up but no less pensive than when I'd first opened my eyes that morning. I don't sleep well. I tend to wake up knotted. I tend to wake up mean. Skipping the workout in my basement gym had only soured an already ugly mood.

Two vehicles were parked in the lot, their noses pointed at the squat cinderblock building. One was a little plastic thing painted an obnoxious green. It was one of those bright little bits that sipped gas and probably handled like a brick on ice skates. The other was a silver BMW with a license plate that read, 'BUSTUUP'. The envelope with the bloody face hadn't been wrong about Buster's routine.

*"He's there until noon, always,"* the note read. *"Tuesdays, he's alone."*

I looked at the little green bit parked next to the BMW and felt myself frowning. No, he wasn't alone. It was a complication. I stood there in the intensifying June heat, uncertain. My cell vibrated in my pocket. I didn't recognize the number. A seven-three-four area code. Somewhere in Michigan, but not Detroit.

"This is Roarke," I said.

The voice that answered was distinctly feminine. Soft. Casual and sunny. It got my attention.

"Oh, hi," she said. "I thought I'd get a receptionist or something."

"I can pretend if you want, say he's in an important meeting and can I have your name and number so he can get back to you."

She chuckled. It seemed genuine. Even if it wasn't, I still felt that lift a man gets when a woman favors him with a trilling, china-bell sound of amusement.

"My name's Savannah Kline. I was hoping to talk to you about a personal matter. An investigation, I mean. Or, really,

2

a…not an investigation. A family matter. I sound like a dimwit, don't I?"

"How did you get my name?"

"Oh. Jack Reinhart. The FBI man? He gave me your name and number. Would it be possible to meet? Today, I mean. Its urgent."

The envelope with the bloody face stuffed inside it was in my pocket. I stared at the entrance to Simonson's Gym and silently debated which way to go. I hadn't agreed to work for whomever had placed the envelope in my mailbox. I'd found it the day before. Stared at the battered, tragic face of a young woman. Read the note telling me where Buster would be. Counted the seven hundred dollars in mixed bills.

It wasn't a contract. It was a plea from a stranger. *Do something about this.*

"Mr….?"

"Just Roarke."

"Can we meet and talk today, Just Roarke?"

"Not for a couple hours."

"Because you're in that important meeting?"

"Something like that."

"Is Ypsilanti too far? I'm in Ann Arbor and need it to be somewhere I can get back from on my lunch break."

Ypsilanti was as agreeable as anywhere else, so she told me where to meet her. A college hang-out with an Asian salad that was to die for, she promised. I didn't mention I was as close to a pure carnivore as a human being was like to be, so we agreed on a time and hung up. I looked at the clock on my phone. It was a hair after nine in the morning. I needed to get to business if I was going to have time to shower and make the drive out to meet her.

I slipped the cell back in my pocket. Pulled out the envelope with the bloody face stuffed inside it. Extracted her from inside. Unfolded the page. Stared for a long moment. Lips swollen like purple balloons. Eyes mashed to black swirls under the hands of a man trained to punch with ferocity. Swollen. Deformed. Rent into something hardly recognizable as human. Underneath the awful injury I could see the humiliation and sorrow. The heartbreak. I didn't know her name. I didn't need to.

*Do something about this.*

I stalked into the boxing gym.

*

She had mocha-rich skin, the fragile beauty of a runway model, and she didn't smile when I appeared in the doorway.

"You can't be here." Four-inch heels click-clacking. "Come back after eleven."

To my right, some sort of manager's office with its walls full of trophies and framed photos of fighters. Ahead, past the frowning beauty, the gym. Three heavy bags hung in a line on

4

the left, one of them still gently spinning on its chain from a recent beating. The floor was littered with medicine balls, skip ropes and sawdust. On the right, four speed bags dangled like brown, over-ripe gourds.

In the center of the gym floor, the square circle. Buster was up there in the ring, alone, punching the air. He moved smoothly in little half-circles, huffing loud bursts of air as he threw out combinations at an imaginary opponent. Myself, I didn't need much imagination to picture the woman in the envelope up there with him, reeling, crying out, shrieking as he worked.

The mocha-skinned beauty was right in front of me now, stern, arms crossed under her breasts. She was draped in folds of earth-toned silk. Her eyes were the shape of almonds. The perfume that hung around her smelled pricey. She wore it lightly, too lightly to eclipse the stink of sweat and toil that permeated the dim interior of the old boxing club.

"Mister Simonson never mentioned he had a new heavyweight in his stable," she said after I made no sign of leaving. She peered up at me like she was appraising a cut of meat.

"I'm too old," I said.

"I've seen them older."

"Maybe tune-up guys but not contenders."

"Sure. The bums. Like that."

"I'm not one of those, either."

5

"Yeah, okay. The gym's closed to the public until my man's done. He rented the whole morning. You want a workout, go somewhere else."

Buster kept punching the air. His pale, freckled back was shiny with sweat. I wondered where his trainer was. Maybe he didn't have a fight lined up and was just keeping himself in form. I hadn't bothered to check any of that out before heading over. I follow the fight game pretty regularly but Buster wasn't a talent I'd kept track of. He was local. Young. A prospect who might get his day in the sun a couple more years down the line.

If he stayed healthy.

"I guess you're his girlfriend," I said, keeping my eyes behind her, on Buster. He had good footwork. He moved well. His head was on permanent swivel and he kept his chin tucked nice and tight. Whoever his trainer was, he had the kid going in the right direction.

"So?" she snapped. "Ain't your business who I am."

"You ever met his wife?"

"Mister, you need to go."

Her pretty mouth was an impatient scowl. She watched me take out the envelope. When I held it out, she made no move to take it from me.

"You won't want to stick around," I said. "Maybe take that cute little car of yours and get the tires filled. The rear driver's side is low enough you've probably been wondering why everything is shaky when you get it over forty-five. Or don't. But go somewhere else."

She sighed and snatched the envelope out of my hand like she was humoring a pest. I watched her pull the photo of a bloody face out. Watched the impatience drain right out of her as she stared at it. All her composure went with it. Her eyes bugged and she listed on her feet. I put a hand on her shoulder to keep her steady.

"Time to go," I said. "Take that with you. When you get out to your car and you maybe think you should come back in here and stop what's happening, look at it again. Then go home. Change your locks. Change your number. Cut him out of your heart."

She was dazed and I didn't blame her. What a man with Buster's skill set can do to a prone, unguarded human being is a shocking thing when you've never seen it before. I reached in my pocket and came out with one of my business cards. The card had my name and number printed on it, nothing else. I pressed it into her palm and closed her fingers over it. She stared up at me suddenly, maybe recognizing the life line I was tossing her way.

"He won't be up to coming around any time soon," I said. "But later, he might. He might try and talk you out of everything you're thinking right now. Guys who do this, they're good at talking you back to them. If you're smart, you'll call me."

Slow, almost mechanically, her head pivoted around to look at the muscled fighter in the ring. His sharp bursts of exhaled breath punctuated each blow he landed on his invisible opponent. His circling footwork brought him around, facing us but not seeing us in the unlit gloom of the doorway. He fired a furious combination of hooks our way, ducked back, spun away.

"Are...are you sure?" she whispered. Her lovely face was drawn, suddenly exhausted, suddenly heavy with dread.

"That he's the guy?"

"Yes."

"I'll make certain before anything else happens."

She peered down at the bloody face in her hand. Without looking up, she softly said, "He's the guy."

"I know."

"She doesn't know about me. He talks about her. The things he says...the *way* he talks about her...he's the one."

I didn't have anything more to offer her. There's nothing worth saying to someone stuck in a moment like that. She could go a lot of different ways. If she started sobbing, I'd have to act. If she raced toward Buster with her hands balled into fists, I'd have to act. I didn't want that. I wanted her out of the room for what came next.

"Where is she?" she said after a long silence. "Which hospital?"

"I don't know."

Her face was hard, a line of tension running through her jaw. She'd made it out of the moment of indecision. A choice had been made.

"This is what you do? Muscle work?"

"Sometimes."

"His best is the right hook upstairs. Watch for it."

It was her last bit before she stepped past me and marched shakily out into the sunlight and whatever decision she'd made about where to go and what to do. I stood still as the door swung back shut. The sunlight was sealed away and I was alone with Buster Long.

*

The girlfriend told the truth about the right hook upstairs. When I closed on Buster, it was his first impulse. I took it on the cheekbone. Felt it. Then I got my hands on him and he realized we were going to the ground. He flailed a bit. Said something I didn't hear. I heaved him sideways and followed him down to the canvas.

There were no more upstairs hooks after that. I weighed half again what he did. I had the strength that comes with size, the strength that comes with a strict, punishing daily workout, the strength that comes with furious indignation.

9

His hands were useless, trapped inside his gloves. He spit his mouthpiece out and blurted a confused, panicky noise at me.

I gave him what he'd given the woman in the envelope. His lips split like soft fruit. I worked deeper until red-slicked teeth fell away into the black gap of his throat. I moved up. His nose buckled, caved down, flattening into the plane of his cheeks. A gurgling moan escaped him, full of surrender, but I kept on. I worked on his left eye with short, straight blows, superimposing the image of her photograph over his face until the orbital bone fractured and I was certain their injuries were twinned.

All of what he'd given her, I gave back to him.

When it was done, he was a length of spasms and shallow wheezing. I hadn't touched his right eye because he hadn't touched hers. It swam incoherently amid the wreckage. I got on my feet and climbed down out of the ring. I didn't have anything to say, never spoke a word to him. I'd delivered the exact message I'd been paid to deliver. It wouldn't help the woman in the envelope. I wasn't kidding myself about that. Mangling the monster wouldn't sooth her heartbreak or heal the trauma of having a loved one turn on her so savagely. The best it could do was keep him away, keep him scared.

If it didn't, if another envelope appeared in my mailbox, I'd deliver the message again. Sometimes that's what I get. I get hired to do the mean thing, the rough thing. I have a reputation for it. I don't mind it. I'll do it. But I prefer the jobs that require a little more out of me beyond muscle and meanness.

As I jogged back to my home in midtown, I was hoping lunch with Savannah Kline was about that other sort of job.

*

I met Savannah Kline at the Tower Tavern, on the edge of Eastern Michigan University's campus. It was clean and well lit. The customers were college kids and university faculty. I ordered the house steak and a Labatt's. Savannah ordered an Asian chicken salad and a water with lemon. The kid who took our order rushed off. He had big hoops of black metal sunk into his earlobes. I was disappointed they didn't whistle as he walked.

"You don't look like I imagined," Savannah said once she got tired of me not saying anything. I don't mind being silent for long stretches of time. I'd grown used to it. Sometimes it was easy to forget how it bothered other people.

"What did you imagine?" I said.

"Hmm. Can I be honest?"

"Sure."

"Someone rumpled and unshaven. A guy with a big belly who used to be a cop and now he's pretending he still is."

Savannah Kline was trim, smartly dressed, and had thick coppery blonde hair that went down to her waist. It was tied back from her face with a black ribbon. I thought she was nice to look at. Most people probably would have agreed.

"You haven't asked why I need to hire someone...like you," she said.

"I thought you were working your way up to it."

"You do look more like a cop."

"Ouch."

She smiled, so I figured the day was won. Our food came. She was precise with her salad. She'd stab some lettuce, then a piece of chicken. She chewed slowly and took her time. I sawed at my steak and ordered another Labatt's.

"You weren't ever a cop?"

"I was a parole officer for about a minute. Is that close enough?"

"You're kidding."

"Nope."

"Why did you stop?" She finished her salad and pushed the plate to the edge of the table. She folded her hands neatly in front of her.

"It wasn't all I'd hoped it would be," I said.

"What did you hope it would be?"

"Noble."

"Oh. I'm sorry."

"I was, too."

Savannah sipped her ice water with lemon. She watched me over the rim of the glass. I didn't mind.

"Brute," she said. "But not brutish. Does that make sense?"

"I might have preferred cop."

"Your shoulders are huge."

"Wide."

"Okay, but *you're* huge."

"Not so loud. The professors will scold you for objectifying me."

That got another smile, this one a bit more genuine. Her eyes crinkled at the edges and I guessed we were both enjoying ourselves. When the waiter came back, Savannah ordered a whiskey sour. I almost asked him what he thought his earlobes would look like if he ever had the metal hoops removed, but decided against it. It would have made me sound old. No man wants to seem old in front of a woman who looked like Savannah.

"My niece has been kidnapped," she said, once the waiter was gone.

"When?"

"Two days ago. Chelsea's mother called the FBI. He gave me your number. Agent Reinhart. He told me you were honest."

"Where does Chelsea's father live?"

She looked surprised.

"How did you know it was her father?" she said.

"The FBI handles all kidnappings ever since the Lindbergh baby. If Reinhart sent you my way, it means it isn't a kidnapping. Not legally speaking. When I think kidnapping, but not legally speaking, I think divorced dad with shared custody."

Savannah smiled at the waiter when he set her drink on the table. She took a sip of her whiskey sour and said, "Why did you really stop being a parole officer?"

"I lacked objectivity."

"That's vague."

"I attacked a parolee inside the Wayne County Jail."

"Yikes. Really? Why?"

"He described what he'd done to an eight-year-old girl the day before."

That got me something better than a smile. She blinked three times, quickly, putting me in a clearer focus. I knew I was hired.

"Is what you do now a better fit?" she said.

"So far. I like the freedom."

Something passed over her face, like she was considering whether to voice what was behind her eyes.

"So…freedom. That's important to you?" she said finally.

*Reinhart.*

He hadn't just given her my name and a recommendation after all. He'd thrown my biography at her. I decided not to bite. If she wasn't going to ask the question directly, I wasn't going to give the direct answer.

14

"How old is Chelsea?" I said.

"She turned thirteen last month."

"Is her father violent?"

Savannah took another sip of her whiskey sour. She looked like she was choosing her words carefully. Or she was getting ready to lie to me.

"He's a violent man," she agreed. "But not with her. At least, he never has been before."

"How do you know?"

"I'd know."

"What's his name?"

"Paul Gullins," she said. She set a manila envelope on the table between us. "I wrote down everything I could think of that might be important. Do you want to read it and see if there's more I need to write down?"

"Is your number in there? If I have questions I'll call you."

Now her smile was knowing. She put her elbow on the table and cupped her chin in her palm.

"Is that a strictly professional inquiry?"

"Let's say it is, even if it isn't."

"It's in there. How much do you charge?"

I told her my rate. She didn't throw her drink in my face, so I assumed we were still on good terms.

"Why isn't Chelsea's mother hiring me?"

Her playfulness vanished. She curled her lip and rolled her pretty eyes dramatically to let me know what she thought of Chelsea's mother.

"Donna's a train wreck. That's the way it's been since we were kids. She's two years older, but I was always the big sister. So I did what I always do and decided to take charge while she falls to pieces."

"Where do you think he took Chelsea?"

"Up to Two Pine, without question," she said. "That's where his militia buddies are. Sovereign North? You've heard of them?"

"No," I admitted. "But I don't get up north very often. Does Chelsea's father live up there?"

She nodded her head.

"Paul took her out of school when he knew Donna would be gone. They aren't divorced, though. I mean, they split up a few years ago. But neither of them ever filed. It wasn't as bitter as some break ups. He got sick of her junkie drama and just moved north without any big to-do. He was still involved with Chelsea. Now and then he'd take her up north for a week or two. There's a program for girls up there, a two-week camp in the woods where they build fires, learn first aid, basic survival stuff like the Boy Scouts do. Self-esteem stuff. He seemed like he was going to just be a pretty good weekend dad, I guess. Now, out of the blue, he does this."

I guess I was silent a little too long, because she tapped her nails along the table and said, "What? What's the matter?"

"I can't just grab Chelsea from her father. That actually *is* kidnapping."

"I know. I'm not expecting that."

"Then what is it you want me to do?"

Savannah's eyes got hard. I wondered if this was the first time I was really seeing her. Some beautiful people look ugly when they're angry. Savannah Kline just looked more lovely, like fine china transmuted into marble.

"Convince Paul to give her back," she said, biting each word off. "However you have to do that."

"Oh. You mean like a brute?"

"If it has to be that way."

"There's probably a smarter way."

"Like what?"

"Donna could go to family court and ask a judge to order Paul to produce Chelsea," I said. "If he doesn't, the judge can get law enforcement involved by issuing a warrant."

Savannah nodded her head, the way you do when you're hearing something you already know.

"I told her that. She's not going to. Paul has her scared. *I'm* scared of Paul, and I don't frighten that easy. Sovereign North is full of scary men. Are you having second thoughts?"

"Because of the scary men?"

"Yes."

"No."

She arched one neatly sculpted eyebrow.

"They have a lot of guns up in Two Pine."

"Lucky for us, I'm bulletproof."

"You *really* don't seem like a private investigator."

"I'm not. People with problems hire me. That's all."

She finished her whiskey sour and we settled the tab. I took the envelope with me. When we were on the sidewalk she crossed her arms under her breasts and squinted up through the sunshine at me.

"I love Chelsea. My sister would tell you I don't like kids, but that's not true. I made different life choices than Donna. I earned a Masters in finance and went into banking. Having kids didn't fit in. But I love Chelsea. She's the best thing in my life. Can you get her back?"

"I can try."

"Even if there are a bunch of militia goons standing in the way?"

"Even then. But I'll need to talk to Donna first."

Her eyes went half-lidded and I knew it wasn't what she wanted to hear.

"I understand," she said after a moment. I wasn't convinced.

"If she wants me to go find Chelsea, I'll do it," I said.

"You're going to try and talk her into seeing a judge, aren't you?"

"I don't know yet. Maybe."

"You'd talk yourself out of a job?"

"Money isn't everything. Whatever happens, it needs to be because it helps your niece."

"That makes me glad I called you."

We said goodbye. I started off toward my car. It was a clear June afternoon. Summer semester coeds bopped about in shorts and skirts, their cheeks sun-kissed, their futures still untroubled.

"Hey," she called.

I turned around.

"You'll call me when you know something?"

"I will."

She cocked a hip and held her head to the side so her hair spilled down. It made her look absolutely adorable. There was no doubt in my mind that she knew it.

"Or even if you just feel like calling me?"

"And here I was going to surprise you."

That was good enough for her. She turned back around and walked off, her coppery-blonde tresses swooshing in time with her hips. I watched her until she rounded a corner and was gone.

*

When I pulled away from the curb and started heading back toward Detroit, prison was on my mind. Savannah had poked around the edges, but she'd never gotten up the nerve to come out and ask me about it directly.

Reinhart. He'd sent her my way. Told her I was honest. It was a recommendation. Still, he was a cop. He wouldn't gloss over a prison record. He'd put it out there in the air because, for him, it was always an asterisk trailing behind my name.

That was fine with me. I didn't hide who I was.

But I wondered. I wondered if my three years in Jackson was maybe the reason Savannah had hired me. If it was, it meant she wanted somebody mean, not somebody smart.

Had Reinhart mentioned my exoneration? I doubted it. Cops see humanity as divided into a trinity: cops, citizens, and criminals. You can be in the citizen box and move to either of the other two. You can be in the cop box, but move into the criminal. Retired cops are still cops, not citizens.

Once you're in the criminal box, there is no moving. You never get out.

A judge overturned my conviction. A jury awarded me a settlement after I sued for the three years I'd lost. That settlement and the outrage I'd felt at what had been done to me got me through enough schooling to secure a job looking after other guys cycling out of prison. Working as a parole officer meant I'd been a state agent for a while, a first cousin to actual law enforcement. But for Reinhart, who'd shared beers with me in my living room, those facts would never move me entirely out of the box he had me in.

I'd been inside. It was that simple.

*

I was eastbound on I-94 when I suspected I was being followed. A blue Ford Explorer had been behind me ever since leaving the Tower Tavern. I changed lanes a few times, watching in the rearview as the Explorer either sped up or slowed down enough to keep a car or two between itself and the Stratus I was piloting.

Since hiring myself out to people who needed the kind of help I could offer, I'd been followed and confronted plenty of times. A lot of the work is sitting on people, watching them, following them. Sometimes, they're sharp enough to notice you. When that happens, it can go either way. They might just rush away and hope you didn't see what you were looking for, or they might get their courage up and come at you.

Snooping into people's business is an invitation for conflict.

I took the Belleville exit south onto Rawsonville Road. A half-mile past the strip malls and fast food joints, it turned rural. I checked the mirror again. Blue Explorer. Tinted windows.

I hung a left. A quarter-mile down, the pavement ended and I was crunching over gravel. I pushed the accelerator down and stopped watching the Explorer. Farmsteads sped by on either side. Nothing had grown much, this early in the summer. I could see far in all directions and didn't have to worry about some farmer's hound bounding into the car's path.

The Stratus ate a mile of gravel. I looked again. Through the cloud of dust I'd kicked up, the dark mass of the Explorer was still visible. Whoever he was, he'd figured out I knew he was there. He was matching my speed.

Another mile whipped away before I hit a length of road where the nearest farmhouse was way off in the distance. There was nothing but wide, deep ditches and soybean fields on either side.

I let off the gas and braked hard enough to bring the Stratus to a fish-tailing halt. I had a Sig Sauer P232 out of the glove box and in my hand when I bolted out of the car. The dust cloud I'd kicked up rushed over me. I crossed the road, not looking back, putting several yards between me and the car. The Explorer was loudly chewing gravel. I heard it come to a stop behind the Stratus the same moment I plunged down the steep bank of ditch. Wild grass and cottontails. Behind me, a car door opened, then slammed shut.

I pivoted, training the Sig ahead. Crouching, I could see just over the lip of the ditch. One man was standing a few feet in front of the Explorer's grill. He was wearing camouflage overalls and big rubber boots. A blue Tigers' cap was pulled down low over his eyes. His hands were cradling a hunting rifle across his chest.

"Shit, big man," he called out. "You sure spook easy, you know that?"

I had the Sig's sights on him, center mass. His chin was covered in a shaggy black goatee, but that was all I could make out under the baseball cap's brim.

"What's the matter? You don't want to shoot the shit? Come on outta there, big man. Let's get a look at you, tough guy."

The standing water in the bottom of the ditch was soaking through to my socks. I ignored it and kept the Sig trained. Behind him, it sounded like another person was speaking from inside the Explorer. I heard him say "relax" to whoever his passenger was.

"You seemed to like chit-chatting with that whore," he shouted in my direction. "Maybe you're all chit-chatted out. Maybe you're just gonna run on home and not listen to anything whores have to say. You think maybe so?"

I watched him take two steps forward. I kept the Sig on him. He pointed the hunting rifle at my car, holding it low down at his hip. The rifle cracked and the rear driver-side wheel of the Stratus made a clapping sound as it burst.

"Yeah. I guess maybe you're done with whores, buddy. You go on home and be smart. Do that and you won't have to learn how sovereign men settle their disputes."

I watched him climb back inside the Explorer. He put it in reverse and made a show of shooting straight back, kicking a load of gravel ahead of him. The Explorer whipped around. Its horn sounded two sharp barks as it drove out of sight.

*

I climbed up out of the ditch.

I looked at my shoes, then at the tire. Both were ruined.

I stuck the Sig in my waistband at the small of my back and hauled the spare tire out of the trunk. I started jacking up the Stratus and replaying the last few minutes.

What I had was the sound of his voice, the license plate on his Explorer, and a general idea about his height and weight.

I wrenched three of the lug nuts off, setting each one in the basin of the plastic hub cover. I stopped long enough to reach into the car and get a pen out of the console. I wrote the Explorer's plate down on the outside of the envelope Savannah had given me. Then I got back to changing the tire.

Sovereign men, he'd said. Savannah hadn't been exaggerating. That was the sort of grandiose title a militia group would assign themselves.

24

*

Once I was back on 94 and headed east, I called the number I found for Savannah inside the envelope. It rang once and went to voicemail.

I had doubted there was much use for my services after hearing what she had to say over lunch. Having a child yanked away by an ex-spouse had to be the worst feeling in the world. I didn't have any children of my own, but I believed Savannah when she talked about how close she was to Chelsea.

Still, you assume a situation is typical until it proves itself otherwise. And typical in a situation like that was that the kid gets returned pretty quickly. The ex-spouse sobers up or calms down or has a chance to think and they decide to do the smart thing and get the kid back to their primary caregiver. Sometimes they don't wise up fast enough and a judge orders them to bring the kid to court. That was where my head had been going before spotting the Explorer tailing me.

A gunshot straight out of the gate earned Savannah something more than just talking Donna Gullins into getting in front of a judge. That gunshot was all the evidence I needed to assume that Chelsea was in real danger.

I was nearing Dearborn when I decided to call Jack Reinhart of the FBI. He answered on the second ring.

"Roarke. Is this about the cute blonde banker I steered your way?" he said.

"Yeah. Can we meet?"

"If there's food involved, sure. I'm off at seven. You know the Gas Light downtown?"

"Yeah. The place that looks like an old Bavarian inn."

"You can buy me a couple beers and thank me for the blonde. How'd that go?"

"Somebody shot my car and told me he was a sovereign man."

"That's exciting. Did you shoot back?"

"I didn't think lethal defense of auto would fly in court."

"In this town? Don't be so sure. Let's say eight."

He hung up and I took the West Grand Boulevard exit into Detroit.

*

I don't get romantic about this city.

Some guys defend her every chance they get, like they're sticking up for a woman with a sketchy reputation she doesn't deserve. I wasn't one of those guys.

Detroit is failure, through and through—a sagging, broken down and worn-out old hag. Her decline has made her spiteful, and she'll lash out at you if you give her the chance. Even if you love her because you find some sort of savage beauty in her decay, the bitch will never love you back. She might let you hang around, sure; maybe even long enough to start feeling like you've made a home. But sooner or later she'll turn on you, guaranteed.

I knew that firsthand. I'd been born in Detroit. After eight years in the Marines, I came back to her, thinking I was returning home. She set me straight with a single night of mindless violence, before sending me off to a cage for three years to lick my wounds and learn my lesson: there is no sanctuary in her.

*

There was a tire and oil change franchise on Livernois. It was still early afternoon and I had plenty of time before I was to meet with Reinhart. While I waited in the little customer lounge for my tire to get replaced, I read through the contents of the envelope Savannah had given me.

Most of it was all type-written by her, a kind of stream-of-consciousness attempt to get down everything she could think of that might be important. Two photographs were attached to the pages with a paper clip.

The first was Chelsea's eighth grade class photo. Like Savannah, she had blonde hair, but cut to just above her shoulders. Her face was heart-shaped and heavy with freckles.

27

Smiling into the camera, she had that awkwardness everyone gets when they're stuck between being a kid and being a young adult.

The second photo looked like it was taken in the hospital after Chelsea was born. A bland, brown-haired, and exhausted-looking woman was sitting up in the hospital bed with a swaddled newborn in her arm. I could see the resemblance to the older photo of Chelsea. Both her mother and she had soft, round faces that kind of swallowed their eyes.

The man leaning into the frame with his arm around the new mother's shoulders was slight, stooped, and bald. He had a neat little mustache and a receding chin. With his paunch and his spindly frame, there was nothing about him that screamed sovereign man.

I flipped the photo over. On the back it said *'That's Paul. Sorry, it's literally the only photo I have of him.'*

I looked at the guy again. The camera had caught Paul looking comically baffled, like maybe he'd just that moment woken up to the reality that his entire life had changed with the arrival of a newborn girl. He could have been an accountant or a middle manager at first glance.

I tried to picture him in head-to-toe camo, shooting guns in the Two Pine wilderness and spouting militia-screed. I didn't have the imagination to pull it off.

I was starting to read the attached pages when the counter jockey called me over. He was young and clean. The man beside him was wearing dirty overalls and his hands were black from working on the cars all day. They both looked perplexed as I walked up.

"What's up?" I said.

The counter jockey looked uncertainly at the mechanic like the older man might be a lifeline. The mechanic shrugged and held his hand out toward me. There was a spent, mashed bullet sitting in his blackened palm.

"Neat," I said. "But you can keep it."

# T W O

Home is a two-story red brick house at 55 Willis Street in midtown. It sat abandoned ever since the 1967 riots accelerated the on-going flight of money, business, and panicky white people out of the city.

The city government was so desperate to get human beings to come back, they were offering abandoned houses for as low as three hundred dollars. Mine had a full basement, a detached two car garage, a mature apple tree in the front yard, and maybe the single greatest selling point to a sane buyer: a nine-foot-high brick wall enclosing the entire lot. I bought the place for a little over two-thousand dollars.

That, by itself, is everything any outsider needs to know to understand Detroit. When houses are being sold for pocket change, there is no renaissance on the horizon.

The wall's iron gate slid away on its track when I touched the remote clipped under the visor. I put the car in park and got out to check the mailbox bolted on the wall just to the left of the gate. Neighborhood kids had torn off or destroyed seven of my mailboxes so far. At eight months old, this one had already exceeded its life expectancy.

The gate purred shut behind me and I parked the Stratus in the garage. My ruined shoes and socks went in the plastic trash bucket in one corner. Barefoot, I took the mail and Savannah's envelope with me and strolled over to the apple tree. It was a Golden Delicious—a thick and gnarled old-timer with gray bark that was as rough and resilient as a suit of armor.

I bought a book on apple trees after I moved into the house because the Old Soldier had been in rough shape. His leaves had been coated in an ashy moss and the years without any tending had left him a tangled mess. Three years of careful pruning, nutrient-rich watering, and tying his limbs out of each other's way had him back in top form.

I checked him over for a few minutes before giving his trunk a solid slap. He was doing fine, so I took a seat in his shade and started sorting the junk mail from the legitimate. It was all junk mail, so I settled back and finished reading what Savannah had typed out for me.

When I was done, I knew Paul was a tax lawyer and accountant. He'd only lived in Two Pine for two years since splitting up with Chelsea's mother. Before that, they'd lived together in Plymouth. Savannah had given me phone numbers for all of them. The note said she'd called the cell phones for both Paul and Chelsea several times since he'd taken her out of school. Nobody was answering.

Sitting there against the trunk of the Old Soldier, I knew I was going to Two Pine. I was going soon. I considered calling off the chat with Reinhart and just hitting the road. Eventually, I settled on promising myself that I'd pack a bag, meet Reinhart, and head out after that.

Still, I was anxious. I looked at the class photo of Chelsea. I thought about the man in the Tigers hat who'd come at me after I met with Savannah.

Directory Assistance got me the number for the county sheriff. I called their non-emergency number and a man answered on the second ring.

"Crawford County Sheriff's Department. Is this an emergency?"

"Maybe," I said.

"How can we help you?"

"There's a thirteen-year-old girl who's been taken out of her school down here in Plymouth by her dad. He took her up there to your neighborhood and her mom's worried. She can't reach either of them by phone."

The man on the line was quiet for a second and I heard keys tapping. When he came back on, he sounded like he was reading off his screen.

"Does the father have legal custody of the minor?"

"Yep."

"Has the minor been threatened?"

"Look, he's in some militia outfit up your way. The mother is scared for the girl's safety. We were hoping maybe an officer could drive out and check on her."

Another pause. He was talking to someone, but I couldn't make anything out.

"Are you related to the minor?" he said.

"No. Friend of the family."

"Has the father made threats? Has there been violence?"

"Nope. Not yet."

I started gathering up my papers and heading in to pack an overnight bag. It was obvious where this was going.

"Well," he sighed, "that's a complicated situation, sir. Unfortunately, because he has legal custody of his child, and there's no threat of violence against the child, we'd need a judge to--"

I hung up and walked inside my house.

*

The wall enclosing the property was the clincher when I bought the place, for a couple reasons. Sure, it would help keep street kids from burglarizing the house or stealing my car. But primarily its existence allowed me to do the top-to-bottom renovations the house needed when I bought it.

One of the reasons people aren't lining up to spend pocket change on houses in Detroit is that they all need extensive repairs after lying derelict for decades. Well, good luck finding a contractor willing to park a truck stocked full of tools and building materials on a Detroit street.

Having the wall allowed me enough peace of mind that I could stack lumber in the driveway and not be looking over my shoulder constantly.

Now, three years in, I'd nearly completed all the work I intended to do. The roof was new, and all the drywall. New stairs. New fixtures and appliances. New windows. Furnace. Hot water tank. Everything, really.

Two thousand got me in the door. Making it habitable was the real expense.

*

Showering and packing a bag didn't eat much time.

I padded down the stairs to the living room and sprawled out on the couch. I called Savannah's number again. This time, she picked up.

"That was fast," she said around a chuckle. "I was worried I didn't make an impression."

"Someone followed you to our meeting. A man in camo, driving a blue Ford Explorer. He shot my car and called you some unwholesome names."

She was silent. When her voice came back, she sounded frightened.

"Paul?"

"No. He was bigger than Paul. He had a black goatee and a Tigers cap. I think there was another person in the truck with him."

"I don't know any of his militia buddies. That could be anybody. Are you alright?'

"Peachy. I was worried about you. Why would Paul have someone following you, Savannah? Why would he want to do that?"

"Roarke, I have no idea. I'm stunned. I don't know what to even think."

"You should check on your sister," I said. "I'm meeting with Agent Reinhart at eight. After that, I'm going to need to talk with Donna before I head up to Two Pine."

"You're going to go there tonight?" she said, relief in her voice.

"It looks that way."

"Good. That's great. Yes, I'll go see Donna and check on her. I'll make sure she's in a condition to talk with you."

"What does that mean?"

"What it sounds like. She's a junkie. Most of the time she can't carry on a conversation."

"Alright. If you think anyone is following you, call me."

Her playfulness returned. Her voice dipped into a silky whisper.

"You'll protect me?"

"Until the check clears, sure."

"You're no fun."

"Sometimes I am."

I hung up and paced off into the kitchen. I sat back down on the couch with a glass of water and turned on the television. I flipped channels and wondered about Savannah. I wondered if maybe she knew exactly why the Sovereign North would think it prudent to follow her around. I wondered at the way she could effortlessly shift from concerned aunt into playful tease.

Mostly, I wondered what her lips tasted like. That was the most intriguing question, so I let it occupy me until it was time to go meet Reinhart.

*

Jack Reinhart was one of those guys who'd been dealt a winning hand from birth. He was big and blond, with a face that could have earned him work in Hollywood. People liked him because there wasn't any excessive self-love evident in the way he treated everyone else.

When he sat down next to me at the bar in the Gaslight, his tie was tugged loose, his collar unbuttoned. We shook. His handshake was firm but not obnoxiously so. He ordered a beer and we wasted a little time with meaningless talk before getting around to it.

"Sovereign North," I said.

He gave a noncommittal shake of his head.

"I couldn't find squat," he said. "If they're real, they're a needle in a haystack. Last time I saw someone count heads, there were forty-nine militia groups operating in Michigan. Only state with more is Texas, with something like fifty-seven. And they have three times the population as us."

"What do you mean 'if they're real'?"

"Maybe they're just a bunch of buddies shooting guns on the weekend. There's plenty of that. Giving your social circle a silly name doesn't make you a real militia, you know?"

The bartender appeared with a basket of fries and set it between us. I reached for the ketchup.

"Have they ever shown up on anyone's radar?" I said.

He shook his head and said, "Nope. I asked around though, after you called. Wayne County has one of their members up on a felony murder charge." He reached in his blazer pocket and came out with a little notepad. He flipped through it until he found the page he wanted and said, "Jeffrey Tombs. Young guy. But that seems like it was a drug deal gone south and not related to the group."

"How's that?"

"Someone pulled a gun, so Jeffrey Tombs pulls a gun and, presto, you've got a dead guy and a pick-up truck full of marijuana. Detective I talked to says he thinks the kid's some backwoods hayseed who thought he could just drive down to Detroit and ask the first person he met on the street if they wanted to buy all the weed he'd grown in his basement. They put a deputy pretending to be another inmate in his cell with him. That's what jogged the detective's memory when I mentioned the Sovereign North."

"Why'd they put a cop in his cell?"

"See if he'll mention other people. Maybe he's just a courier. Could be he bought the weed from someone else and was just looking to turn it over for profit. Maybe he'll drop names and do the prosecutor's work for him."

"Is he?"

"Dropping names? No. But he's identifying himself as a militia member. Apparently the kid won't shut up about his bestest-buddies back home and how they'll come roaring down here with their guns out once they hear how the kid's rights are getting trampled. Dipshit talk. Other than him, I couldn't find anybody who'd ever had dealings with Sovereign North."

"Not even the sheriff up their way?"

"We're friendly, Roarke," he said with a smirk. "That means I'll ask *my* guys. Doesn't mean I'm calling up locals and doing your job for you."

"Fair enough."

He ate a few fries and swallowed some beer. He looked like he was trying to figure out a way to say something.

"You told her I was locked up," I said, beating him to the punch.

He nodded once and looked me in the eye.

"I guess you think that was out of line," he said.

"No. I don't hide it. But it isn't the whole story, is it?"

"That depends on how you see the story."

I ate a fry and looked at our reflections in the mirror behind the bar. He was blond and bright. We were both a little over six foot, but I was larger, my frame thicker and heavy with muscle. Some of that was genetic, some got added on in the Marines, and the rest of it was from the prison workout I'd kept up with even after my release. 'Brute', Savannah had said and I couldn't think of a much better word.

"Look, I don't want to sugar coat anything with you, Roarke."

"Then don't."

"Alright. Wrongful conviction doesn't mean a man didn't die under your fists. Provoked or not. Railroaded or not."

"I got it," I said and hated how I could hear my voice get lower, thicker. I didn't want him to hear that, to know that the subject meant anything to me at all.

"And," he pressed on, "you flamed out of the parole officer shtick when it took three deputies to stop you from doing it again to that child molesting piece of shit. You know, I'm right there with all the other guys downtown when they talk about pinning a fucking medal on your chest for that."

I finished my beer and looked at the door. I wanted to throw some bills on the bar and walk out. I wasn't interested in hearing a cop run down his idea of who I was.

"So, yeah. When a lily-white citizen wants to take you on, the prison bit comes up. I'll give them your name because I know you're straight as they come when you give your word. But also, they need to know—you've got violence in you, Roarke. *Real* violence."

"Not you, though?" I said softly, so no emotion could get out. "Not you and every one of your brothers in blue?"

"I don't mind violence, Roarke. As long as it's pointed in the right direction. The day ever comes when you're pointing it the wrong way, at people who don't have it coming, I'll be at your front door. But not for beers."

"You done?"

"I'm done."

It was quiet between us for a little while. I couldn't find fault with him. That didn't mean I had to like it.

"What was your read on Savannah and the mother?" I finally said, when it was clear he was done with the subject of me and the lens through which he saw me.

"Mother's a pill popper," he said, sounding as ready to be off to other topics as I was.

"Kid going missing might push someone to that."

"That wasn't the feel I had. She's got that used-up look. Whatever her drugs of choice are, she's been doing them long enough to look a lot older than she actually is. Next to the blonde, you wouldn't guess in a million years they were sisters."

"The mom seemed concerned, though?"

Jack grinned humorously and shook his head.

"Hell if I know. She was zonked out on the couch when I made the house call. The whole place stank like cat piss and dirty laundry. The blonde was taking care of her. Embarrassed as hell, you know? To be associated with a wreck like that."

He took a long pull of beer and shrugged his shoulders.

"And that was it. I asked the good-looking one a few questions but there wasn't anything there I could use. I dropped your name and she seemed agreeable."

We talked a little while longer but he didn't have anything I didn't already know. When we shook hands and said our goodbyes, he made a point of putting a hand on my shoulder and

41

giving it a squeeze as if to say *'Yeah, you're a convict in my book. But we're good, right?'*

Sure.

It was dark when I got back on the road and headed for I-94. It was a thirty-minute drive to Plymouth. I kept the radio off and the window down, letting the wind in my face remind me that I was here, in the world, *outside*.

\*

The night I beat Freddie Esposito to death, I was just back from the Marines. I was young and full of the bravado of a warrior. I'd given them eight years of my life. They'd spent that time building me into something they could put to use. I enjoyed that half of it. It was work and it was a purpose. Go where we say. Do a thing with precise, orchestrated violence. Return. Continue training until we tell you to go somewhere else.

That's a simple, pleasing rhythm. But somewhere in there, I started rankling at the control system. The bureaucracy of it all. The little petty details. I cashed out and headed home without a plan in the world or an idea what would come next.

For me, what came next was Freddie Esposito.

\*

The car's GPS guided me to Donna Gullins' house on Clement Drive. It was a residential street with wide, maintained sidewalks and a single large elm tree planted in front of every house.

I parked on the curb and stared up at the two-story, canary yellow house the GPS assured me was Donna's. None of the lights were on.

Savannah Kline was sitting on the wide cement porch, under the shingled overhang.

When I got out of the car she lit a cigarette, the ember an orange dot in the gloom of night. I hadn't smelled cigarettes on her when we met earlier that day. Usually, I can pick that up like a neon sign. I'd been a smoker before I got locked up. I didn't miss it often, but my nose seemed to always be on the look-out for the stink of tobacco like a lonely soul hoping to run across an old flame.

"I don't know where she is," she said as I walked up the drive toward her. "I've been calling but she doesn't answer."

I peered past where Savannah's car was parked. There was a detached garage in back, a blue Saturn sedan parked inside it.

"Is the Saturn hers?"

Savannah blew smoke and chewed at the edge of one of her nails. After a beat, she nodded her head.

"Well, Paul's, technically. He bought it. But she drives it."

"Do you have a key to the house?"

"No. I told her I should. All the time. She doesn't listen."

I looked at her sitting on the steps. She'd changed into cream Capri pants and a black cotton top that hugged her slim frame. The sandals on her feet were open-toed, showing off nails painted an earthy clay hue. Beside her, a large black duffel bag rested on the porch.

She saw me looking at it, and stood up.

"I'm going up there, too," she said, in what I guessed was her professional tone, the one she used on people she outranked. She didn't look like how I'd imagined a bank manager. She looked too beautiful to have ever needed to climb a ladder of that sort.

"I thought you said these were dangerous people."

"They are."

"Then you're not going. Have you tried the door or windows?"

I walked past her, up onto the porch. I pulled the screen door open.

"They're all locked," she said behind me, her voice impatient. "Look, I want to be there for Chelsea. You're going to get a room, right? Or were you going to go confront Paul at five in the morning?"

She was right about the door. I pushed up on a couple of the windows. She was right about the windows, too.

I turned back around and looked at her. She cocked a hip in a defiant pose.

44

"Don't you think you'd like my company?" she said, shifting into playfulness like it was a comfortable, oft-worn shirt.

"Someone already took a shot in my general direction," I said. "If you're with me I have to split my attention between keeping me safe and keeping you safe. I'm not going to be responsible for you."

"You wouldn't be," she said. "I'd stay at the room. I just want to be there once you've got Chelsea back. Look at you. To her, you'll be a gigantic, strange man. She'll be terrified. She needs to see a loved one and know she's safe."

As she was talking, I climbed up on the porch's railing. She held her hands out at her sides in bewilderment.

"What on earth are you doing?"

I grabbed hold of the overhang's lip and pulled myself up.

"Checking on your sister," I said.

"Someone's going to call the cops."

I crawled to one of the two second floor windows and tested it. It shimmied up, so I shimmied inside. Behind me Savannah said something that sounded sharp, like a curse word, but I couldn't make it out.

*

I flipped the wall switch and found myself standing in Chelsea's room. It was neatly kept. I scanned the trophies and

45

framed photos arranged across the top of her dresser. She was a track athlete. Her smile was wide and enthusiastic in the framed team photos.

I lifted one of the frames off a shelf and peered at her. She was sitting cross-legged in the shade of a tree with a textbook opened across her lap. One pale and bony knee was starkly visible, poking out from her jeans. An active kid, the sort who wore the knees of her jeans away. She looked like the photo was a surprise, capturing her as she glanced up from her reading. Her cheeks and nose were touched with sun and the rims of her nails were dirty.

I set the photo back down and kept looking around.

The bed was as smartly made as my own had been in boot camp. The carpet was clean, free of even a stray sock or note from class. I opened a dresser door. Neatly folded clothes.

A laptop was open on a desk near her bed. I touched the mouse and the screen came to life. A user password was required, so I left it alone.

In a shallow walk-in closet I pulled the cord for the light bulb and found myself staring at my reflection. Along the top of the wall-mirror Chelsea had taken a kid's alphabet stickers and written a daily reminder for herself.

*'smile it won't always be like this'*

I pulled the cord again and walked out into the hallway, softly calling "Hello?" as I turned on lights.

Reinhart hadn't been wrong about the disarray throughout the house. Every room except Chelsea's was littered with stray dishes, dirty linens and cast off litter. The carpets looked like they hadn't been vacuumed in months.

When I got downstairs, I found Donna's nest: an overstuffed leather couch piled with blankets and pillows. Potato chip bags and pop bottles were strewn all around it. Spills had gone untended, so that a half-circle of carpet in front of the couch was a sticky, cola-colored shell. I peered down at the coffee table. Among the food wrappers and dishes were three sandwich baggies containing pills. I poked around and found a baggie of marijuana in a ceramic cup. An ashtray was struggling to contain a heap of cigarette butts and wads of chewed gum.

I checked the kitchen and the laundry room. More clutter and mildew-stink but no Donna Gullins.

I loitered in the kitchen because I hadn't decided what I was going to tell Savannah. I hadn't met Chelsea's mom or even spoken to her but Savannah was out on the porch expecting me to race off and snatch a minor from her father. I *was* going to Two Pine, no question. The gunshot and sovereign men speech had guaranteed that much.

Beyond that, I had no plan.

*'smile it won't always be like this'*

I looked at the piled dishes in the sink. The trash can near the door was overflowing. My shoes made sucking noises on the sticky, fading linoleum. The house was chaos and neglect. It stank of dysfunction and surrender. One floor up, Chelsea's room was like a shrine— an ordered and bright corner of her own where she could try and fend off the calamity surrounding her.

I entertained the notion that maybe her father had stood here, amid all the signs that Donna Gullins was not a functioning person, and felt the same sympathy for the kid I felt. Hell, he was her father. Whatever I felt for Chelsea's plight, he could be expected to feel a hundred times keener.

Maybe he hadn't snatched her. Maybe he'd rescued her.

I walked back through the house, turning off all the lights again. I locked Chelsea's window, went downstairs, and opened the front door.

Savannah was still standing with her hip cocked to one side and her arms crossed over her chest. I couldn't make out her face in the dark, but I assumed it was registering impatience. I thumbed the door knob's button into the locked position and pulled the door shut behind me.

She snatched her duffel bag up off the porch and slung the strap over her shoulder. We both walked down the steps and onto the lawn. Out in the moonlight, her pale skin was as white and rich as milk. She smelled like scented moisturizer and not cigarette smoke.

"If you're coming with me, the deal doesn't get negotiated later," I said. "You stay at the hotel and don't argue about it once we're there. I'll go and talk with Paul in the morning. If I bring Chelsea back, she'll need you to reassure her everything's alright."

She arched a brow.

"If?"

"That house is a nightmare. If Paul owns a broom and knows how to flush a toilet, I'll probably be tempted to give him my blessing and call it a day."

I stashed her bag in the trunk next to mine. She eased down into the passenger seat beside me. I felt an unexpected thrill in my stomach. That's just the way of it, I guess: no matter the circumstances, hardly anything beats a beautiful woman riding next to you in your car.

I rolled my window up and turned the car's fan on low, letting the smell of her walk around the joint. After we'd been on the road for several minutes, she reclined her seat and curled up on her side, like she was ready to fall asleep.

"You'll bring her back," she said, and closed her eyes.

I turned onto I-94 eastbound, and wondered who the gorgeous blonde beside me really was. She seemed earnest enough in her concern for her niece. But there was another side of her she kept hinting at; a toying, flirting Savannah that seemed every bit as real as the other.

She stretched in the seat beside me, half-turning, and her sleek black shirt rode up, exposing the flat plane of her stomach. A small silver hoop was pierced through her belly button.

I was looking at her, at the perfect shape of her, when her eyes opened. I caught the slow grin spreading over her lips as I fixed my eyes back on the road.

"See?" she teased. "You're already glad I came along."

*

"That FBI agent said you killed a man."

I'd been driving two hours up I-75 when she said it, putting to rest my curiosity about whether she was asleep. In the periphery of my vision, her face was a pale moon amid the darkness of the car's interior. I wondered if she'd been watching me in silence all that time. I was used to being quiet and still for long spells. I wasn't used to it in other people.

"Is that why you hired me?" I said.

The Stratus' headlights swam over the exit sign for Standish. The smaller blue signs that recommended places of interest told me Lake Huron was only a handful of miles to the east. I'd never seen any of the Great Lakes except Lake Erie. I'd never been on a boat, or gone fishing.

Rolling along north, cutting a line through the great sweep of forest and lakes, it occurred to me that I was as much a foreigner

50

to Michigan as anyone could be. I knew Detroit, and I knew the sprawl of suburbs surrounding it, and not much more. Any of the conservative, rural homesteaders north of Flint probably would have answered, "Then you don't know Michigan, buddy", and they'd have been right.

"What do you mean?" she said.

"Forget it."

"I didn't mean to make you mad," she said in a little girl's voice.

"You didn't," I lied.

"I'm sorry. Was it bad to ask that?"

I rolled the window down a few inches and kept my eyes on the road, moving forward, carrying us into tomorrow even while my mind was falling back to yesterday.

\*

I was in the Honey Horn bar on Michigan Avenue because it was a jazz bar and the type of place my presence would go unnoticed. The older folks who frequented the Honey Horn wouldn't mind a young white man sitting at the bar sipping beers and keeping to himself. Or, if they did mind, they wouldn't raise the issue with me. Some of the joints in Detroit, skin matters a lot, just like it does in plenty of rural white towns all across this country.

People from other places hear someone from Detroit refer to it as a 'black city' and they get all pucker-faced and indignant with accusations of reverse racism. The reality is, all the money was swept away on the steady tide of white exodus, leaving a minority population left to run a broken, abandoned system. If you aren't prepared to venture within the city limits, much less work or live there, you've got no business criticizing. Yeah, it *is* a black city. I didn't resent people claiming ownership of a place nobody else wanted anyway.

The Honey Horn was full of old men with their ladies, come to see live jazz. They were working people and pensioners. People who'd spent their lives on assembly lines, who lived for Friday nights when they could dress to the nines, see a show, drink some drinks, and smoke themselves hoarse.

I was only three months out of the Corps and still busy spending everything I'd managed to save during the eight years Uncle Sam was providing for all my needs. The only life plan I had was to get through a few more beers and slouch back to my rented room above a second-hand store a few blocks away.

Up on the stage, a dark brother as large as a refrigerator was managing to play the trumpet and nimbly juke around at the same time. The crowd was raucous, leaving their work week stress there, getting rid of it and forgetting it.

I was thinking about cashing out when I heard the woman's scream.

She broke from the floor of crowded tables, toward the door. The few of us at the bar all looked. She was a young black beauty in a tight silver party dress. I saw one of her feet twist down as she lost her footing in her four-inch heels. She pitched forward on the twisted ankle, her long weave spilling forward.

Her momentum halted when a slim little Latino man in a red silk shirt and black slacks grabbed hold of that weave and yanked back. He was shouting something, but the horns on the stage drowned it down. The trumpet man was still juking and jumping up a storm, oblivious to the world, lost in his moment.

As the girl struggled to pull free, I saw her face clearly for the first time. Her eyes were bulging with panic, comically large. A three-inch line of red stood out on her left cheek, gushing blood.

He grabbed hold of her face with one hand, squeezing and pinching her mouth into a pucker. He had her pinned now, up against the wall near the restroom doors that read "Cats" and "Kittens". He was shouting in her ear, his narrow face a mask of rage.

Locked down and frozen, only her eyes could get away from him. They saw the group of drinkers at the bar, searching, desperate, until they settled on me. We were looking right at each other while he squeezed her bloody face like a sponge and shouted venom in her ear.

I don't remember getting on my feet.

I only remember her eyes, growing in mine.

\*

I was on autopilot, lost and brooding, when I felt Savannah shift and lean her head against my shoulder. I checked the mile markers. I'd driven seventeen miles through the darkness and silence without being there for any of it.

Her hand slid over, down, coming to rest on my crotch. I sucked in a sharp breath, the perfume of her, so near, filling me. She squeezed once and found the zipper.

"Savannah."

"Shh." She tilted her chin up and her lips touched my ear. Her voice was a low murmur. "I made you angry with me. I was bad."

"It's not like that." My voice was thick, a groan.

"Shh. I want to."

She brought me out, squeezing at the base, rhythmic. With her free hand she touched the radio and something silky rumbled up out of the speakers. She kept her lips against my ear and began to whisper.

"Am I still being bad? I am, aren't I?"

"Savannah…"

"I want to. Just drive."

The road kept on and so did she.

A horn called out mournfully from within the song she'd summoned, and I saw the trumpet player's sweat-soaked face again. He was still jiving full tilt up there, massive and inexhaustible. He mopped his brow with a white rag and went right back at it, his cheeks ballooning as he strained to make the horn speak his name.

When I grabbed hold of the skinny little Latino, there wasn't a coherent thought in my head. All I could see was the terror in the girl's eyes and the silent pleading they'd shot my way. He was small and light. I heaved him off her, lifted him whole from the earth.

He shouted something in surprise as he found himself in the air. He crashed down and I was spinning around, keeping myself between him and the bloody-faced girl. I was reaching out again. As I got hold of his shoulders, I didn't have a plan. I didn't know if he was going to get thrown up and down again, or if I was going to drag him outside. He was just a thing I was going at, an offensive object that had to be kept at bay.

I didn't feel the knife go in my stomach the first time. It was too fast and too sharp. Freddie Esposito, I learned later, had done time in a Florida prison. He used the slim little stiletto blade on me the way inmates do on each other: rapid, furious stabs to the abdomen.

Pain came, but it wasn't what pushed me over the edge into a killing frenzy. The pain was real but dull, far off. It was lagging

55

behind in the race to get to my brain and sound the alarm. What got there first was a purely animal impulse. That signal, primordial and nameless, knew that I was in mortal danger. Its single, elegantly simple command: kill.

"Please. Please *stop*."

The girl behind me, sobbing the words out.

My hands bunched up into hammers and I watched them begin to beat Freddie Esposito to death. The pain in my guts flared for real, but it was too late to signal any sort of order to retreat. I mashed his face into a red smear. When it wasn't a face anymore, I wrapped my hands around his neck and squeezed until there was nothing under me but a limp body. I collapsed forward, a dark exultant wave washing over me, whispering, telling me this was what triumph felt like.

"You like to be bad, too. I know you do."

Savannah squeezing, chuckling darkly in my ear as we whipped across deserted blacktop. She bit the lobe of my ear and slid away, down, sensing the climax. I saw Freddie Esposito's broken body as the other drinkers hauled me off him. Saw the girl, shaking like she was in shock, staring at me in horror.

Savannah's mouth slid over me, a melting sheath. The battered girl fell to her knees, spent, her face running red. The trumpet player summoned his last ounce of juice and blasted a fevered chord to herald the end.

# THREE

Morning grew hesitantly, a shy sun in an iron sky.

We drove through a high forest of marching pine, down a cleanly paved county road just south of Two Pine. Savannah was curled into herself beside me, asleep, her heap of copper curls hiding her face. One hand still rested lightly on my thigh as if to remind me of the intimacy she'd so brazenly initiated back on that night-shrouded highway.

Daylight dispelled that fever dream, bleaching away the unsettling mixture of dread and exaltation she'd summoned inside me. I touched the buttons that sent both our windows down and let the summer wind kiss me awake with false promises of a fresh start.

*

The woman at the front desk of Home Among the Pines was short, plump, and had a Dutch boy haircut. When I walked in, she appeared from a back room, dressed in jeans and a man's flannel shirt with the sleeves rolled up to her elbows.

"Morning," I said.

"Sure is. What can I do for you?"

"You guys have any cabins?"

Her nose crinkled and she looked surprised.

"No reservation?" she said.

"Nope. Is that a problem?"

"Heck, no. This time of year? We don't fill up 'til the fourth of July. After that, we're packed all the way through gun season. Let me get a map, you can have your pick of cabins."

She disappeared in the back again. I looked around. All the surfaces and the furniture were pine, the whole place designed to look like a rustic settler's cabin. An antique musket was hung on one wall. A stuffed wolverine was hung on another. Behind the reception desk, there was a series of framed photos. They all depicted her and a fit, short-haired woman posing over freshly downed game—deer, elk, moose, and a brown bear. The two of them looked deliriously happy in the photos, beaming smiles, their cheeks wind-burnt and pink.

She came back and spread out a map of the property on the desk. We both leaned over it and she started to point out different sites before stopping and sticking her hand out.

"Rhonda," she said.

"Roarke."

We shook hands and she got back to it. There were thirteen cabins. Two of them were four-bedroom monsters designed for large hunting parties. The others were either one- or two-bedroom cabins.

"Just you?"

"Me and one other. Let's go with that one," I said and pointed at a two-bedroom set furthest away from the others.

We went through the process, and I paid for one night after she assured me it wouldn't be a problem if I wanted to extend the stay longer than that. She gave me two keys.

"Me and Sharon keep coffee and tea stocked," she said. "But if you want to use the cabin's kitchen for more than that, we've got a little store in the back. The nearest real grocery store is out in Grayling. I can give you directions, if you want."

"Two Pine doesn't have a grocery store?"

Rhonda snorted and shook her head.

"You really didn't plan this trip out, did you?"

"It was kind of impulsive, yeah."

"Well, Two Pine doesn't have anything. I mean, it never had much to begin with, even when it was still alive. We used to have a couple machine shops supplying the Big Three. They folded, and that was the end of things. It's a ghost town. That's not me exaggerating. If you and your friend want to go out on the town, you'll be driving half an hour back and forth."

She put her hands on her hips and shook her head ruefully.

"Did I just talk you out of it?"

"Nope. We're still good."

Rhonda smiled and rolled her eyes.

"Thank God. My better half would skin me alive if she found out I'd talked someone out of a stay. Sometimes I talk too much."

*

Savannah disappeared into one of the two bedrooms with her big duffel bag, leaving me to look the place over. The cabin's living room had a slider door that opened out onto a deck. I stepped outside. There was more of the pine furniture on the deck—four chairs and a round table with an umbrella on a post in the middle of it. A tarp-covered grill was in one corner. I walked to the rail and stared out at the sweep of forest. We were on the crest of a hill. The tops of the nearest trees were eye-level. They plunged away sharply with the land, so that I was staring out at a valley of green.

I counted three hawks spiraling lazily in the morning sky. As I watched, one of them dipped suddenly, pulled its wings in flat against its body, and disappeared into the trees. The two others followed, chasing down toward what the first had spied.

"I feel like we're honeymooners," Savannah said behind me, and appeared at my side.

One of the three hunters surfaced again, breaking past the tree tops and pushing hard into the sky. Something small squirmed in its beak.

"Roarke?"

The other two reappeared, set on a pursuit course. I hoped the first bird, the one who'd spied the meal far below, was the one in the lead. It didn't seem fair to think that one of the others had snatched his game away. They wheeled around in the sky, the two trailing the first as persistently as dog-fighting pilots. Eventually, the meal was gulped down whole by the first, and all three settled into their previous, lazy circling. They were partners in the hunt again, their cooperation likely to continue until another meal was spotted.

After that, all bets would be off.

Beside me, Savannah was bristling.

"What?" I said.

"It was a fucking blow job. It didn't mean anything. You don't have to get awkward on me."

"It's not like that."

"What is it like?"

I didn't have an answer to that. All I had were questions. Savannah Kline didn't make sense to me. I understood her when she was telling me she wanted her niece back safe and sound. That was a client I could comprehend. That was a different woman than the one who had ridden beside me through the night.

She'd whispered dark seductions in my ear and coaxed me to climax, all of it done with a casual ease.

Some women like a guy like me—the big quiet man who doesn't have a single pick-up line or any sort of manufactured charm. I knew what I looked like, and knew when a woman was interested in the blunt-faced and big-shouldered sort. But I'd never met a woman who shifted gears as fluidly as Savannah. It didn't ring true. I felt like the seduction she'd performed out there on the dark highway was her way of managing me. I'd been handled.

I just didn't know why.

"I think maybe I should call your sister," I said.

Savannah's china-fine face sharpened, her beauty turning cold and severe.

"Yeah?"

"I need to know more about what this is."

She was silent for a beat and I knew I was right; she was staring at me like a tool that wasn't performing its promised function. She looked me up and down, hunting for the flaw in the design. I kept my expression flat, giving her nothing.

"Fine," she snapped. "You do that. I need a shower."

She marched back inside.

*

When you get locked-up, advice is the first temptation they dangle in front of you. Your cellmate starts in first. He'll lay out the rules of the room: who has top bunk (him), whose personal effects can go on the little aluminum shelf above the toilet (his), and who has to keep the place spotless at all times (not him).

Once that's squared off, he'll start coaching you on the rules outside the cell. This is where everything stops being free. Advice on how to stay un-fucked in prison is just like any other commodity—it costs.

My first minute inside my cell at Jackson was spent listening to my cellmate run all that down. He was a young white guy, like me, but that's where the similarities ended. He was short and narrow, with a bald head and Aryan Nation tattoos. A freshly inked lightning bolt stood out on his neck.

He told me his name was David.

He told me he was down for at least another five years of a fifteen-year bid for selling large quantities of methamphetamine to undercover cops.

He told me he was with the Nation, and that meant I was going to be with the Nation, too.

He told me I'd blow him nightly, and that was the last thing he told me before I picked him up by his throat and held him against the wall long enough for the dynamics of our relationship to become crystal clear to David.

He miscalculated with me, but it wasn't his fault. I was fresh, a brand new convict on his first bid. By all rights, I should have been easy to manage. I should have been so full of fear and panic that he could get me to do just about anything so long as he dangled out the promise of my survival.

David understood his mistake later, once the word spread that I was second generation Jackson Prison. My old man was inside. He'd been there for twenty-one years. In that cement hell, he was legendary. He was never getting out. I'd visited him exactly one time during my childhood, before my mother died.

"They try to corner you in here," he told me from the other side of the Plexiglas barrier. "They find out what you want, what you need, and they use it to get at you. Understand, boy? There's exactly one way to do time as a man on his own, with no crew. You can't need anything. Need *nothing*. So don't take it hard when I tell you this: don't you ever come back here to see me. I don't want you, Roarke. I don't need you, and I don't need anything you think you got to give. Cut me out of your heart. I've already cut you out of mine."

It was the only conversation I'd ever had with my father as a kid, and it turned out to be the most useful thing I'd ever been told.

If they find a way *in*, people will use you up.

So when Savannah dangled her seductions in front of me, and then soured when her performance on the highway didn't have me sufficiently at heel, alarm bells sounded.

*

Once I heard the shower running, I opened Savannah's duffel bag and carefully began picking through everything she'd brought with her. There were a few changes of clothes and some decidedly imaginative lingerie that suggested there was nothing impromptu about her behavior the night before.

In the bottom of the bag, I found a thick manila envelope. Inside the envelope were rubber-banded rolls of hundred dollar bills and a passport. The passport was Savannah's. It was unmarred by any travel stamps. I checked the issue date. Two years old.

I put it all back in the bag and didn't take the time to count the money. A rough guess had it at around a hundred-thousand dollars.

In a little side pocket, I found a Ruger SR22 pistol. I popped the magazine and thumbed all the bullets out onto the bed's comforter. I checked the chamber, making certain I hadn't left one in the weapon, then put the empty gun back in the bag where I'd found it. The bullets went in my pocket.

Five minutes later, I was rolling out north on the county road that lead to Two Pine, letting the GPS point the way to Paul Gullins' address. Savannah and her go bag could wait. I needed to lay eyes on Chelsea Gullins and know that she was alright.

It would give me time to work out an angle for getting the truth out of Savannah. When you discover someone is lying to you, the immediate impulse is to confront them. If you wait, if you let them carry the lie out a little longer, there's no telling what inadvertent truths you'll learn along the way.

I rolled my window down, tossed the bullets to Savannah's gun into the wind, and kept going. I was plunging into something unknown. As the road vanished under the Stratus' wheels, I thought about my father and the second time I'd met him.

I thought about the warning he'd offered me.

*

The guard who collected me that night and led me out to the prison's recreation yard was named Puckett. Short and barrel-chested, with Popeye forearms and a brush mustache that made him look the picture of a fascist, Puckett didn't tell me where we were going in the darkness while the rest of the prison slept. He just called for the doors to open on his shoulder microphone, then shoved me ahead of him when they obediently slid open.

Throughout the seven months I'd spent as a convict, I'd only ever seen the rec yard in daylight and full of other prisoners. When Puckett guided me out through the last door and into the empty, night-shrouded yard, that emptiness made the yard seem much larger than ever before.

Moonlight lit the aluminum bleachers on either side of the basketball courts. A single bulb illuminated the interior of a looming guard tower. The prison itself was a black, geometric pool that the moon's glow didn't seem to touch. I shuffled along in the direction Puckett prodded me, the only sound in the world the clank of the chain between my ankles.

We passed the weight pits, crossed the northern curve of the jogging lane, and approached the north-east corner of the yard that, during the day, was Aryan Brotherhood territory. I'd never stepped foot here before.

Puckett brought me to a stop as I spied the lone figure sitting at one of the concrete tables near the fence.

"Give me the hands," the guard said. He unlocked the shackles on my hands, but left the leg irons alone. He leaned in close enough I could smell his aftershave, and said "You get half an hour. Sit on the bench across from him. If you get up before I come to get you, or you do anything besides sit there, it's a bullet in the back. I promise you that."

Puckett faded off into the darkness, leaving me to shuffle up to the concrete table and take a seat across from my father. Above us, the razor wire shone bright in the light of the moon.

We both looked each other over in silence. He hadn't seen me since I was a little kid come to get a look at the monster my mother assured me was my father. My memory of that prison visit was as clear as if it had just occurred.

He was draped in night's obscuring cloak, but I could make out some details. To me he looked no different, as if time was powerless to diminish him. He was taller than me by nearly half a foot and his shoulders were a mountain range. His face was a fun house mirror's reflection of my own—there were hints of the recognizable in the structure of bone and the arrangement of features, but the rest was a stranger.

The one startling change was his left eye. It was gone. A pale white scar ran down his forehead, over that destroyed eye, and continued down, finally stopping in the curled flesh of his upper lip. He wore no patch and when he shifted in the moonlight, I caught a glimpse of the eyelid, sewn shut over the wound.

As he looked me over, I felt like that little kid on the other side of the Plexiglas barrier again. Throughout my life, I'd grown accustomed to other men regarding me with trepidation because of my stature and size. Staring up at the dark mass of my father, I could empathize with them now.

"I can see me in you," he said after a long while. "When you came the last time, I didn't see it. I thought maybe your mother had lied to me."

I didn't know what to say to that. The idea of a real connection between us was an anguished scream inside my head. I kept myself still and didn't say anything.

When I was still in the womb, my father robbed an after-hours high stakes poker club on Telegraph Road in Dearborn. It was an illegal casino so I guess he saw it as an easy mark.

The building alarm got tripped and he found himself surrounded by cops. The easy stick-up job transformed into a hostage situation. He started making demands with a strict timetable attached to each one. When those deadlines weren't kept, he executed two men before the cops realized they were dealing with an authentic madman. They stormed in and he managed to execute three more civilians before they put enough bullets in him to kill any normal human.

It took Henry Ford Hospital eight months to rehabilitate him sufficiently enough to sit upright in a wheelchair and answer the judge's question.

"Guilty," he hissed into the microphone. "I'm guilty as all hell. So let's get this shit-show on the road, right?"

Now, as I regarded him from across the table, both of us dressed out in prison orange, there was no sign that the hail of bullets had managed to have any lasting impact on him. All that remained to hint at his murderous brush with death was a second scar on his face. Unlike the knife-line that had robbed him of his left eye, this second scar had been present when I visited him as a kid. It was round and puckered, an inch below his right eye. Its edge was raised, the center recessed. It looked like a crater on the face of the moon.

He caught me looking at it.

"The other six got me in the torso and guts," he said. "You ever been shot?"

"Stabbed. In the guts."

"The guards say you're in on a manslaughter charge."

"Yeah," I agreed. "That's what it is."

"Manslaughter. Huh. Bar fight?"

"More or less."

High up in the guard tower, a single body passed in front of the light bulb, the rifle in his hands standing out like a needle in the sky. Behind me in the shadows, Puckett muffled a cough.

"Tell me about it."

"About what?" I said.

"About how you ignored the one thing I ever told you."

I guess the confusion on my face must have been acute, because the giant across from me grew an ugly grin. There was no warmth in it, nothing but a cruel mocking. It was the closest thing to an emotion I'd seen him manage.

"I told you to never come back here, Roarke. Not ever. So tell me how in all hell you managed to fuck up that one simple thing."

"Because I should have listened to my father? Is that a joke? What is this? What am I *doing* here?"

Behind me in darkness, the snap of a Zippo wheel on flint and the slap of its lid flipping shut. Puckett noisily exhaled. After only seven months quit, the odor of his cigarette smoke was like the perfume of a long-lost lover to me.

The giant shadow in front of me sneered at my whispered outburst.

"Tell me how you come here," he said.

"Forget it. I've got nothing to say to you."

"Then tell me about your sad childhood and your momma dying on you and boo-hoo. Is that what you want to do? See if I pity you? I don't. I don't have any pity in me, Roarke. Not one drop."

"You think I don't know that?"

"How'd you get put in the box? How'd you wind up in here?"

"She died when I was fourteen," I said. "Did you know that? Drank her way into a hospice. She was yellow in the end. A yellow, wasted...thing. The last words she said to me was her begging me to get her a drink. Then it was foster homes."

He shifted, a monolith settling. Above him, the moon and the stars, and he looking as eternal and inscrutable as them all.

"Alright," he said. "You got it out of your system. Good for you. Now answer my question."

I told him about the night at the Honey Horn, all of it that I could remember up to the point when the dumbstruck onlookers snapped out of it and pulled me off the corpse of Freddie Esposito. He listened without comment.

When I was done, my father rubbed his knuckles in silence. I waited. Up in the guard tower, the rifleman continued his pacing, passing back and forth in front of the single bulb's light. Puckett was silent, but I knew he was nearby.

"You made the easy mistake. The easiest for men, anyway."

I squinted into the looming void of my father, trying in vain to spot something human upon the surface of him.

"What does that mean?" I said.

The moon went away behind a burst of cloud cover, equalizing the darkness of my father and the world around us. For a span of several heartbeats I was alone in a silent nothingness, until his raspy voice returned, rendering his verdict about me and my folly.

"You tried to save the girl."

*

Rhonda hadn't lied when she called Two Pine a ghost town.

I sat at the single defunct traffic light in the center of town and looked around for a minute. Two Pine had been of those little Midwestern towns that never built up any bigger than a single stretch of road. Michigan is full of towns like that, where everyone is spread out in rural homesteads, and the only thing to do in town is buy groceries, get your car fixed, or pay a ticket.

I looked through the empty storefronts, and up into the dark windows of the second floors, and inwardly thrilled at the emptiness of the abandoned town. It was nearing noon, and I might have been the only man in all the world. Even in prison, you aren't alone. The presence of the other convicts is always there—the press of them, the lonesome static of their human noises, the stink of bodies languishing in dry recycled air.

Two Pine was bereft of life. I was the most alone I'd ever been.

I checked the time on the dash clock and waited, watching the intersection and the road behind me. Ten minutes passed in silence, and not a single car appeared, from any direction.

Part of me wanted to just step out of the Stratus while it was still idling in park, and walk around the desolation like a post-apocalyptic scavenger. I wondered if the grocery store on the corner or the clothing shop a few doors down still had any artifacts within them, or if they'd been picked clean in the days before the last man rode out of town.

I put the Stratus back in drive and drifted past the last quarter-mile of buildings. A sun-bleached A&W was the final derelict. The old-fashioned speakers were still mounted beside each parking space, dumbly waiting for some soul to drive up and make a request.

Once I was past the edge of town, the marching forest returned. I gained speed and wondered why a tax lawyer and accountant like Paul Gullins would move out to an area where the tax base had been swept away.

*

"What the hell, Roarke?" she snapped in my ear. "Where'd you go?"

The GPS found Paul Gullins' driveway at the same time Savannah called me. I held the phone to my ear and rolled slowly up the gravel lane that wound into the woods. I passed a little wooden sign tapped into the earth at the side of Paul's lane, maybe twenty feet past the entrance.

In black letters, it read "PRIVATE: TRESPASSERS WILL BE SHOT ON SIGHT".

"I'm at Paul's," I answered. "We can spar when I get back."

A little silence from her after that. I could see the peak of a roof through the trees ahead. As I got nearer, I could see the house was big, made of logs and cedar shingles, with a sweeping wood deck all the way around it.

A red Chevy pickup was parked in the shade of a pine tree.

As soon as I spotted the Chevy, I stopped the car. I didn't think I was visible to anyone who might be looking out from inside the house, but if there was a human behind the tinted windows of the vehicle, they had a clear line of sight to me.

"Roarke, listen…"

"Maybe later," I said and turned off the cell.

I backed the Stratus up slowly until the gravel drive curved enough that the Chevy was no longer visible. I grabbed the Sig from the glove box, holstered it at the small of my back, and got out of the car. I didn't hear anything other than the click of insects in the woods, so I walked into the tree line.

When I crept closer to the house again, I could see the front door was standing wide open. I scanned the windows but there was nothing moving inside that I could see. I looked back at the door, at the little corner of hallway I could see beyond it.

I took my cell phone out again and dialed the number Savannah had given me for Paul Gullins. It rang three times.

On the fourth ring, a rifle shot cracked through the woods.

\*

I was already sprinting hard for the doorway when it registered that the gunshot had come from behind the house. The Sig was in my hand. I stared in all the windows at once, adrenaline surging, pushing me up onto the deck and inside.

I hugged the wall, checking corners, and resisted the urge to nudge the door shut behind me. If I needed out fast, the time it would take to yank it open could mean the difference between a bullet in the back and getting out whole.

Paul Gullins' house was all yuppie-rustic—lots of sturdy furniture that looked hand-crafted but was really just pricy inventory ordered through a catalog.

Nothing made a sound inside the house. It occurred to me that the rifle shot could simply have been a hunter straying too close to private property...hell, it could have been Paul taking a potshot at an out-of-season doe for all I knew.

I remembered the Chevy pick-up and pushed away the urge to lower my guard.

The kitchen was all stainless steel machinery and butcher block counters. On the big, restaurant-grade refrigerator, a pinned photo of Chelsea dressed in her track uniform and holding a little trophy up in her hands. Her head was cocked to one side, her smile bashful and hesitant around her braces. She looked awkward, guileless.

When I passed the window above the sink, I saw the body sprawled in the grass behind the house. It wasn't Chelsea. By the size and shape, I knew it was a man. I stood there looking at the dead man for only a moment—but that was one moment too long.

"Drop the pistol on the floor, tough guy."

A man's voice, full of easy authority. I didn't know was how he'd managed to get behind me so noiselessly.

"Do it now or I pull the trigger. Last warning."

I tossed the Sig. It clattered across the stone floor tiles.

"Good boy. You hold real still, just like that."

The dead man was Paul Gullins, I decided. Outside, the wind gusted, making the thin hair atop his head dance. I couldn't know if Chelsea was lying somewhere nearby in a similar, final pose. I'd only heard the one rifle shot. I clung to that fact and told myself she wasn't here or, if she was, she was alive and curled up in some impromptu hiding spot.

It was the most reassuring idea I could manage, so I held onto it until the sovereign man soundlessly closed the distance between us and pressed the barrel of his rifle into the small of my back. Low. He was holding the weapon down near his hip.

It was a loose, swaggering sort of thing to do. Stupid.

"You're a big son of a bitch," he said, jabbing the barrel into my back like it was an exclamation point. "Not a cop though, are you? What're you doing here?"

I took one fast step to the left, at the same time swinging my left arm back to slap the barrel away to the right. The rifle barked a round out into the air. A leaping fear ran up the length of me, but if I was shot my body didn't know it yet.

He was backing away, as startled by the gunshot as I was. Facing him now, I slapped the barrel a second time with my left hand, took a step, and buried my right fist in his mouth.

I felt a sharp biting in my hand. He didn't make a sound. His eyes went vacant, swimming in his head, and he crumpled to the floor. My hand felt like it had been stung by a wasp. Looking down at it, I saw one of his teeth was sunken into the flesh between two knuckles. I ignored it and snatched his rifle up off the floor.

It had a strap, so I slung it over my shoulder and retrieved my Sig from under the kitchen table. Through the glass slider door, I could better see Paul Gullins. A dark blotch stood out on the back of his white cotton shirt.

Behind me, a low moan.

I stood over him as he came around. Dressed all in camo. He had a full head of close-cropped black hair. His face was angular and tan, like scalpel-sculpted clay.

He blinked several times and squinted up at me. I pulled his tooth out of my hand and tossed it in the sink. It made a clattering noise as it disappeared into the mouth of the disposal.

"Get up on your feet," I said.

"Fuck you," he spat, then winced. His mouth was a red mess and he gingerly probed at it with one hand while he kept his eyes fixed on me.

"You swaggered too much. You should have put the barrel between my shoulder blades," I said. "Talk is talk. Kill is kill."

He curled his upper lip and a chuckle burbled out through the gap in his teeth.

"Yeah? Give me that rifle back and I'll give it another go."

"You had your chance. It's my turn now. Get on your feet."

He did, and I marched him out through the slider door. Close to me now, he stank of sweat; skunky, pungent, and dank. It hung all over him.

The deck back there had a table and chairs very similar to the room I'd rented at Home Among the Pines. I gestured for him to take a seat. I sat across from him and kept the Sig leveled at his torso.

"You ain't going to shoot me."

"Depends."

"You might be a big scary looking dude, sure. Doesn't mean you're a shooter. Maybe I can just stand up and walk out of here. You think?"

He put his hands on the arms of the chair, like he was going to push himself up. His eyes were full of his dare, moving back and forth between me and the Sig.

I leaned forward and set the Sig on the table between us. I settled back and watched the daring in his face become confusion, then understanding, and finally a sullen sort of doubt. He sat back down heavily and sneered.

"Bullshit," he whispered. "That's bullshit, bud."

"Then go for the gun."

"The hell I will. I saw how fast you are."

I shrugged and folded my hands over my stomach.

"Yeah, you did. But maybe you'll change your mind later. We can talk for a bit while you think it over."

"We've got shit-all to talk about."

"Where's the girl?"

"Which one? I know lots of girls."

I took the Sig up off the table, fast, and he flinched. I smashed the butt of the gun across his cheek. He yelped and threw his arms up to ward me off. I put the gun back on the table between us and settled back into my chair while he probed at his welting cheek.

"I guess I should have told you the rules," I said. "That was my mistake. Every time I ask you a question, you tell me the truth. If you don't, I give you a little tap like that. You're a reasonably tough man, probably. You can take a few of those, sure. But not too many. They'll add up fast. Pretty soon your face is going to start falling in on itself."

He was coming around now. I saw it in his eyes; the loss of challenge in them. He slouched, rubbed his cheek, and stared at the Sig.

"Or…" I said.

"Or?"

"Or you can end the game."

"Let you gun me down, is what you mean. I reach for it and you get to tell yourself it was self-defense, right? No, man. I ain't doing that."

"Where's the girl?"

He stared at me with a stubborn intensity, his jaw clenched shut. His whole body was rigid and he didn't blink.

"Where's the girl?"

He was ready for me to repeat what I'd done. Instead, I left the gun alone and pounced straight at him. He got his hands up. I pulled his arm down with my left hand and hammered him twice on the same spot where the gun butt had purpled his skin.

He howled under me and balled up. I shoved him back into his seat and sat back down.

"Where's the girl?"

Slowly, he un-balled. All the rigid resolve was gone. He slumped in his chair and stared at his hands. His cheek was split open, blood running down and mixing with the blood smeared around his mouth.

"The Reverend has her," he bleakly muttered. "How come you don't know that?"

"The Reverend?"

"Yeah."

"What's your name?"

He was quiet a beat, and I thought maybe we were going to have to go at it again. I was getting ready to snatch the gun up when he limply shrugged in surrender.

"Wade. Okay?"

"What's the Reverend's name?"

"Are you fucking serious?"

"Don't I seem serious, Wade?"

"Sure you do."

"So answer the question."

A whining guitar solo leapt into the air. Wade's breath hitched in his chest and he held suddenly still.

"Van Halen," I said, and leaned forward. "Panama, right?"

He stayed still, so I pulled open the Velcro flap over his breast pocket and plucked his cell phone out. The caller on the display read "002". I thumbed the green answer tab, the guitar solo died, and I settled back down.

"I only want the girl," I said into the phone.

"Wade?"

"Hold on," I said. "I'll get him."

I held the phone out between us. Wade looked at me warily, like it was a trick. Eventually, he reached out and took the phone, careful to move slowly.

Careful to make it clear he wasn't going for the gun.

"The hell do you want me to say?" he whispered.

I shrugged. He scowled and held the phone to his ear.

"Hey. I don't know. Just some guy. Yeah, right here. Well I guess he drove. Hell, I don't *know*."

I yawned, Wade's side of the conversation reminding me that it had been a long time since I'd slept. I didn't feel tired but I knew that was just adrenaline from being jumped in the kitchen.

Somewhere in the woods behind us, a bird called out. Another answered. They began repeating it again and again, the first one plaintive, as if playing the avian version of 'Marco Polo' with the second.

Wade's face reddened and his voice dropped an octave.

"Because he's holding a fucking gun on me. Huh? I don't *know*. He's asking about the girl. Uh-huh. Yeah, okay. Hold on."

Wade held the phone out. His cheek had swollen up something fierce, and the skin under that eye was starting to go purple.

"He wants to talk to you."

"Who?"

"The Reverend."

I took the cell and watched Wade lean back. He folded his hands in his lap and looked at his feet. Bloodied up and cowed as he was, I might have felt some sympathy for him if Paul Gullins wasn't sprawled back-shot and dead out on the lawn.

"Give me the girl and I go away," I said into the phone.

"Well if this isn't a pickle," the Reverend answered. His voice was lilting. It had a genteel twang in it that made me think of a southern gentleman dressed all in white, sipping sweet tea on his porch and lamenting the loss of free labor.

"All I want is Chelsea Gullins," I said. "Nothing else."

The Reverend chuckled good-naturedly in my ear.

"Well, shoot. You get to the point in a direct fashion, don't you?"

"Is Chelsea alive?"

"What's your name, friend?"

"Roarke. Is she alive? She needs to be."

"Roarke, my name's Reverend Wayland Graves. Now how about we get together, you and me, and talk this out face-to-face like two men ought to do."

"Or maybe I just call the cops and let them come get your friend here."

Again, the easy-going chuckle in my ear, like we were side-by-side on his porch, jawing about the weather or politics.

"Hell, Roarke, you ain't going to do that. No, sir. You didn't drive all the way up here just to get the law involved."

84

"Paul Gullins being a dead body might've changed my plans, Reverend."

"Nah. You're Savannah's man, ain't you? Sure you are. That little peach isn't going to tolerate any lawmen. Unless you're the sort to sell out your meal ticket. Naw, let's not carry on about the law no more. Let's figure out how we both get what we want."

Across from me, Wade wasn't stirring at all. He wasn't touching his chin or his cheek. His hands were flat on his knees. Only his eyes moved. They darted here and there, always coming back to the pistol on the table. He'd stare at it, catch himself, and look quickly away.

It was just a matter of time.

"Roarke?"

"I'm still here, Reverend."

"What we need is a meeting. We'll do it tonight. Just the two of us. So we can sort this nasty business out."

I opened my mouth to answer him.

Wade went for the gun.

# F O U R

He tensed for just a second before lunging and that was all the telegraphing I needed.

I swept the Sig away, knocking it to the deck's floor as he furiously groped for it. His eyes boggled, but he kept on with his forward motion, too committed to stop now. I brushed his clawing hands out of my eyes and gave him another straight punch in the mouth. He didn't lose any more teeth, but his lips both split wide like overripe fruit.

He collapsed, spent and dazed. I stood over him long enough to watch his eyes gloss over into unconsciousness, then picked the Sig up off the floor.

Behind me, the cell phone was lying next to my chair where I'd dropped it as soon as I knew Wade was making a go at the Sig.

I waited a beat, then picked up the cell and put it to my ear.

"Still there?"

"Is Wade alright?" he said, all of his easy friendliness gone. "What was that?"

"Your man seems like a slow learner, Reverend."

He was silent for a little while and I figured he was weighing the situation in his head. I didn't mind. I didn't have anywhere else to be.

Wade made a low, incoherent noise at my feet. The Reverend cleared his throat, his tone conciliatory.

"I reckon we really should get together. Don't you? We can sort this out without any more violence. I want you to have the girl. I do. I know her mama must be beside herself. But I need something in return."

"Okay."

"I need something from that willful blonde girl sent you up this way. Something rather vital to my interests."

I thought about Savannah's seduction game with me, and about the go-bag she'd brought with her. With a new passport and a small fortune in bills, she was ready to run. I just didn't know where or why.

"What is it you need?" I said.

Silence.

"Reverend?"

"Hmm? Oh. Hold on just a tick, won't you?" All easy, warm molasses again.

Wade coughed a wad of blood onto the deck and rolled sluggishly onto his side. I saw myself in the glass slider door, standing over him. Behind me, Paul Gullins on the lawn and the pine forest beyond that. I listened for the two birds that had been calling to one another earlier, but there was only silence.

The Reverend's twang came back to me.

"I do apologize for that. I know we're talking serious business here."

"What is it you need from Savannah?"

"Well, that's the thing. I think I'll just go on down there and get it from her directly, if you don't mind. You strike me as a volatile sort. No offense intended there. I can be a bit volatile myself, mind you. But a man who can handle Wade as easily as you seem to have done…well, that's a man I'd just as soon not have in the same room with me."

"You're wasting my time," I snarled.

"And that's a crying shame," he agreed with a sympathetic cluck of his tongue. "Seeing as how you don't have any time left."

In the slider door, a reflected spot of light from within the tree line. Sunlight on glass.

I managed to drop forward and down when the crack of the rifle leapt up out of the forest. The slider door held for a split second as a sheet of spider-webbed glass, then plunged, a glittering cascade. I lunged through it as it came down over my shoulders and back, an animal urgency hurling me through, onto the kitchen floor.

Another whip snap sound from outside. A corner of the butcher block counter above me splintered and flew apart.

I got up to my hands and knees, the open front door of the house the only thing in my mind. I started moving forward to get around the island counter when Wade wrapped his arms around my right ankle. He bear hugged my leg and stared up at me: within that mask of blood and purpled, swollen skin, a determination in his eyes to hold me there until the assassin in the woods could finish his job.

A third shot rang out and a bullet buried itself in the cabinet inches above my head.

Wade hissed something that might have been "son of a bitch" through his mashed and broken mouth. Pink saliva bubbled out after it.

I pointed the Sig at the ruin of his face.

I pulled the trigger.

A hideous transformation.

He slumped, dead, and I jerked out of his grasp. A fourth rifle shot snapped through the air. I didn't know where it landed. I was pushing forward, past the kitchen. In the living room, I got to my feet again and sprinted until I was out of the house.

The lawn sloped down to the wood line and I didn't slow. If there were more shooters positioned around the house, they were free to take their shots. I barreled on, into the pine, pushing through brush and briar, the wild apprehension of having a scope trained on my back keeping me at full throttle.

The fear didn't abate until I was behind the wheel of the Stratus and grinding gravel in reverse. I whipped out onto the road and came to a stop. The world was suddenly silent again. Nothing moved in either direction down the road, and the driveway to my right was empty.

I saw Wade's face as I killed him, the determination in his eyes winking out as he came to an end. I heard my father's admonition in the darkness of night, his verdict as to what had undone me.

"You tried to save the girl."

I put the car in drive and moved forward.

A quarter of a mile down the road a police car was pulled up into the weeds on the shoulder. I rolled slowly past it, the Sig in my lap, my right hand holding it, ready to go.

It was a nineties-era Crown Vic that was so heavily coated in road dust that I would have believed it if someone told me it hadn't been washed since rolling off the assembly line. Its body was beaten and dented. Some violent event in its history had left it with only one headlight, the other nothing but a dark socket ringed in crumpled metal. The faded police markings were green and read "Two Pine Police".

As I rolled past, I kept my eye on it the whole way. It was empty and there was no sign of anyone around.

90

Across the back of the filthy old beast, along the length of the bumper, someone had stenciled a legend in bright red paint. The letters had run like bloody wounds, but I could still read what it said.

*THE LAST WATCHMAN STILL RIDES.*

I sped up and let the advancing rows of pine on either side of me dissolve the adrenal fear. My hands steadied and I grew calmer the farther I got from the assassin's rifle scope.

I'd gone three miles when the gunshot wound below my right shoulder announced itself. It came on all at once, a throbbing agony. His first shot, the one that had shattered the slider door, hadn't entirely missed its mark.

I groaned against the pain and mashed the accelerator down.

*

When I shuffled into the cabin, Savannah was in the little kitchenette wearing a pair of slim-tailored jeans and a red t-shirt cut high enough to leave her pierced belly button bare. Her hair was down, cascading over her shoulders. She was swirling a metal whisk around in a large ceramic bowl and looked up with a ready, expectant smile.

It died when she got a look at me.

"Oh my God. Roarke. What happened to you?"

The big candles Rhonda and her partner had decorated the place with were all lit, lending a warm glow to the living room. Something sweet was baking, a comforting scent filling the place.

I sat heavily in one of the cushioned pine-frame chairs and winced as pain flared through my right arm. Savannah stood over me, fretful, like she wanted to reach out and touch me but didn't know if she should.

"I don't have Chelsea," I said. "So the happy homemaker thing you've got going here is for nothing. The candles are a nice touch, though. Very calming. I'm sure they would have put her at ease. Enough to be manageable, anyway."

It all slid over her without effect. She knelt down on her knees and put her hands on top of mine. I stared into her lovely face, grown lovelier with faux concern.

I wanted to slap her and demand answers.

I wanted to taste her and hold her against me.

"You're bleeding," she whispered. "Roarke, what happened? Is Chelsea alright?"

"I think so. That smells good. What is it?"

"Orange cake. Roarke, you're bleeding."

"Where'd you get orange cake?"

"They have a little store attached to the office. It doesn't matter. Talk to me. What can I do?"

I leaned forward enough to unbutton and shrug out of the left sleeve of my shirt. I let out a grunt when I started to try and do the same for the right. She took hold of the collar and gently began pulling the shirt down and off me.

"Get me a mirror," I said, watching her ball the bloody shirt up. She put it against the wound and guided my other hand over to it. I nodded and pressed down despite the surge of bright pain that shot through me.

I watched her. She was calm, her lovely mouth a straight and focused line. There was no panic in her as she marched away to find a mirror.

She came back with a round cosmetics mirror and held it for me so I could get a clear view of what the Last Watchman's bullet had done to me. The wound was a freely-bleeding mess, but relief washed through me as soon as I could see its reflection. The rifle shot had gone in a few inches south of my shoulder, shallow enough to miss the bone, and come out again before shattering the glass slider.

There was torn muscle for certain, and two ugly holes that needed to be sewn shut, but the bone was spared. I pressed the ruined shirt back over the wound and closed my eyes. Fatigue was barreling down into me.

"Roarke, what do you need?"

"Hard liquor."

"Don't kid."

"And needle and thread. Understand?"

I forced my eyes open to see if she did.

"You need a doctor," she corrected.

"There are two dead men at Paul's. He's one of them. The other has a bullet from my gun inside his skull or in the wall. Personally, I'm fine explaining all that to a cop. Are *you*?"

Savannah didn't contemplate it for long. She shook her head once, then leaned in and kissed me. Lightly at first, then harder. Her fingers ran over my scalp, brushing my hair back off my forehead. Her lips were soft and full, the way you dream a woman's mouth will feel, and I kissed her back even though I knew her seduction was to bind me closer to her. It was little more than tugging a dog's leash to remind it of the order of things.

I pushed the idea away and breathed her in, drunk on her.

It was over too soon. She whispered, "I'll be fast", and marched out of the cabin with her purse slung over one shoulder. I watched her leave, heard her lock the door behind her, and closed my eyes.

The pumping throb in my shoulder became the whole world.

Soon even that fell away, pulling me down with it.

# FIVE

Dreams of madness tore themselves into pieces as I came awake.

Fragments lingered.

The beaten police cruiser creeping silently through the abandoned crossroads of Two Pine. A shadow lurked behind the wheel. When I tried to see the driver, the shadow around him only deepened. Chelsea running, a pale blur in her track uniform…running, running, but never getting farther away. The Last Watchman hounding her, the single eye of his steel steed casting a hellish light across the blacktop. An engine roar and Chelsea running in place, her blonde hair whipping, her head turning to stare at me. Savannah's face, smiling, blood in the spaces between her teeth.

My father's voice rumbling out of the murderous shadow behind the wheel.

"I have no sympathy in me. Not a drop."

I blinked several times until the dream world was out of my eyes. The pain in my shoulder was a muted throb, steady and rhythmic but bearable. I sat up in the bed, giving myself time to let reality sink in. I was in my bedroom in the rented cabin. A moose head was hanging on the wall across from me, just above a flat screen television. Its glossy brown eyes looked like buttons. Beyond the open door, I could see a corner of the living room. As I watched, Rhonda's short, robust form crossed from the kitchen to the back of the living room. She had a cutting board heaped with meat in her hands. I heard the slider whisper open, then shut. Female voices sprang to life outside, chattering incomprehensibly.

I got on my feet and went to stare at myself in the bathroom's mirror. Someone had stripped me down to my boxers. My shoulder and upper bicep were neatly wrapped in white bandage. I stared at it for a little while as the smell of cooking meat began to waft around the room.

Further down, my stomach was a mass of scar tissue. I'd killed Freddie Esposito, but not before he left a permanent signature on my flesh.

*'Snakes,'* I thought. *'Looks like a nest of little white snakes.'*

I chuckled and watched a wide smile bloom in the mirror. That's when it registered that I was drugged. The muted pain and the detached musing about the mass of scars across my abdomen had failed to alert me of the opiate-fog.

But the smile; the goofy, unabashed smile…that was foreign enough to get through to me. I was pumped full of something. I experienced maybe two seconds of alarm at the realization before the concern melted away and was forgotten.

A minute later, I was sitting out on the deck wearing nothing but my undershorts and a big, friendly grin for the three women whose conversation died all at once as they watched me appear. To their credit, none of them laughed out loud.

They fed me steak and glasses of ice water. Rhonda's partner, Sharon, was mostly silent, even after I told her I liked her short, spiky blonde hair. At some point I admitted I liked lesbians, but "not in a sexist way", and there was a chilly argument between the couple. Whatever was said after that was just a blur of feel-good on my end of things, a cottony state of disconnect while I happily chewed steak and asked for beers they refused to get for me.

At some point, a decision must have been reached by the three of them because I found myself being helped back to the bed. Rhonda and Savannah were each supporting an arm. I craned my head around and told the sour-faced Sharon that I really *did* like her hair a lot. I saw her roll her eyes and then I was plunging back down onto the mattress.

The women went away, their chatter resumed outside, and I was sure we were all great friends as I sank back into the ether.

\*

97

It was dark when I woke again. Savannah was curled up beside me, still dressed in the clothes she'd been wearing earlier. Her hair smelled like the smoke from the grill Rhonda had been overseeing. I shifted, trying to ease off the bed without waking her. Her eyes opened and she grinned.

"I wasn't sleeping," she said.

"What time is it?"

"I don't know. Really late."

In the bathroom, I got a fresh look at myself. The pain killer haze was dissipated. My arm ached, but when I began raising it and rotating it around, the pain was manageable. Savannah appeared in the doorway, crossing her bare feet at the ankles and leaning her weight against the jam.

"Can I get you anything?" she said.

"No."

I ran my hand over my stubbled jaw and reached for my little toiletry bag on the counter. She rushed in and snatched it up. She smiled into my frown as she fished out the razor and travel-sized bottle of shaving lotion I'd packed.

"Let me, okay?"

"I can manage it."

She hopped up on the counter, resting her butt on the edge, her knees on either side of me. She dabbed some of the shaving lotion into her palm and wrapped her legs around the small of my back, pulling me closer.

"You're right handed," she teased. "You'd cut yourself. I want to anyway."

She began rubbing the lotion on my cheeks and chin. Her fingers were soft and small. Her belly ring was a sapphire. She saw me staring at it.

"You like it," she said, not a question.

"I guess I do."

"You like *me*."

"The jury's still out, Savannah."

"Hush. Don't move."

She started running the razor carefully over my skin, pausing occasionally to lean around and wash it off in the sink. This close to her, and with nothing to do but stare, I noticed for the first time a light array of freckles across the bridge of her nose and just under her eyes. She nibbled her lower lip as she scraped under my chin. Her teeth were small, even, and very white.

"What did Paul say?" she asked, not pausing, like it was an off-hand and trivial question. I reminded myself about her go-bag and what the Reverend had said about her. I forced myself to stop looking at her.

"Nothing. He was dead."

"Who killed him?"

"A guy named Wade. You know him?"

"Uh-uh. Wade is who you shot then?"

"Yeah."

"And he shot you?"

"No. Someone else did. I don't know who."

I saw the Last Watchman again as he'd appeared in my dream—a shadow behind the wheel of his roaring patrol cruiser. He'd have had me, whoever he was, if I hadn't caught the shine of sunlight off his rifle's scope. I wondered who he was and what the legend he'd painted meant.

When she was done, Savannah wet a hand towel with hot water until steam was rising out of it, then began pressing it against my cheeks. I closed my eyes and marveled at how luxurious it felt. I didn't bother to tell her she'd performed the operation of shaving in reverse, for fear she'd stop.

"You put on quite a show for Rhonda and Sharon, you know."

"What did you give me?"

"I gave you a couple pain killers."

"What were they?"

"OxyContin. Donna gave them to me for a headache once. Which is nuts. They're way too strong for me. Are you mad?"

"No. You bandaged the wound, too?"

She made a scoffing sound.

"Yeah, *right*. No, Rhonda did. She seemed to know exactly what to do. I like her. Sharon too, but Rhonda more. They were guessing how you got all those scars on your belly. Rhonda thinks you were mauled by a bear or a big cat. Sharon said she thinks you did it to yourself and that you have mental problems.

100

It didn't help your cause when you started talking about approving of lesbians. I don't think they're open about it. At least not with half naked, muscle-bound men."

"I acted like an ass, I guess."

"You weren't so bad. I thought it was cute."

The towel was losing its warmth. Savannah took it away and I felt her legs tighten, pulling me in closer to her. Her lips found mine and we kissed for a long moment.

When she drew away, I opened my eyes. She pulled her top up over her shoulders and tossed it in a corner. Her breasts were small and pert and perfect. Constellations of pale freckles dotted her shoulders.

"You owe me," she said, matter of fact.

"How's that?"

"Let's see…" She started ticking off fingers as she counted. "I gave you a stellar orgasm in the car. I kissed you and got you emergency medical help. I served you steak when you were high. I shaved you very expertly. And I kissed you again. You owe me."

She hopped off the counter and slid out of her pants. She stood there in the doorway naked, her head cocked to one side, letting me stare at the slim, milky perfection of her. The sight of her was doing its job-- I felt my pulse leaping ahead. The wound under my shoulder flared back to life, but I didn't care.

"Come on," she said and held out a beckoning hand.

I wanted to. God, I wanted to.

"Savannah…"

My voice was a growl; the effect she had on me.

"Mmm. I like to hear you say my name. I'll say yours, too. Over and over again."

"It isn't that simple. I have a lot of questions."

"So ask them," she sighed. She flipped her hair in an arc as she spun and paced into the bedroom. "But do it after we fuck."

I watched the swing of her hips as she walked away. I took one step, ready to surrender to her. In the mirror, I saw myself standing there. The white bandages wrapped tightly around the gunshot wound. The nest of scars across my abdomen.

"You tried to save the girl," the stranger who said he was my father had told me, there in the darkness of the prison yard. He'd said it with amused contempt, as if that simple statement could explain my doom.

I wanted to push him away, push it all away, and just sink into her. I could lose myself inside her, I knew. I could just get drunk on all her charms and see where she guided me next.

But Chelsea was still running in place in my fragmented nightmare, running, but never getting away. The shadow behind the wheel of the Last Watchman's hellish cruiser was my father, warning me away from the girl—warning me to be like him, to cut off all sentiment and let nothing inside that might lash out or wound.

I walked into the bedroom.

Savannah was splayed across the sheets on her side, watching me with a playful smirk.

I reached down, snagged my pants off the floor and started putting them on.

"You're kidding," she said.

"I've got questions. And you're going to answer them or I call the cops and wave goodbye to whatever all this is."

Her face got hard, turning to marble. She pulled the sheet up over her, suddenly modest now that it was clear I wasn't in the market for what she was selling.

"You're not going to do that."

I grabbed a red short-sleeve shirt from out of my bag and carefully guided it up over my right arm, then all the way on.

"Go ahead and put on some clothes," I told her. "When you're done, you can make us both something to eat while we talk about what exactly it is Reverend Graves thinks you owe him."

Her lip curled into a snarl and she got to her feet, the sheet held around her.

"Screw you," she hissed and started to march past me, her chin up in the air as if her dignity had something to do with all of this. I grabbed her arm as she passed, bringing her up short.

Fast, without any hesitation, she lashed out. Her palm slapped against the bandages on my arm and a white wall of pain appeared there.

103

"Get your hands off me," she spat, and raised her hand back as if to strike out again.

I yanked the sheet away from her and watched her reflexively cover herself with her hands. The agony in my arm was as real as anything had ever been, but I kept on despite it, letting my outrage push through.

I blinked and she was against the wall, my left hand pinning her there, fingers splayed wide just above her breasts. Fear finally appeared in her eyes, as if she were seeing me for the first time. I sucked a deep gale of air in through my nose, clenched my teeth down, and punched the wall beside her head with my right fist.

Drywall fell in, making a hole. She cried out in surprise. My arm went dead, the pain spiking past the point where it could be processed.

"You see me?" I whispered, our eyes locked.

"What...?"

"Do you *see* me?"

She swallowed and nodded her head. I felt my chest heaving, the heart within it thundering a furious beat.

"Say it."

"I see you."

She did. It was there in her unblinking, frozen expression. Whatever breed of attack dog she thought she'd bought, I wasn't it. I was something else. She was trembling under that realization, pale and naked and beautiful beneath my hand.

I let go of her and tangled my fingers in her hair. When I kissed her, her lips pressed tight against one another and her hands balled into fists against my chest. She tried to squirm away and muttered something I couldn't hear over the thrum of blood in my ears.

I lifted her up off her feet by her buttocks and brought us both down on the bed. The wound was furiously alive, but the pain it pumped was a fuel now, feeding the roar of blood running through me. I was between her, spreading her thighs with mine and pinning her wrists to the mattress with my hands.

She started to say something again, but it drowned away as I kissed her. I drank like that for a long moment, holding off as long as I could. She turned her head to the side, breaking the connection, and whispered thickly in my ear.

"Do it, bastard. What are you scared of? Do it."

I groaned and she pulled her hands free. She watched me, not blinking, as she jerked my fly open and tugged me out.

"Do it with this, bastard," she dared, and squeezed down hard. I groaned again and pushed the full length of myself inside her.

Savannah cried out and bit down on my ear. Her hips writhed under me and I obeyed, matching the rhythm she dictated. Our hands slipped together, fingers intertwined. Soon, she was gasping again, shuddering.

"Roarke."

I groaned at the sound of her voice, at the exquisite vision of her beneath me, naked and prone.

She said it again.

"Roarke. Bastard."

Her eyes went vacant, sightless. I didn't slow as she came. She rose and crested with the orgasm, and I kept on. She whispered a plea.

I kept on.

*

Morning carried the rich smell of cooking sausage to me.

Blood on the sheet beneath my arm. I sat up and inspected the bandages. They were hard and dark, crusted over. However our exertions had re-opened the injury, it seemed to have closed off again. Outside the room, I could hear the sizzle of the meat in a skillet. A cupboard door opened and shut.

I showered, careful to keep the bandaged area out of the water spray. I dressed in jeans and a blue cotton dress shirt, rich snapshots of Savannah playing through my mind the whole time. I heard her say my name again, just before she began to tremble under me.

I took a moment, just standing there and knowing she was one room away. She was out there, and she'd be every bit as beautiful as she had been in the night. I pushed her out of my eyes and told myself it couldn't go the same as it had last night. I couldn't afford to fall back into her and get lost.

Chelsea couldn't afford that.

I stared at the hole my fist had made in the wall. Letting my emotions run away with me around her was a sure-fire way to end up in bed again, or dumbly following her lead.

The knuckles of my right hand were raw and skinned. I flexed my fingers and felt ashamed. I saw her as I yanked the sheet away, starkly naked, vulnerable. I felt the blood rushing again, the hunger to sink into her and to shake answers out of her both reviving themselves inside me.

Before either impulse could grow strong, I tamped it down and pictured myself standing in Chelsea's little bedroom closest, framed in the mirror.

*'smile it won't always be like this.'*

I made my face a blank and walked out into the living room.

\*

Sharon was standing at the stove flipping sausage patties. She was lean in an athletic way, with a sturdy frame. She had on sandals, khaki shorts, and a white cotton t-shirt. Her calves were round balls of muscle and she was very tan, which made her bleach-blond shock of spiked hair stand out all the more.

107

She glanced at me as I came into view and the wrinkles at the corners of her eyes and mouth told me she was middle-aged, though everything else about her looked young and hearty.

"Where's Savannah?" I said.

Sharon started using the spatula to spoon sausage patties out onto a plate that had a sheet of paper towel laid over it.

"Rhonda took her to Grayling," she said. "They think you need more supplies to tend to that gunshot wound." She turned off the burner and fixed me with a flat, challenging stare. "I told them to call the sheriff to haul your ass away, let him worry about your boo-boo. Since you're still on my property, I guess you can figure out who won that argument."

She set the plate of sausage on the counter that separated the living room from the kitchen. I sat on a stool.

"Why the sheriff?" I said. "Why not the Two Pine P.D.?"

A suspicious frown passed over her face. She wiped her hands on a little green cloth towel and said "You take anything with your coffee?"

"Cream and sugar."

She poured out two mugs and soon we were sitting across from each other, nibbling sausage and sipping some sort of French roast. Her nails were shorter than mine and looked ragged, like they'd just been chewed down. I looked for other signs of nervousness in her, but found none. Her arms had the sort of taut muscle that comes from hard work. She had piercing holes in her ears, but no earrings or any other jewelry except a simple silver band around her wedding finger. The watch on that wrist was black, big, and looked like it could probably tell me the barometric pressure and wind speed.

"Two Pine is dead," she said after a while. "They don't have a police department. They don't have anything, since there is no 'they' anymore."

"But the Last Watchman still rides," I said. "Doesn't he?"

I watched the slow crawl of apprehension across her face. Her eyes hardened, and I couldn't tell if it was fear or anger that my words had elicited. Either way, the mention of the blood red legend scrawled across the shooter's bumper seemed to push her to a decision. Sharon set her fork down, folded her hands in front of her, and looked me in the eye.

"The two of you are leaving today," she said. "Rhonda's bringing back drywall and mud for that hole you made in my wall. When you're done patching it, I want you and Blondie Sweet Tits out of here. I don't know if I can make it any clearer that you're not welcome."

"Seems pretty clear," I said and sipped the coffee. "I'll fix the wall."

"Uh-huh. So you're that kind of man? Is that her thing, too? Or do you get tough with every woman you're around?"

I saw Savannah pressed against the wall, her expression a mixture of apprehension and arousal, trembling, waiting for me to just give in.

"It wasn't like that."

"If you give me any shit, I *will* call the Sheriff."

"You won't need to. I'm going to see him as soon as we're done eating."

I washed the dishes and the skillet in the sink while she watched me in silence from her stool. Outside the little window above the sink, the morning sky was clear and vibrant.

I put on my shoes, got my keys, and opened the front door.

"I apologize about the wall," I told her. "And about anything I might have said out on the deck. I wasn't myself."

She didn't seem to know how to take that, because she just kind of shook her head in bewilderment and shrugged her shoulders.

"What are you doing up here, exactly?" she asked. "The blonde makes up pleasant lies when I ask. She says you think a hunter took a wild shot and it just happened to hit you when you were taking a leak on the side of the road. Which is bullshit. And you aren't honeymooners. So what are you?"

"Out of your hair. Thanks for breakfast."

It didn't satisfy her, but there was nothing I could do about that. I closed the door behind me and went off to find the Sheriff

110

so I could tell him I'd shot one of his citizens in the head point blank.

# S I X

I found the Crawford County Library and paid for a couple dollars' worth of time on one of their computers.

The internet has made the notion of privacy quaint, like the stories old people tell about getting a gallon of gas for ten cents or how milk used to be dropped off on the porch in little glass bottles. Youth may nod along politely to the sentiment, but it's hard to feel a sense of loss for something you never had.

I'm no exception to the rule that everyone, to varying degrees, can be found out on the web. More than a dozen papers and their accompanying websites ran a blurb or a story about Freddie Esposito dying in the Honey Horn bar. The Michigan Department of Correction's OTIS prisoner databank had my intake photo and my criminal conviction up for public consumption until that conviction was overturned three years later. The appeal was big news again because it highlighted police corruption in Detroit.

My firing from the parole officer gig was covered on some of the tackier Detroit news outfits because it involved me, the killer who'd won his freedom and sued the city for a jackpot. One

Detroit blog ran me as their 'D-Town Hero of the Month', as if trying to squeeze the life out of a child molester was something all potential parole agents should have to perform before getting hired.

Anyone who was curious about me would find a digital mosaic that, viewed as a whole from a distance, suggested a highly volatile and dangerous human being.

Seated in front of one of the library's computers, I began looking for whatever was out there for a Reverend Wayland Graves. I wondered if he'd had anyone do the same search on me since his failed attempt to have me taken out of the picture. Did he know who he had tried to kill?

I hoped so. I hoped he found it all, and that it gave him some pause to think that I was out there in the world with his name on my mind.

\*

A narrow, slope-shouldered man with a flesh-colored hearing aide in one ear greeted me at the service desk of the county recorder and assessor's office. When he looked up, I saw that one of his eyes didn't track with the other, the pupil steadfastly refusing to stop loitering in the corner.

Once I'd asked to see the survey maps for several parcels of land in Two Pine, he had me sign in on a little clipboard.

"How long do you think you'll need?"

"A couple hours at the most."

"You know, we're on-line. You can find it all on our site. It's a lot easier that way if you want to print maps."

I didn't get the impression he was trying to shoo me away, so much as fill me in on what he saw as common knowledge.

"I'm an old-fashioned guy," I said and smiled before adding, "I won't be troubling you to make any duplicates."

"That's fine. No trouble."

He led me behind the desk, down a short hall, and into a room filled with several large filing cabinets. The drawers were long and deep, designed to hold over-sized property maps without the need to fold them or roll them up.

The clerk pointed at a large three-ring binder stuffed full of pages, sitting on one of the cabinets.

"That's the master index," he said. "It has every plot in the county. But if you have some street addresses, I can probably find what you need a lot quicker for you."

"Nah, I'll be fine. The hunt is half the fun."

He nodded absently, seeming to notice my arm for the first time. He stared for a beat, frowning.

"You're bleeding, mister."

"It looks worse than it is."

"What, um...how'd that happen?"

"Kicked by a mule."

"You're kidding."

"He's an old mule. Name's Reggie. Stubborn as a cuss."

He didn't look particularly convinced, but he nodded again and walked out of the room. I read through the index's legend and instructions for a few minutes. Soon enough I was pulling maps out of drawers and looking them over. A church and its plot on the eastern outskirts of what used to be the township of Two Pine. Two homesteads, one near the abandoned town center I'd driven through yesterday, the second out in the rural deep near the church.

A vast ocean of state-owned forest abutted that second homestead, the Reverend's. That state forest in turn abutted the county-sized Huron National Forest. I'd already printed out trail guides and a few mini-maps I could find online regarding the state land. Most of it, though, was utterly untouched, with no ready maps or trails to be had. Serious hunters likely knew that land well enough. The sort of guys who hike a full day away from civilization, on the look-out for good swamp land where an ancient, wary buck might at long last be felled.

I carefully photographed all the maps with my cell phone's camera, holding it close and doing a segment at a time. When I was done, I slipped the maps back where they belonged and strolled back out to the front desk.

The clerk looked up from his computer.

"That was fast."

"Thanks for the help," I told him and walked outside.

It was time to bring the cops into this.

*

I pulled into a strip-mall's parking lot across the street from the county courthouse and the Sheriff's office. I felt a sick little thrill in the pit of my stomach over the very real prospect that I wouldn't be walking free from either building any time soon.

I saw Wade again, one side of his face swollen and purpled, his mouth a smear of blood. I hadn't hesitated to pull the trigger on him. I'd watched him die in an instant and moved on, animated with white wild terror that any moment a rifle shot would cut all my wires and turn the world off.

I'd been poking around my interior ever since for a hint of remorse over killing Wade, doing it unconsciously, like a tongue that can't stop prodding a rotten tooth. But there was nothing there, at least not yet. Instead, I felt only vaguely energized. Not even the opiate fog of the pill Savannah had given me was able to fully dull the electric hyper-reality that had descended on me after escaping Paul Gullins' house. I'd fought through that fog enough to scarf down heaps of red meat while babbling enthusiastic nonsense at the women around me. I'd raged against Savannah's duplicity and pounded a hole in a wall with an arm

116

that should have been as useless as dead wood. I'd taken her on the bed, furious and frenzied.

It had been as clear a case of legal self-defense as I was ever likely to see. Wade had murdered Paul Gullins and held a gun on me. When a second gunman took aim, he'd done his best to pin me down and give the Last Watchman a clean shot.

Still, knowing a thing to be true was cold comfort in the face of convincing a bunch of cops of the truth of it. I was a stranger from the infamous pit of Detroit, one whose incarceration would still show up when they ran me through the Law Enforcement Information Network. And Wade? Wade was a local boy. One of theirs, to at least some extent.

I stashed my cell phone and my keys in the glove box with the Sig and got out of the car. If I was getting caged for killing Wade, they'd get me, the clothes on my back, and nothing else.

*

The deputy behind the service window had a long face, made longer with the boredom that comes from being fixed to the same spot for an entire shift. When I asked to see the Sheriff he wanted to know what it was about.

"I need to report a crime."

"That's vague. What's wrong with your arm?"

"I fell down a well. Is the Sheriff in?"

117

He wasn't, but the long-faced deputy said he could have me talk to someone else. He had me empty my pockets and walk through a metal detector before he buzzed me past the front desk and lead me down a short hallway covered in cork boards that were plastered with all sorts of the missives and memos a modern bureaucracy generates. We turned left and he had me hold up while he rapped his knuckles on an office door and peeked inside.

"Got a guy wants to report a crime."

"Alright."

The deputy made a slight ushering gesture and walked off. I stepped into the office.

The man behind the desk was obscured in the bright afternoon sunlight pouring in through the window behind him. He raised an arm toward the chair across from him, so I sat down. The sun disappeared behind his head and I could see him better.

His department uniform was cleanly starched and ironed. The man inside it was long and lean, with that tight and compact shape that suggested a practiced, dedicated fitness routine. His face was all hard edges and straight lines that suggested he rarely smiled. His hair was gray and cropped into a rigid flat top. His glasses had thick frames, like the ones the military issues.

I glanced at the framed articles hanging on the wall around him and noted several of them that featured him, younger, in Marine dress. Others were more recent photos in his sheriff's

118

department dress uniform. He was alone in all the photos I could spy.

"You have a wound," he said, without alarm. His voice was even and inflectionless, almost mechanical. His eyes were gray, flat, with no hint of who lay behind them.

"I was shot."

"That doesn't look like a hospital job. You're still bleeding, I think."

I glanced down at the red wrap around my arm. That arm had stiffened considerably since I woke, and I knew punching the wall was finally yielding its reward: the wound flared with a stinging ache whenever I attempted to move the arm.

"It'll be fine for now," I said. "I need to fill you all in on some killings. And a kidnapping."

"You do?"

"Yeah. They happened yesterday out in Two Pine. My name's Roarke."

I produced my wallet, pulled my business card, and held it across the desk toward him. He stared at me a moment while I held it out between us, his expression utterly impassive. Finally, he leaned forward and took the card from me. As he leaned in I could read the little metal nameplate above his breast pocket. *Dpty Rezner.*

He scanned the card I'd given him without any real sign of interest and handed it back to me. His nails were clipped short and clean.

"This business with the killings, you say they happened yesterday?"

"That's right. In the afternoon."

"Why are you only reporting it now?"

"I was shot. I needed to have it tended."

"But not at a hospital. Who patched you up?"

I could feel myself getting irritated, but I kept it off my face and out of my voice. There is no profit in getting blustery with the police. If his questions eventually lead to what really mattered, I could go along with it.

"I did," I said. There was no reason to mention Rhonda, or risk roping her into the possibility of being charged as an accomplice after-the-fact, if that was how things were going to turn. "It was shallow and didn't touch the bone."

"Where'd you learn to tend a wound?"

"In the Marines."

"You're a Marine?"

*Are*. Not *were*. The general rule is 'once a Marine, always a Marine'.

"Yeah."

"But now you're out?"

"Yeah."

120

"What've you been doing since then?"

"Different things. Why?"

He rubbed idly at his chin and his eyes narrowed, appraising.

"Way you hold yourself," he said. "Way you stare. I see it on guys. You know what I'm saying. Don't you?"

I kept staring, stubborn, unwilling to be the one who put it out in the air.

"You've been in prison," he said. "Haven't you?"

Nothing changed on his face as he said it. He was as inscrutable and blank as when I first sat down. I felt like I was talking to a human-shaped recording machine, an automaton that took in all information diligently, but without the ability to discern the merits or importance of any of it.

We stared at each other across the gulf of his desk. He seemed to get farther away, as if that gulf was widening with the revelation that we were on opposite ends of the spectrum. I was exquisitely alone in that moment.

A convict again.

*

Puckett appeared out of the murk, just behind my shoulder.

"Wrap it up," he whispered.

Up above, the rifleman in the guard tower was invisible to me, but I knew he was still there all the same. If either I or my father

121

got up suddenly or made any gesture that might seem remotely threatening, one of us would drop dead before the sound of the shot reached our ears.

I'd only been inside a few weeks when a young, strutting black convict had started a heated argument with one of the Aryans in the weight pit. Words turned to shoves and the rest of the inmates shuffled away from them quick. They knew what the black kid had forgotten in his rage over whatever slight had started the whole thing: there were always eyes above you in the yard.

The first rubber bullet took the black kid in the small of the back, and he was down. A writhing mass on the ground. The second dropped the Aryan, and every last one of us in the yard went down flat on our bellies. The siren rose up, as shrill and piercing as a banshee's wail. Guards poured into the yard like locusts.

Whoever had been on the tower that afternoon must have decided the black kid was the instigator, because he fired a second round into him like an exclamation point driving his message home. It hit the kid in the chest, drawing the ugly sound of cracking bone out into the yard. I never saw him again and never asked after him.

Sitting there across from the shadowy mass of my father, I knew it wasn't rubber that would be fired into us if we moved the wrong way.

His one good eye regarded Puckett as he sneered at the guard.

"I'll say what I came to say… *fucker*," my father hissed, his tone turning venomous with unveiled hatred.

I felt Puckett bristling at my side, and I was certain he was going to order us both down on the ground. More guards would appear and we'd be escorted back to our cells. That was all fine with me, in that moment. I hadn't asked to be reunited with the monster who'd planted the seed out of which I'd grown. When I'd heard from other inmates that he was a permanent resident of the solitary holes, all I had felt was a dull relief that I could forget about him and not have to deal with him in the yard or the mess hall.

But Puckett didn't bark, much less bite. He stood rooted and frozen for a second, then slid back into the darkness behind me without a word. All I could do was sit there, silent and stunned, while my father unblinkingly watched the guard slink off.

When he was satisfied that Puckett was back where he belonged, my father spit into the grass and looked at me again.

"Don't ever trust a badge. They're rats. All of 'em."

"I don't need advice. Not from you."

"Tell me how you come to be here, then."

"I just did. We just went through it. What *is* this? I never asked to see you. I never even think about you, understand?"

"What you laid out sounds like self-defense to me. That little spic pulled a knife on you. You can kill a man, he pulls a weapon."

I sighed and gave in. It seemed impossible to get at him or turn him away from what he wanted to know. My options were to either give him what he wanted, or go back to my cell. The night air and the dome of stars were enough to keep me rooted there, even if I had no stomach for this man whom biology dictated was somehow connected to me.

"Only the prosecution witnesses showed up," I said.

"No shit."

"Nobody showed up. Not the guys who witnessed it. Not the girl I dragged Freddie off of. Only people who testified were the cops and the medical examiner. They floated the theory that it was mutual combat between two drunks. It was a Detroit jury looking at a white kid who beat a colored person to death inside a black-owned bar. It took them seventeen minutes to find me guilty."

He nodded and ran one giant hand over his jaw in a contemplative fashion. I felt a queasy recognition as he did it. It was like watching someone pantomime one of my own habits. I had to look away, down at my hands bunched into knots on the cement table. I didn't want to see anything in him that looked like me.

"I know this story," he said.

"What?"

"Detroit," he said, like it was an answer.

"Okay, thanks," I drawled and sighed deep, growing tired of him and his questions.

"Look at me, Roarke." His tone had gone flat, just like that, as if draining every hint of himself out of his voice was as simple as flipping a switch. It was a chilling thing to hear, and it got my attention. I looked at him.

"You think I'm a man to take a smart lip? You think I'm a man to take it from anyone, even my blood?"

I saw him in my child's imagination, calmly executing human beings inside a Dearborn bank, for no other reason than that a cop had negotiated in bad faith.

"No," I said, feeling like that child again, haunted by the dark, mythical visions I'd had to concoct around my father as a substitute for actual memories.

"That's right," he agreed. "I don't take it off any living man. Not even an inch. So when you say 'okay' like you just did, like you're sneering at me, it's not a small thing that I don't reach across and snatch out your tongue. It's not a small thing by any measure."

I wasn't going to apologize. He was a stranger to me, unknowable, inscrutable, but an instinctual wisdom in me knew for certain that the only thing more noxious to him than an insult would be an apology. More than that, I couldn't do it for my own sake. There was no version of me that could look in the mirror, every day throughout the future, knowing that I had ever asked forgiveness from the malignant thing that, through nature's wicked jest, was my father.

I let the silence grow long enough between us that he eventually accepted that there was no argument forthcoming from me on the topic of what he would or would not put up with. When he spoke again, the deadly emptiness in his voice was gone.

"The Detroit Shuffle," he said. "That's what some of the old spades called it. I never had much use for them. I didn't mix. It's different now. I get some yard time once in a blue moon. I see how the whites are like the blacks, now. They say they're Aryan and talk about white power and all that bullshit. But if you see how they move and listen to the way they talk, it's all spade, through and through. Wasn't like that in my time. Not at all. But I come up in Detroit, all the same, so I had to deal with blacks every day. Anyways, the story went that the Detroit cops had a problem getting witnesses to take the stand. Blacks don't cooperate. They catch hell from the neighborhood if they testify against another one of their own. That's where they got us beat, I figure. A white man will roll over soon as you rub his tummy. Not a black. A black'll make sure he's somewhere else when it comes time to get up in court and point a finger at one of his own. So the cops, they have to find a way around that, see? The courts ain't happy. The white rich people ain't happy, because too many niggers are skating free on serious charges. That can't be allowed. So these cops, they come up with a brainstorm. The Detroit Shuffle."

As he laid all that out, I wondered at the bizarre racism he so casually revealed. White supremacists, apparently, were to be scorned because they weren't white *enough*, while black men were to be admired only for their cultural aversion to cooperating with law enforcement. Was there any group my father could have called his own? Or would he have felt contempt for anything that might dare suggest it could contain all of him within its scope?

"I don't see what this has to do with me," I said.

"The cops started locking up the witnesses," he explained. "If you're a little black mama on the street and you see some brother shoot someone, the Detroit cops decide maybe their only way of getting the conviction is to grab your ass up and hold you until the courts call you up to testify. You can't disappear on them if you're cooling your heels in the lock-up. Family members might come around looking to get you out, sure. But that's the *shuffle*. They'd just 'lose' your ass. Move you from one precinct to another and never put it on paper. Keep you shuffled until the court needed you on the stand. And you know what? It worked. For a while, anyway. If the choice is point the finger on someone or stay in a cage with no charges and nobody working to ever get you out, even a spade will look after their own interest eventually."

"Yeah, that sounds like Detroit cops."

"Sure. They pulled that for years and years. Shit takes a long time to get out of Detroit, to stink hard enough that the outside world starts taking notice. Finally, the feds came in and put a stop to it. Or pretended they have. I guarantee it's still going on here and there, when the cops figure they can get away with it. Detroit doesn't change. It might slink down into the shadows when the light's being shined on it. But it don't change, not really."

I sat there and thought about what he'd said. He seemed content to let me. He was a great shadow among shadows, watching me, seeing if there was a sign of intelligence inside me. Behind me, the little whir of a lighter's flint and Puckett's rich cigarette smoke teasing me like a lover long lost.

"Okay," I said after a while. "But that's not what happened with me. My witnesses *didn't* show up."

My father's answering chuckle had all the mirth of the sound a bat's wings make as they beat against the night air—a soft, predatory sound not meant for human ears.

"You know yin and yang," he said. "Don't you? The symbol I mean."

"Yeah."

"Black is white. White is black. The same. That's what it means, right?"

"Sure. Yeah, okay."

"So...tell me what happened to you, Roarke."

I thought on it a bit and it came to me shortly.

"You think the cops kept the witnesses *off* the stand," I said. "A reverse Detroit Shuffle. They locked them up until my trial was over to make sure I went down on the charge. That's what you're saying."

"Yeah," he said and if there was any satisfaction in seeing his son puzzle out what he was getting at, he kept it buried deep enough that I couldn't spot it.

"That's a stretch," I said.

"Not in Detroit. In Detroit, it's standard procedure. You got done. One way or another, you were had. And here you are, rotting in this pit with me. I'm *supposed* to be here, Roarke. That cell I live in? It was waiting for me. Ever since the day they built it, it was meant for me. I know that. I was never going to stay free because I won't tolerate another man's will. I just *won't*. I was born to end bloody or get put in a cage. A man has to know himself. You? You've been had. You got rolled and tagged and made the sucker. And I guess you're okay with that if you never asked these questions before now."

Six months later, I would learn he was right. A volunteer group of appellate attorneys would make contact with me and take up my cause. They were a well-meaning and earnest bunch of kids from privileged backgrounds, fighting the good fight against the abuses of the system. They came to my rescue after a beautiful young black woman with a four-inch scar on her cheek walked into their offices and told them the Detroit cops had muscled her into silence.

Portia Jefferson. That was her name. I'd dragged Freddie Esposito off her, saved her from whatever further cruelty he would have subjected her to.

But that was still six months in the future. Sitting there in the dark across from my father, I didn't know that Freddie's older brother was a Detroit police lieutenant. I didn't know that the entire scheme to keep Portia and the other witnesses off the stand would be revealed by a bunch of volunteer do-gooders. I didn't know I would be free in a couple years or that a civil jury would drop a heap of cash in my lap for all my troubles. All I knew was that a monster whose face looked like a distorted reflection of my own had sought me out and arranged a private meeting in the dead of night.

I remembered the first lesson I'd learned in prison: everything has its price. I wondered what my father had been forced to pay in order to arrange this midnight rendezvous.

He must have seen the confusion playing across my face, because he chuckled again, a low and ugly noise.

"Never trust a badge," he whispered, like it was a fundamental truth of existence.

# SEVEN

"Yeah, I was in prison. Three years in Jackson. So what? I'm reporting a missing girl."

Deputy Rezner's implacable, machine-like disposition didn't seem to register the irritation in my voice. He was a Marine, alright—still and focused, with that inner calm some of the guys get after they've had their rough edges hewn away. If you get with the program the way the Corps intends and give yourself over to being made anew, what survives is hard and polished smooth.

I'd gotten with the program well enough that I still kept my living area squared away, still rushed mechanically through the morning ritual of toilet, shave and shower. I kept fit religiously. But my mind wasn't Marine. They'd rented my head for eight years and as soon as my contract was up, I'd reclaimed it and gone home.

Deputy Rezner looked to me like a man who had never left the Corps, even after his career there had ended.

"Jackson was a serious prison before they shut it down" he said. "What were you in for?"

"Involuntary manslaughter. It got overturned. If running me through LEIN will get us off this topic, feel free."

He ignored the suggestion and was silent for a second, as if contemplating.

"Jackson assignment for involuntary, huh? That's a pretty high security rating for the offense."

"You can run me, Deputy. I really don't mind."

"Was it the psych exam that got you assigned there?"

I knew what he meant. When you get convicted of a felony and sentenced to prison, you're handed over to the custody of the Michigan Department of Corrections. They hold you in what they call quarantine. Beyond checking you over for communicable diseases, they run a series of psychological evaluations on you. The most famous and widely used of those is the Minnesota Multiphasic Personality Inventory, though there are plenty of others. Mostly they try and evaluate your disposition for violence and whether you have impulse-control problems. If you score far enough in the wrong direction, far enough that you seem like someone prone to extreme acts of unwarranted violence, you'll wind up in a high security prison even if your crime alone didn't warrant it.

I'd killed a man in what amounted to a bar fight gone wrong. Even with potential defense witnesses getting the Detroit Shuffle treatment, nobody at my trial suggested that Freddie Esposito had been attacked without provocation, or that his death was premeditated. I had a belly full of stab wounds, three surgeries, and a two-week hospital stay as proof of that much.

With no prior record, the most likely assignment for me would have been a medium security site, not a maximum pen like Jackson.

"I have no idea why I went there," I said. "They don't share the results with inmates. They sent me there, so I went. The girl's name is Chelsea Gullins. Her father was killed yesterday and a local militia outfit is holding her. Sovereign North. Am I boring you with this?"

"I'm trying to get the whole picture."

"Should I be talking to the feds or the state cops instead?"

That, finally, got something that might have been called a reaction out of him. He blinked twice and nudged his glasses up on his nose.

"No. You came to the right place. What were you hired to do, exactly?"

"Find Chelsea Gullins and get her back to her mother."

"Her mother hired you?"

"No. Someone else did."

"Uh-huh. So this someone else hired a killer Marine to drive another person's kid home, huh? Nothing else? Nothing a little rougher, maybe? Like scare somebody or hurt somebody, like that?"

I felt the throb of blood in my wound, and knew I was losing whatever composure I had. Part of me knew I should just keep answering questions until the Deputy got around to the one that actually mattered. I didn't listen to it.

My hands bunched up into fists in my lap and I felt my face going red. I began barking the words out.

"I'm trying to tell you I *killed* a man, Deputy. And another man is also dead, murdered by the man I killed. A little eighth grade girl is being held against her will. The only question is what are you going to do about it?"

The man in the sharply pressed uniform stood up. His expression remained unchanged—flat, calm, verging on disinterest.

"Sovereign North," he said. "Those are just some local men. They tend to mind their own business."

"Yeah? That's what you call armed militias these days?"

"Civic pride's a crime now?"

"Civic...? What?"

His lip curled and he said, "North of the rifle line the word 'militia' isn't a pejorative. This isn't Detroit. Up here, a free man doesn't have to apologize about being free. But I think I do have a file on them. While I'm gone, you really should look around."

It was a bizarre offer, and I didn't know what to say to it. He walked briskly out of the room, leaving me with an unsettled certainty that it had been a mistake to seek out the attention of

135

law enforcement, though not for the obvious reasons. I'd known there was a real chance of being detained or arrested once I mentioned the bullet I put in Wade's head. That was a real apprehension, one grounded in reality. Whatever this new fear was, it was the result of Deputy Rezner's strangely detached reaction to everything I'd been trying to get out.

I stared through the open door to his office at the empty hallway outside, waiting for him to reappear with whatever file he was intent on finding. When he didn't come back straight away, I looked over the framed photos of his time in the Marines and, later, as a sheriff's deputy. He was alone in almost all of the photos and always posed with a deliberate, formal look about him. In the few photos where he was with another Marine or deputy, that stony formality was still present. He looked like a man who was so wrapped up in the idea of duty that he'd submerged any sign of a personality.

I'd known guys like that in the Marines. They were the ones who saw themselves as lifers, married to the role of soldier. They came to boot camp having already mastered the ability to breakdown and reassemble their rifle, able to easily bear the slog of long marches because they'd been doing them at home for months before signing up. They made for good soldiers, I guess. But they were useless for companionship, the last kind of guy you'd ever want to fill out a card game or come along on a weekend of carousing.

136

His desk drove home the image of him I had in my head. There was nothing personal there, nothing beyond the department-issued computer, a phone, and a file organizer. No coffee mug with a pun written on it, no photos of family, no magazines or food wrappers—just the tools of his trade and nothing more.

Minutes ground away. Out in the hallway, nobody passed by. A phone rang somewhere in the depths of the building and stopped after the third ring. I sat. The bandage was dry again. I touched it here and there, gingerly, but my fingers never came away red. I needed antibiotics. Soon, I knew, I would need more pain medication. The opiates Savannah had fed me were entirely gone from my system, if the sharpening knife of pain deep in the shredded muscle was any indication.

Enough time slid away that I finally stood up, anxious, torn between the idea of calling out for Deputy Rezner and the notion of marching through the department until I found someone who would take me seriously. I'd been alone in the little office too long. Either Rezner wasn't coming back, or when he did it wouldn't be with a file on the Sovereign North. Were they watching me, somehow? Sweating me like a suspect, waiting for me to show keen agitation before waltzing back in and starting in with hard questions?

It occurred to me that they might have already found Paul Gullins and Wade. They might have already been on the look-out for a killer. Maybe Deputy Rezner's cool, matter-of-fact demeanor and lack of curiosity was because he already knew about the bodies in Paul Gullins' back yard. Maybe, while I rambled at him, he was just taking his time in deciding how best to go at the killer who had wandered in and sat down across from him.

It was a lot of maybes. I wanted out. Amid all the questions and anxieties, that was the one impulse that shone through. I was going to just walk out. The desk officer would call out to me as I passed, but I wouldn't slow. I'd be out in the sun, then down the walk, into the lot, the car, behind the wheel, rolling, out and away. That was exactly what was going to happen.

I took the first step on that journey.

And stopped.

It was one of those rare events in life when something just on the periphery of your vision seizes your attention, when you can't say why or how, but some quality in the indistinct corner of your eye screams out to be seen and recognized.

I turned and stared at the expanse of wall that had been at my back ever since sitting down across from Rezner. A sub-zero fear grew in the base of my skull, an arctic ache that slowed every rational impulse, froze them and left me unable to do anything but stare.

There on the wall, a slightly younger Deputy Rezner stood, framed behind sun-kissed glass. I stepped one pace to the side, blocking the sun, staring into the snapshot of yesteryear. A rifle was resting on one of his shoulders and, unlike the other photos displayed around the room, here Rezner was smiling. Three elementary school-aged boys crowded around Rezner's legs, all of them in summer shorts and sneakers. Behind them, Two Pine's A&W restaurant, only here it was alive with cars parked in the lot and a waitress frozen in mid-stride with a tray of root beer floats in her hands. Other summer-farers were milling on the sidewalk. A woman had a camera in her hands. A man lapped at a large ice cream cone. It was a moment in time when Two Pine still thrived.

Deputy Rezner's cleanly-pressed uniform had changed colors. The sheriff's browns were now green, as green as the needles of the trees the town had been named after. It was the uniform of a Two Pine police officer.

A little white business card-sized rectangle of paper had been slipped in between the photo and the glass, resting at the bottom of the frame. Typed across it were the words, "TWO PINE HERITAGE FAIR 2007".

My eyes continued to scan, seeking to put a name to the icy dread that had paralyzed me. Another photo, smaller, hung beside the larger. The Two Pine Police Department was a narrow brick building crowded on either side by a hardware store and a tailor's shop. Parked on the curb, a department-painted Crown Victoria. Its skin was clean and shiny, and there was no sign of an injury to one of its glass eyes. Still, I knew it was the same. And it was Rezner's.

*'You really should look around,'* he'd told me before ghosting away out of the room.

He had wanted me to know: I was in the lair of the man who came half a second away from shooting me to death a day before. I'd neglected the advice my father tried to impart to me years ago in the darkness of a prison yard. I'd dismissed his warning about men who pinned badges to their breasts the same way I dismissed everything else about him—they were the mutterings of a bloody-handed monster, and I wanted nothing of them or of him. So I'd walked into the belly of the beast and offered myself up as a meal.

Deputy Rezner was the Last Watchman.

\*

The desk officer was busy listening to an elderly woman in a floral pink dress when I walked back through the door. He didn't so much as glance up at me, though he could have shouted for me to stop and I wouldn't have slowed down. My legs felt stiff and uncertain, the fear-induced adrenaline howling at me to lose control and just bolt wildly away. I forced myself to walk, to keep my expression calm as I pushed the entrance door open and exited the building.

Sunlight bleached the outside world and I blinked several times. I took a step and stopped. Rezner was there. Down at the end of the steps, becoming real, materializing as I squinted through the afternoon glare.

A Crawford Sheriff's cruiser was idling in park just behind him. The passenger-side door yawned open beside him. In the back of the cruiser something dark stirred. A dog, I realized. Its head rose into view. A German Shepherd, peering through the glass at me. It saw me looking at it and became very still, fixed on me, unblinking. An eager whine rose out of the beast as it locked on me.

Rezner watched me as the situation became clear. There was no tension in him. He stood loose-hipped and at ease, comfortable to let me weigh all the options I didn't have. The traffic on the road beyond us was infrequent. Here and there, a citizen coming in or out of a storefront. Nobody was looking our way. Behind me, the Sheriff's office. Far away, across the street, the Stratus was parked where I'd left it.

Any direction I bolted, Rezner could pull his sidearm and empty it. The Stratus was unreachable. Charging back into the Sheriff's office would just buy me a second shooter once they saw one of their own was firing at me. The deputy riding the front desk would execute me and ask questions only after he'd re-holstered his weapon. If I lunged off into traffic, Rezner would calmly correct the mistake he'd made at Paul Gullins' house. I'd' be a back-shot corpse sprawled on the baking asphalt while he was mentally arranging how to word the 'fleeing felon' report his department would rubber stamp. Would there be questions? Sure. Until the bodies of Wade and Paul were offered up, along with the bullet from my gun that was inside Wade's head. Once that shoe dropped, Rezner would never have to buy his own beer again and I'd be remembered as the Detroit Lunatic who earned himself some country justice.

The German Shepherd barked once, as startling as a sudden gunshot. Rezner made a casual gesture with his right hand and the dog obediently sat on its haunches and fell silent. Its eyes stayed trained on me.

I looked at the open passenger door. Rezner cocked his head to the side and nodded once, acknowledging the truth of every bloody scenario that had played out in my mind. A thundering indignation threatened to drown out whatever sense of self-preservation I owned. It was the storm of outrage that, to one degree or another, had always been with me. It insisted I should take my chances and throw myself at the cop. It told me to risk the first shot from his gun. To damn the realities of the situation and gamble that I could wrest that gun out of his grip and turn it into a hammer against him.

It must have been obvious. My face must have screamed what was going on inside me, because Rezner shook his head once and said, very softly, "She'll go in the ground if I have to clean you up."

The idea of that was enough. I saw a slight, milk-pale child in the earth, lost to time and memory for no reason other than that I couldn't tame my own impulses. Rezner watched as I stepped heavily forward and dipped down into the passenger seat of the cruiser.

"Good," he said, and tossed a set of handcuffs in my lap. "You keep following simple commands, this can all resolve itself. Put those on."

He shut the door without waiting to see if I obeyed. Behind me, I felt the Shepherd's breath huff hotly against my ear as it pressed its snout against the metal grate separating us. I remembered my first walk to my cell, how the other convicts strained against their bars to get a look, some of them hooting vicious predictions, some braying like animals.

"Solidarity, brother," I whispered to the agitated beast, and snapped the handcuffs in place.

*

Once Rezner turned onto the same county road I'd followed into the derelict town of Two Pine, I stopped keeping careful note of the turns we made and spared some time to look over the handcuffs clasped around my wrists.

143

Rezner thumbed his shoulder mic, opening his duty radio's channel, and spoke into it.

"Sean? I've got a personal thing. You okay to run the show for a bit?"

"Yup," someone answered, in a bored tone that suggested there wasn't much of a show to handle.

The stylized and encircled 'S' and 'W' logo for Smith and Wesson was stamped into the face of each cuff. The chain had two links between each cuff's eyelet. Not as indomitable as the modern hinged-cuff. With a classic set of chain-linked cuffs, you've got more range of motion. Still, that was scant help. Steel is steel. Human strength, even when fueled with desperation and adrenaline, pales to insignificance.

"They're new," Rezner said beside me. "A rampaging gorilla couldn't snap out of those, so just sit there and forget the fantasy."

His voice stirred the dog behind us to alertness. I heard him whine in answer and felt the warm jet of his breath on my ear.

"Shush," Rezner muttered.

"Maybe he doesn't like what you're doing."

"Wagner? Forget it. He's a warrior, through and through. Best partner I ever had, in the Corps or out. You have any dogs?"

"Never have."

"Well color me shocked. Detroit probably uses them for soup, right? Feed the homeless, keep the bottom feeders from dying off so they can still vote the rest of our freedoms away, like that?"

I could feel Wagner begin to pace around behind me. Rezner pushed a button on his door. I heard a window in the back whisper down. Wagner's nails made clacking noises as he climbed up to stick his head out into the wind. The cruiser barreled on, a heavy, well-engineered machine that ran smooth. Ahead, the abandoned block of downtown Two-Pine came into view.

When we reached the crossroads and stopped, the light was green. Rezner looked to the left and we just sat there for a long minute while the light changed to red. We were as alone as I had been the first time I'd stopped here and marveled at the bleak and forgotten town.

"I aimed to take you up to Wade's place," he said after a while, his voice low and gruff as he continued to stare away from me.

"Why?"

"To show you he had a wife and a little boy. He was a good man. You killed a good friend of mine, you god damned gutter rat."

"He didn't give me a choice. Neither did you."

Rezner's cheeks flushed with sudden color and he turned to stare at me. For the first time since walking into his office, the man wore his emotions on his face. His gray eyes narrowed into ugly slits. Their black pupils shrank to lethal pinpoints. His mouth curled into a mean, trembling smear. The malice he was directing at me, suddenly naked and unveiled, radiated with an intensity I could feel in the nerves of my scalp and in the base of my spine.

I was certain he was going to lash out at me. He bristled with such abrupt contempt that I doubted he had the capacity to pull his sidearm and put a bullet in my face. No sign of human calculation remained in that murderous expression. He was going to claw at me and rend me apart like an animal. Without consciously deciding to, I crowded against the passenger door and wove the fingers of my hands together. If he moved, I'd batter and pound at him until he was forced to use the gun. If I died, I would not die easy.

Out of the corner of my eye, Wagner, pulling his head back inside the cruiser. His long snout sniffed the air once, and what he sensed in the deadly silence coaxed a low howl out of him. It was an eerie, disturbing song full of sadness and warning; the chilling lament of the wolf.

Rezner's dead stare faltered. He blinked several times, rapidly.

146

"Shush," he snapped, his voice thick as he came back into himself. Wagner's song fell silent, but I knew it had served its purpose. Rezner's composure returned, and in an instant he was self-contained again, sitting bolt upright and staring out the windshield. He took hold of the wheel and put the cruiser in drive. We surged through the red light. Two Pine whispered away behind us and we were cutting through the forest once more.

Wagner stuck his head out the window again. Silence reigned inside the vehicle. I wondered at the vacant-eyed monster I'd glimpsed behind Rezner's stoic mask. I'd seen that face before. In prison I saw it often. Later, I sometimes saw it sitting across a table from me, staring with a freak's intensity while I explained to it my role as parole agent. It was the face of disconnection. Bad wiring. The face of madness.

"You haven't left me any choice, either," the Last Watchman whispered.

\*

Two guards from the Michigan Department of Corrections sat me down in the back of an Economy-sized van when it was time to go to prison. There were no windows in the back, so I spent the ride staring between the two guards, out the windshield. I-94 started urban, then suburbs, and finally rural fields. The dread

147

settled in once we were out there in the country, rolling past flat, empty land. I didn't know the country. It was alien to me. The emptiness was foreboding. Nothing broke the horizon. You could see too far.

Rezner must have sensed that same dread growing in me as we turned onto a rutted dirt and gravel lane. He smirked and pointed ahead at the ribbon of road disappearing into the high pine.

"You know where we are?" he said.

"No."

"Yeah, I guess you don't."

"This is a mistake, Deputy. You--"

"This is an ocean floor, Detroit. Ancient as the world. Then the glaciers. Then the big melt that gave us the Great Lakes. Then the trees grew up and that's how it is now. All this? It goes on and on. We're in the shallows, like if you've gone to the beach. If you go too far, you're out there. You're in the ocean proper. You can't see land anymore. If you don't know what the fuck you're doing, there's no chance to make it back. You'll drift around in circles until you're dead. We're not staying in the shallows, Detroit. We're going in deep, you and me."

"But you know your way back," I finished for him. "And I don't. So don't think of running for it, right? I'll keep it in mind."

We passed a large wood marker on the side of the road that announced we were entering the Huron National Forest. There was smaller print detailing some basic rules of behavior, but I didn't bother to read them. Littering and building illegal campfires weren't likely to be high on my list of worries.

Wagner barked at something out the window and I heard his tail thumping eagerly against the metal grate that divided us.

"He loves it out here," Rezner said.

"Is Chelsea Gullins still alive?"

"You don't need to worry about that anymore."

The rutted lane narrowed and became nothing more than two lines in the earth worn down from occasional vehicle traffic. This wasn't an official entry point to the forest. The cruiser rocked and heaved over the heavily uneven ground. The sun disappeared as the canopy of trees drew in over us. The hum of the cruiser's engine was the loudest thing in the world.

We were already out past the shallows.

The tire-ruts came to an end shortly. The cruiser stopped. Rezner killed the engine and stared out ahead of us for a long moment. His thin lips pursed into a frown.

Two dirt-caked four-wheelers were sitting unattended in the shade of the forest, precisely at the end of the narrow lane. One was yellow, the other blue. They both looked heavily used, their big balloon tires balding, their paint chipped and blackened with trail dust. Beyond them, and on all sides, the world was a thick

149

choke of pine, elm, and oak. The breeze wafting in Wagner's window was heavy with the rich stink of earth.

"I guess we aren't the only ones taking a swim," I said and watched Rezner's face carefully.

"Guess so," he said, casually. "Not that it does you a bit of good."

It didn't work. I'd spotted the keen frustration in his eyes. As he climbed out of the car and shut the door behind him, I knew one thing for certain: he hadn't expected to see the four-wheelers. This was a complication.

My door swung open. Rezner watched me as I got out, his face a blank again. Once Wagner was out and happily sniffing circles around the forest floor, Rezner shut the doors and hit the lock button on his key fob. He pointed off into the trees.

"That way. Start walking."

"This is a mistake, Deputy."

"Yeah. Yours. You never should have come up here. This isn't your home. It's *our* home. It's *our* lives. But here you are. And my friend is dead. Start walking or I bury you here and leave room in the hole for the girl."

He didn't need to put his hand on his sidearm to drive the point home. I'd seen the face beneath his mask. He'd do it. Even if it meant greater risk to himself. Even if it meant some dire consequence I wasn't privy to, he'd execute me and then Chelsea if I didn't promptly comply with his demands.

150

I started walking.

Wagner ranged ahead of us, looping happy arcs, sniffing, watching everything. When Rezner issued a short, sharp whistle, the German Shepherd obediently darted back to us and fell in with our pace. I spared a glance over my shoulder. The dog remained a pace ahead of his master, between us. His watery brown eyes fixed on me and didn't look away before I did. It occurred to me that there was an equally short, simple command that would tell Wagner to sink his jaws into me. He wouldn't think twice about it. He'd obey the command that had been drilled into him.

As with the awful drive to Jackson Prison, I was being escorted to the unknown by *two* cops, not one. I adjusted my thinking accordingly as we moved deeper into the wild.

*

When I cycled out of the Marines I dumped the soldier mentality as soon as I was on the bus back to Detroit, but I didn't toss the things I'd learned on Parris Island or the skills I'd acquired over the eight years I did ugly things for Uncle Sam.

The sun tells you plenty, right away. I kept track of it as time wore on. Its position will tell you the time and it'll tell you where the points of a compass invisibly lie across the land. Before noon, when you face the sun your shadow will spread out

151

behind you. Raising your left arm straight out will approximate the direction of North. After noon, you face the sun and switch to the right arm. The sun shifts in the sky depending on the season, but a lost man can always get a general sense of north with that basic process.

I didn't really need the sun to know north. That was born into me, something inherent in the genetic soup of my forefathers. It wasn't part of a skill set. If you raise a Robin from an egg in an artificial setting and then set it free into the wild, that Robin will build a nest identical to all the other Robins that grew up naturally. It's hard-wired into them. True north and not getting easily turned around was hard-wired into me.

Still, the Marines had taught me plenty. A human being's walking gait is typically four and a half miles per hour. But that's on even, open ground. My forced march through the Huron National Forest was often halting and uncertain. The land sloped up, then down. Brush thickened and choked our progress. I stumbled several times on purpose to reinforce Rezner's preconception that I was an utterly befuddled city-dweller. As I kept track of time with the sun's path across the sky, I marked our distance by estimating we were moving around three and a half miles an hour.

By my measure, we'd gone nearly two miles on an eastward trajectory when Rezner announced it was time to stop.

"Have a seat, Detroit."

We were in the middle of a shallow depression. I sat with my back against the trunk of an old elm tree and watched Wagner watching me. The dog sat on its haunches beside his master. Still locked on his earlier command. The best partner he'd ever had, Rezner had said.

"You keep fit," Rezner said, grudgingly. Peering down at me, standing loose-hipped and laconic, he looked at home. "I thought you might be worn to hell by now, but you aren't. You run, don't you?"

"Yeah."

"Every day?"

"Pretty much."

"Weights, too, from the look of you."

"So what?"

"So none of that means shit all when I put a bullet in you."

"We didn't have to march this far for that. You could have killed me halfway here and still been sure nobody would find my grave."

"You don't know a god damned thing."

I wriggled my hands in front of me and the chain in between them rattled in the silent wood.

"I know you need me," I said softly and grinned up at him.

Rezner pulled his sidearm. A smooth motion, practiced to the point of becoming a reflex. He took two steps forward and pressed the end of the barrel against my forehead. Wagner walked a quick circle, whined, and sat back on his haunches.

I stared up the length of the gun, into Rezner's gray eyes. They were calm and seemingly sane. But I knew what lie just behind them. I'd seen his mask of humanity fall away.

There was no profit in pushing him to that place again.

I pointed back west, the way we'd come. A tall pine stood apart from its brethren at the base of the depression's rim. He didn't follow the finger with his eyes, but I knew he was aware of what I was pointing at. A single yellow dab of paint stained the trunk, a few inches up from the base of that pine, a faded circle from a spray can. I'd seen several of those marks since starting our march.

"We aren't going to a kill spot, Deputy," I said. "I thought maybe we were, until I started seeing those paint markings every few hundred yards. Whoever rode those quads in, they're waiting for us at the end of those marks. Whatever you and the Sovereign have going on out here in the middle of nowhere, you're taking me there."

His eyes narrowed and the gun stayed where it was. It occurred to me that I wasn't always the best at reading other people. Abruptly exiting the world because I'd goaded a psychopath into doing what came naturally wasn't any kind of death worth having.

"You should take me the rest of the way, Deputy."

"Yeah? Why would I do that?" he said.

"Because Jeffrey Tombs still has a tongue in his mouth," I said. "Sooner or later, it's going to start wagging. Even if he swears it won't. You're a cop. You know the score. Everyone talks. That's why Paul Gullins took a bullet in the chest, isn't it?"

I don't know how long he remained as he was, with the barrel of the gun pressed against my skull. A jumble of intentions vied for dominance in my mind, all of them aimed at staving off death. I settled on the idea of throwing my hands up at the gun and lunging forward simultaneously. It was a suicide bid, but it was all I had.

"No more talking," he said. The gun slid into its holster. He took two steps back, his mouth a sour frown of distaste.

We resumed our march. Adrenaline made my legs shaky as we climbed out of the depression. When we crested the lip and the land was even again, I spied another dab of faded yellow paint far ahead. Behind me, Rezner's silent presence was a knife prodding at the small of my back.

Still alive, still whole, I made my way.

\*

Less than a mile since resuming the march, I noticed the small clearings of roughly tilled earth appear around us like barren wounds on the forest's skin. Over the next mile and a half, I

155

counted nineteen of the small clearings, none of them larger than a couple meters on a side.

The next yellow paint mark lead us up a slope of earth heavy in prickly bushes. I scanned for a moment and spotted a foot path up the slope, a narrow lane where people had been coming and going frequently enough to make a channel through the briars.

As we climbed, I spied the first clearing that had actual plants within it. There were a dozen inch-high stalks sprouting greenly up out of the clearing. Further on, another. Then another. The earth flattened out again. More clearings, now with plants three to four inches high.

Reinhart had dismissed Jeffrey Tombs' arrest for the botched drug deal in Wayne County as being unrelated to the Sovereign North. He was wrong.

The Sovereign North wasn't a survivalist militia. It was a marijuana outfit growing its product in some of the most remote terrain in the state. Guerilla growing, the feds called it. Mostly, California was where that action was going down. Mexican cartels were busy planting fields of weed all over state and federal land out there. Michigan wasn't on the federal radar. Sure, you'd hear about little plots of the plant being found here and there, but never in an organized or large scale fashion.

The Sovereign had changed that, I realized.

"Stop walking," Rezner said.

I watched him come around in front of me. There was a folding buck knife in his right hand, the three-inch blade extended and pointing at me. I felt myself bristle, heard my sharp intake of breath. Rezner smirked, a sheen of satisfaction lighting his eyes.

"Don't move, Detroit," he whispered. "Stay fucking still. If I was killing you with this, I'd have run it across your throat from behind. So don't be stupid. This blade's sharp as they come."

When I didn't make a move one way or another, Rezner's satisfied grin broadened. He was finally getting some fear out of me. That was what the thing behind his stoic mask needed, so I stood there and let it feed while Rezner took the buck knife and cut away the left sleeve of my shirt. He started at the shoulder seam, then ran the blade smoothly down the length of it. Quickly, he had the sleeve in his hands.

"You're blindfolded the rest of the way," he said. He folded the buck knife and put it in his breast pocket, just beneath his badge of office.

"What's the point? I've seen your crop. I've seen the markings to get out here."

"You ain't seen everything. Keep still."

Rezner wrapped the severed sleeve around my head twice and tied it tight with a single, torturous jerk at the back of my skull. I winced at the sudden pressure. Blind, my hands bound in front of me, I pushed back at the mounting panic in my gut. I listened.

157

Rezner's boots scuffed over the earth as he came back around in front of me. Wagner sneezed a huff of air and his tail slapped my calf twice. The forest was silent, windless.

Rezner's first punch was a kidney shot. I was prone when it landed. A nova of agony bloomed in my side. I heard myself gasp. My knees went rubbery on me, but I managed to stay on my feet. Wagner started barking, an impromptu cheering section for the sport Rezner was having.

The second blow landed on my right ear. I tumbled through brush and briar. Hit the ground. His boots scuffed along with me, closing. I kicked out and flailed my way back to my feet. When I reached up to tear the blindfold away, it earned me an elbow in my stomach. I staggered away, still blind, legs growing weak again.

"You should have stayed in Detroit."

Wagner kept up his yapping, somewhere behind me. I listened for Rezner's boot falls and willed my legs to keep me up. When he came again, I'd lunge. I'd throw everything into him, all of my weight and all of my hate.

If I could get on top of him, find his throat, push his Adam's apple down into the earth before the dog sank his jaws into something vital...it was a fantasy. I clung to it.

But he didn't come. No more blows fell. No more sounds of his heavy boots plodding toward me. Wagner's barking died away and the dog made disappointed chuffing noises. My breath rattled. Blood in my mouth. I spat it out and smiled fiercely into the darkness.

"You done?" I hissed.

That thing in me, that rider of the storm that had rejoiced in Freddie Esposito's death and that could feel no remorse over blasting Wade out of the world, hoped that Rezner was not done. Death was close if he decided to keep on. I only needed to hear him coming. My hands were balled into hammers. I waited.

"For now," he said, off to my right. I pivoted to face that way.

"Yeah? You sure?" I spat more blood.

"Why? You looking to die, Detroit?" He sounded at ease. Maybe the thing that lived behind his eyes was sated. The next thing I felt was the hard press of his gun in the small of my back. "Let's get this done."

He prodded me forward. I fell three times before we'd walked ten minutes. Rezner chuckled each time while I righted myself and stumbled forward again. When he needed me to change my course, the gun would appear in my back again and push me in the right direction. The world was gone and the sun with it. Tree limbs clawed at me. Thorns took bits of me with them as we passed.

"Watch out," he laughed, right before the ground dipped too suddenly for me to correct myself. I tumbled down the slope of earth. Tasted earth in my mouth, mixing with the blood. The blindfold was wet with sweat. My shirt clung like a filthy, second skin.

Rezner hauled me to my feet and we marched a minute more before someone called to us from ahead.

"Jesus, he looks like hell." A man's voice.

Rezner's gun prodded me toward it.

"Where's the Reverend?" he called out to the other.

"He's been waiting. Worried the whole time you'd lost your temper and maybe done 'something rash'."

"That's what he said? Rash?"

"Yeah."

"Well, look for yourself. He's in one piece, isn't he?"

"Umm, I guess so…"

"Umm, yeah I guess you do."

"Wasn't me who was worried, Mike."

"Uh-huh. So open her up already."

I heard the creak of hinges and a loud clattering. Before I could wonder at what they'd built out here in the center of nowhere, Rezner gave me a single hard shove in the back. I pitched violently forward. The ground vanished beneath my feet and a sickly thrill shot through me as I plunged straight down.

I fell through darkness.

# EIGHT

They dragged me through a humid, skunk-stenching void.

I was still stunned from the fall when Rezner and his confederate took me under the arms. They didn't wait for my legs to start working again. I was a mass of pain and exhaustion, a heap of meat dragging between them.

"Come on, Detroit. Not far now. Suck it up, *Marine*."

Rezner, sneering, contemptuous.

"This guy's a fucking Marine?"

Rezner didn't answer. The other man let go of my arm and I heard a door clatter open. Rezner shoved me ahead. The skunk-stink of marijuana was overwhelming now, thick and wet as I sucked air that had become tropic-warm. A grow lab. An underground crop.

I understood the blindfold, now. Plots of marijuana found in the middle of the forest could not, on their own, be traced back to their owners. A facility was different. A grow lab meant all sorts of physical evidence of human identity. Fingerprints on the machinery, the doors, the walls. DNA. Supplies for the operation that could be traced to their point of purchase.

161

Rezner *had* meant to murder me in the woods, I realized. It hadn't been a scare tactic. But the presence of the four wheelers had forced him to change his plan. I didn't know why. If I had to guess, my bet was on the syrupy-voiced southern Reverend who'd kept me on the phone long enough for Rezner to take a shot at me from hiding. Wade had pegged him as the leader.

Another door, the sound of a deadbolt clacking free. The two of them propelled me ahead. Something caught my foot, their hands let go, and I was plunged face-first into the cement floor. The metal flavor of blood filled my mouth again.

Silence, but for the sound of my haggard breathing. Dust clotting in my nostrils. I gagged and hacked it out in a series of barking coughs. That brought a blooming pain in my side, and in the gunshot wound from Rezner's rifle. My head throbbed and, even blind, the world swam nauseously. I was beat to hell. If they decided to kill me down here, it wasn't going to be a difficult job for them to get done.

In that black silence, I saw Savannah again, as clearly as I'd ever seen anything. Sitting across from me in the Ypsilanti restaurant, earnestly telling me about her niece between tidy bites of Asian salad. Probing at the edges about who I was. Looking to see if I was the right sort of blunt instrument she could wield. And me sitting there, trying to be witty with her, with my knuckles freshly scrubbed of Buster Long's blood. Thinking that wasn't all I was, that I was more than an instrument of violence.

162

She'd seen through my banter about the law and my reticence to work outside of it. She'd sized me up as the hammer she needed.

And now I was here, coughing blood and waiting for the bullet to the head I'd never hear coming for me.

I laughed. It came on sudden and strong. It was a loud, ugly noise. It hurt as it wrenched its way out of me, but I couldn't stop it. And as it filled the darkness, I recognized that laughter. It wasn't my own. It was my father's. It was his scorn for a feral delinquent who thought he was a soldier, his scorn for a killer who pretended to be a citizen, his scorn for an animal that had fancied itself a man. I could hear the gravel of his voice beneath the laughter.

*"You know what happens to animals when they bite, Roarke. They get put down."*

The laughter died as abruptly as it had begun. I lay there, aching and hollowed out. Waiting for the blackness to become whole, for my desperate suspicions to prove out as nothing more than false hope that there was a chance to remain alive.

When the Reverend's genteel twang reached my ears, I knew I wasn't dead yet. He clucked his tongue and said, "Lord, what have you two fools left for me to work with?"

\*

*"We are afflicted in every way, but not crushed."*

Either Rezner or the man who had met him aboveground shoved me into a wall. I tasted blood in my mouth again. Spat it out while the Reverend spoke in a solemn, sermonizing inflection.

*"Perplexed, but not driven to despair."*

Rezner's sidearm ground into the skin above my ear, sudden, and he whispered, "Hold still, Detroit. Almost there." The other one worked the handcuff that bound my left wrist. When it came free, Rezner drilled his sidearm deeper into my temple, driving his point home.

*"Persecuted, but not forsaken."*

Rezner's helper yanked on my wrist. I heard the clack of metal-on-metal and the click-click-click of the cuff locking again. I was affixed to the wall. Pressed as I was against it, it felt like cement—cool, flat, unyielding. The gun went away and I pressed my left wrist around the wall, probing while Rezner's suffocating presence faded. I felt a metal protrusion. Ran my thumb over it, searching for tactile recognition-- and finding it.

I was cuffed to the eyelet of a thick iron bolt that was screwed into the cement wall. Trapped. Secured beneath the earth, blind and beaten.

*"Struck down, but not destroyed."*

"That's enough, Reverend," Rezner groused. I heard him slide his sidearm back into its leather holster, heard the button-clasp snapping tight over it.

164

"Hope is a powerful motivator for a beaten man," the Reverend sighed. "You ought to look into it. Maybe spare your knuckles so much work, Deputy."

"He don't need hope. He needs a bullet and a couple shovels of dirt."

"Maybe. But it doesn't hurt to talk first."

"Five hours on my shift, Rev. You want to try and wheedle something out of him, that's all you've got to work with. If he isn't dead when I come back, you can roll your tongue back up into your head and stay out of my way, preacher."

Abruptly, fingers were bunched in my hair, twisting and yanking me forward. Rezner's breath in my ear as he softly hissed, "It'll be me, Detroit. You go in the ground tonight. Then the blonde and then the girl. All of you in the same hole. You should have stayed where you belong. This is *our* land."

"Rezner," the Reverend snapped. "Enough."

"Sovereign men, you fucking gutter rat. That's who you messed with--"

"Michael!"

He let go of me with a shove. The back of my head bounced off the cement wall. Whirling pinpoints of light burst alive in the black and I felt my knees threaten to go wobbly. Footfalls scuffed. A door opened and clattered loudly shut.

I took a long, deep breath through my nose and waited while the starburst of pain receded, dimmed.

165

"Roarke," the Reverend said after a while.

"Reverend."

"You don't have to wear that blindfold anymore."

My left wrist was shackled to the wall, but my right was arm was free. I reached up and tore the soiled sleeve from around my head. Tossed it away and opened my eyes.

I looked at the Reverend. He was a thin old man in loose-fitting jeans and a red flannel shirt. His long, handsome face was topped with a coarse mane of snow-white hair, uncombed and flaring wildly in different directions. His wintry eyes were bright and alert, full of a youthfulness that the rest of him didn't share.

"I sure am sorry about how this has all gone on," he said without any prompting from me. As he spoke, his lips bent into a regretful frown. He shook his head and sighed and I knew what he was in that moment. An actor. A natural performer. He exuded sympathy, had turned it on like flipping a light switch.

"I'm a little sore about it, too," I said.

"I imagine so. I imagine so."

I scanned the room quickly while he looked down at his shoes and shook his head some more. We were in a small concrete room, no more than eight feet on any side. The ceiling was low, only a couple inches above my head. The door I'd been dragged through was metal and on my right. On my left, another metal door. The skunk-stink of marijuana was ever-present, a cloying thickness in the humid, unmoving air.

"Well, I suppose we should get straight to the business we're in," he said, and turned his back on me. There was a folding chair propped against the wall. He unfolded it and sat down on the other side of the room from me. Just above his head, several electrical lines were secured to the wall in the eyelets of iron bolts identical to the one that I was cuffed to. The electrical lines ran into and out of the room. One of them snaked away from the rest, up to the ceiling and into the ballast of the fluorescent tubes lighting the room.

"It's a bomb shelter, right?" I said.

He smiled and nodded his head.

"You're not just muscle and mayhem, I gather?"

"I've got a couple marbles rattling around upstairs. You didn't build it. Its old."

He nodded and said, "Yeah. It was built back in fifty-five. Army Corps of Engineers poured and built more than a hundred of these underground bunkers on federal land all across the country. Stocked 'em full of emergency supplies. Lots of iodine and dried food and transistor radios for when the nukes started flying. Silly, I guess, in hindsight. But back then we all believed we could live through it if it ever happened. All those supplies were gone when Wade found this place. It was as empty as could be. When we started our little agriculture business, it seemed like a perfect fit out here in the middle of nowhere."

"Sure, until a forest ranger comes wandering around."

The Reverend chuckled and scratched absently at his chin.

"Ain't a forest ranger has us all so worried, friend. Never seen a single one of them out this deep. Naw, only bee in my bonnet is you and the syrup-tongued gal got you roped into this mess. Savannah's a peach, sure. No denying it. But that's a poison fruit, Roarke. I think maybe you're beginning to come around to that way of thinking, too, aren't you? What I mean is, this can't be what you thought you were getting into."

He spread his hands out to encompass the room and my beaten, shackled state.

"This wasn't the game you signed up for, am I right?"

I coughed up a wad of blood and spit it onto the floor. The wound in my arm was trumpeting its existence. The rest of me was a haggard, aching protest. As clear as if it was happening now, I recalled my first real run at Parris Island. Stopping to hunch over in the weeds at the five-mile mark, barking my breakfast out while my Drill Instructor shouted astonishingly creative insults into my ear.

Like then, I hitched myself straight, stared ahead, and pressed on.

"I'm just here for Chelsea Gullins, Reverend. Your pot farm doesn't mean a damned thing to me."

"No, I don't suppose it does. I looked you up. Last night I mean, I searched around on the computer for whatever I could find out about you. Well, no. That isn't altogether right. I asked one of the younger fellas to do it for me. Isn't that a sad truth? When you can admit the world's moved on past you and you need some young nincompoop to point the way for you?"

Behind him, the wall was a wash of old dark stains and I realized that they were tracks of rainwater from over the years. As the bunker had aged beneath the ground, tiny fissures had appeared here and there upon its skin. The wall was dry now, but I could only assume it grew slick whenever a real rain fell. Along the edge where the wall met the ceiling, I could just make out a line of dark green mold.

"Yeah? What did the computer tell you?" I said.

The Reverend leaned back in his chair and crossed one leg over the other. His expression turned shrewd, like a man whose finished his chit-chat and is ready to get down to dickering.

"You've been inside," he said. "And not for nothing. They cooled you off for killing a man."

"What's that tell you?"

"Hold on, let me get it all out. You got a little schooling after that, I guess. Paper down in Detroit had a blurb on you. Said you tried to be a parole officer for a bit. Only that went sideways on you when you tried to kill a kiddie rapist. So they fired you so you can't abuse any more perverts, which I guess is a real crying shame for the republic. Since then, looks like you're listing yourself as some sort of private eye. I used to like a gumshoe novel, back when those were the popular thing to read. Never

169

imagined I'd meet one, though. Always sort of reckoned they were a thing of the past, like rotary phones and ashtrays in cars. But here you are."

"I'm not a detective."

"What are you, then?"

"Whatever I need to be. Right now, I'm here."

Not close enough to reach him. I'd done my best to imagine myself stretching away from the wall and grabbing hold of him with my free hand. My left arm would get me so far, but not so far that I could then reach him with my right. He was out of range as long as he stayed in his chair near the far wall. I kept the idea off my face and continued thinking about a way out of the bunker that didn't include my getting buried out in the woods.

"What do you want?" he said, finally getting to it. He folded his long fingers together over his knee and his wintry eyes searched mine for any sign of falsity.

"Chelsea Gullins set free."

"Yeah? Just the gal? What about money?"

"Just the girl."

"Because there *is* money," he continued. "Never mind Rezner. What if I told you there was a bag full of cash you could take on out of here if you were to do as I ask? The girl, too. She's a good, smart girl. I'd never allow her to come to harm if there was a choice. If you make the right choice, you could drive away with her and a fat nest egg to keep you afloat for quite a while."

"Give me the girl and I go away."

"Shit, you can't really--"

"Give me the girl. I'm not a cop. I'm not a concerned citizen. Keep your money. Give me the girl."

Reverend Graves shook his head and clucked his tongue regretfully.

"It ain't as simple as all that."

"Yeah. It is."

"We need the blonde, Roarke. You have to give Savannah to us. To me. And you have to do it before Rezner gets back down here and blows your brains all over that wall. Because he will. He's going to storm down here and think about all the beers he shared with poor Wade while they talked about freedom and tyranny and the dismal decline of things. And when he sees your face he's going to pull his shiny old *pistola* and empty it into your head, son."

I followed his gaze and stared at the wall behind me, where he predicted the future splash of my head's interior. I scanned up and down, quickly. I stared at the thick iron bolt I was cuffed to. If the shiny new titanium handcuffs were unyielding, the fat iron bolt looked doubly so.

"You can't buy me," I said softly. "You can't scare me with promises of what that lunatic might do. The only thing you can do is find a pair of bolt cutters, get me out of here, and take me directly to Chelsea Gullins." I looked away from the wall, into the old man's wintry eyes, and said, "If you don't, I will break you until you do."

His expression slackened with incredulity. He was silent for a long moment. When he finally spoke again, it was in a disbelieving whisper.

"Jesus...you and Michael, you're just the same, ain't you?"

"Everything I said is the truth. Remember that later."

"Two rabid snapping dogs. Lord, is it too much to ask for a man who can be reasoned with? You...you can't just threaten to tear everything down if you don't get your way exactly the way you want it. You know, the Lord's son was a carpenter first. A man has to be willing to build, Roarke. Don't you see that? Don't you see that you and me, we can build some trust and find a road out of all this?"

"A carpenter," I echoed, but I wasn't in the room anymore. He wasn't going to believe me or do what I told him to. He would keep talking until Rezner came back. When I was dead, he'd keep telling himself their situation was salvageable. Then Jeffrey Tombs, down in Wayne County, would cut a deal and start fessing up about where the pot he'd been caught with came from. Chelsea would go in the same hole as me, just like Rezner had said. And maybe this old tale-teller would keep talking even after that, talk until he got a deal, talk until he had a better sentence than Rezner and the other Sovereign. But Chelsea would still be dead.

So I went away. I drifted back to my first days in my new house. The driveway was heaped with piled lumber and mounds of brick. I was downstairs. In the basement.

"Yes he was a carpenter. He surely was. He knew how to build, Roarke. Later, when he heard the true calling, he turned those skills to building alliances. To building trust."

Down there in the musty basement, that's where I began the months-long labor of refurbishing my home. I stood at the western wall, eager to begin, and stared at the dark stains that made a damp mural across the face of the cement. Years of abandonment had allowed the rain waters to seep over the wall unchecked. Thick green mold framed the mural.

"I'm offering you a chance, Roarke."

There had been a melancholy sort of beauty to that mural of mold and water stains. It was far more dilapidated than the Reverend's bunker—heavily pitted, a rough topography of mildewed rivers and tributaries that swirled and mingled together. I don't know how long I'd stood there, staring at it. But I remember the impulse to reach out. Slowly, I extended one finger and touched the wall. Granules scattered to the floor. I pressed harder. My fingertip disappeared into the mushy skin of the ruined cement.

"You still here? Roarke?"

I came back into myself. I was in the bunker again. The Reverend was squinting up at me, perplexed. I didn't bother to answer him. Instead, I stepped away from the wall as far as my left arm would stretch. Extended like that, I could almost reach the door through which I'd been dragged. The Reverend watched silently as I widened my stance. Spread-eagle now, I wedged my right foot against that door's base.

His eyes swam with confusion, then bulged as the truth dawned on him. I wasn't trying to get away.

I was making sure *he* couldn't.

He rose out of the chair quicker than I would have thought him capable. Backed himself into the corner farthest from me, near the second door that I assumed lead to the bunker's grow room.

"Stop," he blurted. "Just stop. You're stuck, son."

I balled my left hand into a fist and braced myself for the pain that would surely come. Shoulders bunched. The wound flared and burned itself back alive. I heaved on the iron bolt. Felt the slim titanium cuff bite into my skin like a knife's edge. The iron bolt didn't budge.

"This is it?" he huffed in a register somewhere between fear and outrage. "Blind thrashing? God damn it, man, can't you...can't you listen? Can't you just *stop*?!"

Every injury and degradation Rezner had inflicted on me during our forced march announced themselves with renewed fury. I ground my teeth down until I thought they might shatter and pulled harder on the bolt. It didn't move. I lashed my right hand around my left wrist and heaved with a demon's fury. Blood welled out the edges of the cuff.

Somewhere deep and primal, I knew a simple truth: the bolt would yield or I would shear my hand away until it slipped free as a ground and shattered stump.

"Roarke!"

Despite the agony, I peered at him through eyes narrowed to slits.

"Smile," I hissed, a sound of pure, stubborn hate and defiance, "it won't always be like this."

I roared.

I howled and heaved.

Blood ran and swam, swamping the cuff. It filled my eyes until the world was blood and agony, blood and spite, and nothing more.

The bolt moved.

# NINE

"I guess you feel bad about killing that little spic," father said, chewing his teeth contemptuously around the word *'feel'*.

Puckett's cigarette smoke in my nose. The silhouette of the rifleman just on the periphery, pacing, pacing. Time an indistinct notion in the darkness with this giant and his single, hateful eye pinning me to my seat.

"No," I admitted. "I don't feel bad about it."

"Good. That's good. A man threatens you, you destroy him."

"He wasn't just threatening me. He was stabbing me in the guts."

"You heard what I said."

And I heard it again as the iron bolt whipped free of the wall. Storm winds of adrenaline clapped and coursed through me. It registered that the Reverend had slipped through the second door. Warm, skunk-laden air wafted in.

I plunged after him, surging forward on shaking legs. Knocked the door aside. Lurched into the grow room. The adrenal-storm had my fingertips trembling. I felt over-full, over-charged, a balloon brimming with a static charge.

An indoor forest of marijuana plants. Neat, even rows of warmly-glowing grow lamps affixed to the low ceiling. And the Reverend. Twenty paces ahead. Reaching at the far wall. Clamoring to get a hold of something. Turning. A matte-black pistol in his hand.

I charged through the green expanse, kicking potted stalks wildly away. The storm raging inside me was all-encompassing now, as irresistible and complete as when I had crouched over Freddie Esposito and hammered him to death. The storm propelled me and I could not feel the ground beneath my feet. I was in the wind, carried forward, rushing.

Reverend Graves aimed the pistol at my face. The trigger pull earned him a soft click and nothing more. His motions were panicked. Imprecise. Shaking, he pulled the trigger three more times and was rewarded with three more dry, impotent clicks.

He was holding the pistol sideways, fear-saucered eyes searching for the weapon's safety nub, when the storm thundered and hurled me against him. A flurry of biting contact. Bone on bone and the slap of skin. The pistol pin-wheeled away. The Reverend arced through the air, weightless in my fists. I hurled him through the crop. I couldn't hear the sounds coming out of his gaping mouth over the rush of wind in my ears. I seized him again and again he flew.

When he held a shaky arm up to shield his face from me, I seized that arm in both hands and shattered it over my knee.

Then he flew again. Limply crashed against the wall. Stirred on the concrete slab, spasming like a fish on the floor of a fisherman's skiff.

A stutter in time, a moment lost in the maelstrom's pull.

When I came out of it, I was looming over the broken old man, dousing him with the contents of a two-gallon plastic jug of liquid fertilizer and shouting, "Where's the girl!" over and over again.

It registered that I had been shouting it the entire time, ever since the storm seized me. I'd repeated it without pause while I threw him and battered him across the room. It had become a furious chant, as regular as the thunder-beat of my trip hammer heart.

"Where's the girl!"

The Reverend moaned and twisted into himself to keep the fertilizer's acid caress out of his eyes. I drove my foot into his soft side and felt something snap inside him. An incoherent whimper stuttered up out of him.

"Where's the girl!"

When the jug was empty I hurled it against his head and hauled him to his feet and screamed the demand into his broken, ruined face.

*"Where's the girl!"*

\*

Three minutes.

That was how long I allowed myself to pause, to try and get my heart to wind down out of its frenetic pace. I sucked gales of air through my mouth and let them back out slowly. The storm was hesitant to relent. I shook with adrenal palsy.

A hectic and gnawing fear kept threatening to rise, to whip the storm back up into a frenzy. I suppose it was a voice of conscience and moderation, that fear. It wanted to tell me that I'd gone too far, off into bleak and unforgivable terrain, a disquieting badland that only the worst sort of men ever traverse.

I couldn't afford that type of introspection, so I put myself back in Chelsea's room. I looked at the track team photograph I'd found there, while my heart wound down. Saw her unguarded and gentle smile. My hands stilled. I looked at the perfect tidiness of her room, marveled at her desperate need to make her tiny corner of the world a clean and orderly haven. The storm relented and blew itself out. I walked into her closet and read her reassuring message on the mirror. I opened my eyes and was myself again.

On the far wall, from where the Reverend had retrieved his useless pistol, more weapons hung in neat rows. Five hunting rifles. Four shotguns. Maybe a dozen different pistols of varying make and caliber. Thousands of rounds of different ammunitions stacked in their boxes across a low table.

Centered among it all were two HK-416 assault rifles and a Bushmaster ACR—shiny, black, modern monsters.

I lifted the Bushmaster down and looked it over. It was the selective fire model offered only to military and law enforcement operatives. I checked the magazine. Thirty rounds of .223 hollow point death. I slung the weapon over my left shoulder and retrieved the Reverend's pistol from the floor. A Smith and Wesson .40 with a ten round capacity and its safety firmly set in the 'on' position.

Behind me, a series of trilling chimes.

I found the Reverend's cell phone and a small silver key in his pants pocket. A number without a name attached to it appeared on the phone's screen. I let it ring until it went to voicemail, then slipped the phone in my pants.

Crouching there over the unconscious heap of Wayland Graves, Genteel Voice for God's Eternal Mercy and Abductor of Blameless Children, I pictured Deputy Michael Rezner restlessly marching back to his cruiser and his fake life as a peace officer, counting down the hours and minutes until he could race back out here, tear off his mask of humanity, and do the one thing that came naturally to him.

Would he grow so anxious that he'd call the Reverend and demand to know the situation? Of course. Of course he would. And when the Reverend didn't answer? What then? What would his clockwork madness dictate? Would he turn around and race like hell with Wagner to just put an end to the question of me?

Far off, echoing through the deteriorating skin of the bunker, a metallic creak. Heavy boots on ladder rungs.

I stuffed the phone and the silver key in my pocket and scrambled back to the wall of weapons.

The adrenaline storm was an unquiet memory. All the hurt and exhaustion I'd earned was swelling, insistent and real. My joints felt full of sawdust. A hundred points of pain mapped themselves across my body.

I knew there was no relief for that. The storm surge would not return, would not cradle me in its anesthetizing center or assure me that my wrath was an immortal force, beyond injury or fatigue. That sort of madness cannot be summoned at will and, once summoned, is reluctant to return.

I shrugged the Bushmaster off my shoulder, thumbed the safety, and sighted down at the open doorway. The fluorescent bulbs inside the small room where Rezner had trapped me lit everything nicely.

I breathed out slow and imagined a man-sized figure coming through the far door. I made him a white silhouette in my mind's eye, just under six feet, the average height of a man. I froze him there in the center of the door and lined the Bushmaster up with his abdomen, three inches above the navel. Center mass. Center mass means you don't have to worry about missing a bobbing head. Center mass means you take a man out of the fight, even if you don't kill him immediately.

I heard the Drill Instructor in my ear as I sighted down the firing range on Parris Island, his voice syrupy-sweet, like he was extolling a woman's charms, "Center mass is the gift that keeps on giving. That's the sweet spot every time, maggot. Now *show* me."

The door opened.

Someone stepped into my white silhouette of a man. I pulled the trigger and fired a three-round burst of bullets into the space between us. The grow room clamored with the Bushmaster's ugly eruption. The man in the silhouette jerked, spun, and plunged back into the darkness beyond the doorway.

I adjusted my aim, lowering the barrel several inches, and released another three-round burst a few inches from the floor. My ears thrummed, a high whine that made me deaf to all else.

"Get up," I said soundlessly. "Get up and move now, maggot."

In a crouching jog, I left the Reverend and his crop behind. Once I was in the little room where he'd tried to seduce me with promises of money and cooperation, I ducked to the side and approached the far door. Leaning around the jam, I stared down the length of the weapon and saw the dead man in the shadows beyond.

182

The Bushmaster had nearly cut him in half with the first volley. The second had chewed his boots and the feet within them like so much hamburger. I'd been firing jacketed hollow points. They'd transformed him into a dismal and ground-up thing on the floor.

No more than ten feet beyond his corpse, the light from the open ladder-hatch I'd been pushed down made a golden rectangle on the floor. There, in the center of that rectangle, was a cell phone, blown from his hand as the bullets coursed and expanded through him.

I peered down at the dead man's face. He was a scruffy-bearded stranger, a medium-sized man dressed out in camouflage hunting gear. The Reverend's companion, I decided. The one who had ridden out here on the second quad and who had greeted Rezner as he shoved me out of the woods and into this concrete hole.

I looked at the cell phone and imagined Rezner again. Stopping to call the Reverend and getting no answer. Pacing. Growing anxious. Uncertain if he should continue back to his office or turn heel and come back down here.

The cell phone's display lit up and it vibrated on the cement floor like an overturned beetle struggling to right itself. I snatched it up and peered at the screen. An incoming text message. I thumbed it. The caller was listed as *'Sovereign One'*. Beneath that, the message, *'Well?'*

I thumbed backwards to the prior text from the same caller.

It read, *'Check on them.'*

I felt myself smiling as I typed a response.

*'All good. I'll keep an eye on them until you get back.'*

A few seconds passed in silence before an answering text came through.

*'Do that.'*

I shouldered the Bushmaster again and climbed up out of the bunker. Standing at its lip, I stared down at the hole and allowed a moment of satisfaction to wash through me. They hadn't won. I hadn't bent.

"You ain't out yet. Not by far." My father's low, hateful whisper. "You got plenty of enemies out there, son."

I scowled and pushed the idea of him down into the darkness with the Reverend and Terry. I swung the ladder-shaft's steel door shut over the hole. The top side of the lid was covered in a carpet of fake vegetation, real enough that any casual passerby wouldn't notice it among the clearing of wild grass.

He was right, the voice of my Father. This wasn't victory. This had only been survival. Rezner was out there. And when he returned and saw that I'd turned his secret sovereign man's bunker into a bloody mess, he'd race straight to where Chelsea Gullins was being held. He'd kill her. It was the only option. She was evidence. I had to get to her. I had to steal her back before he could try to burn down all traces of what he and the Sovereign had been up to.

High above, the sun told me it was somewhere between four and five in the afternoon. It seemed absurd. Waking and finding Savannah waiting to scold me in the cabin's little kitchen felt like it had been ages ago, another lifetime.

I searched the tree line and quickly spied the first yellow mark of paint that would lead me back out of this ancient expanse.

Exhausted, I forced my feet ahead.

*

A hundred feet ahead, the first smear of yellow paint.

I hefted the Bushmaster, ignored the protests from my wounds, and forced myself to lunge ahead. One yellow mark would lead to another, then another and on, until I was out of the ocean of trees. After that, I needed the topographical maps I'd photographed with my cell phone. If I could get out of the forest and get to the Stratus, I could get my phone. I could read the maps. I could get to Chelsea.

*"My home,"* the Reverend had wheezed, desperate to stave me off. *"Second floor. North...northwest corner. Please...please stop..."*

I hadn't stopped. Couldn't stop. Once he'd told me where he was holding Chelsea, I'd demanded more answers. Answers about Savannah. And he'd told me. Before it was over, before he lapsed into a wheezing unconsciousness, he told me everything.

I shambled up a rise of earth and back down. I saw Savannah again, sitting in the booth across from me when we first met. Telling me just enough to get me to commit to finding her niece. Poking at the edges of my prison history and sizing me up as a brute. A blunt instrument she could aim at the Sovereign. Flirting as we parted. Stirring a hunger in me. Baiting the hook. Using her seductions in the fevered night ride up here to sink the hook deep.

Another yellow smear in the distance. That many steps closer to Chelsea.

When it was over, when the girl was safe, Savannah would be my new priority.

\*

When the last yellow dab of paint brought me to the parked twin quads the Reverend and Terry had used to get out to the forest, I paused and made a vaguely unpleasant decision. I shrugged the Bushmaster off my shoulder and shoved it down in the earth beneath a thick clot of bushes. If I was going to race along the roads of Crawford county, I couldn't risk some concerned passerby calling in a report of a blood-covered madman with a machine gun headed for downtown.

186

The little silver key I'd found in the Reverend's pocket fit the second of the two dirt-caked quads. Once I turned the engine over and heard the satisfying bellow of the quad coming to life, I killed the engine and stepped away.

I looked at the second quad sitting a few feet from the first.

Terry was dead, down in the darkness of the bunker. But the Reverend was still alive. Broken, yes. But alive. There were no more phones down there with him, no easy way to reach out to Rezner and raise the alarm about what I'd done. If he came around and was able, Reverend Graves would have to climb out of that bloody pit with his one good arm and stagger his way out of the forest. It seemed an unlikely feat. But not impossible.

And if he had the foresight to take the quad key Terry likely had on him...

I slipped the Reverend's pistol from my waistband, leveled it at the second quad, and fired twice. The two fat tires nearest me clapped open and deflated in an instant. The quad sank, listing down, inoperable. I pictured the Reverend, wheezing and shattered, shambling his way desperately through the ancient forest, only to emerge here and stare in impotent dejection at the disabled machine.

I climbed aboard the first quad and throttled wildly away from the place where men had failed to murder me.

Every inch of me was alive with pain.

I sneered into the slap of wind and laughed a maniac's laugh.

*

When Crawford's main drag came into view, I zipped passed it and stayed on the side road I'd been following since reaching the edge of town. This far north, even the suburban homeowners of Michigan didn't look twice at a man driving an all-terrain vehicle. ATVs, camo pants, hunting rifles and fishing boats were all part of the landscape.

After a block, I veered south and slowed down. When I came to the next cross street, I paused long enough to peer east and check if I recognized any of the buildings I could spot along the main street. I didn't, so I throttled up until the next block and peered east again. I repeated that process twice more before I spied the courthouse. Hidden from my view, I knew, was the strip mall across the street from the court where I'd left the Stratus.

I guided the quad to an empty spot along the road and left it there.

Half-way down the block, a middle-aged woman picking weeds in her front lawn looked up from her flowerbeds and stared at me. She brushed her hair out of her eyes and frowned with apprehension.

"Sir?"

I kept walking and didn't meet her eyes. On the periphery, I could see her getting to her feet and taking a hesitant step toward me. I stuffed my left hand into my pants pocket to conceal the still-dangling handcuff.

"Sir? Are you alright? Do you need help?"

"Just fine, ma'am," I said and flashed her what I hoped was a disarming smile. I kept walking past her.

"Are you sure? You look hurt."

"Took a nasty fall is all. Going to the doctor right now, thanks."

"But..."

And I was past her house, past her neighbor, still moving. When I was a few houses away from the main street, I looked back over my shoulder. She was still standing there, staring at me with concern and apprehension.

The back wall of the strip mall appeared and I turned down the ribbon of asphalt that ran behind it. I accelerated to a jog despite the pain it earned me and put the woman out of my mind. If she was inclined to call the police and report a bloody, beaten stranger roaming her street, there was nothing I could do now to stop her.

I came to the far corner of the long building and peered around it.

The Stratus was where I'd left it. The evening sun was low enough that it swam in the car's windows, grown a deep orange as it drew closer to the horizon. Beyond the Stratus, across the main street, the courthouse. And beside it, Rezner's cop clubhouse where he masqueraded as a sane human being. I scanned the lot beside the sheriff's office, but couldn't pick out whether or not any of the county cruisers parked there were his.

It didn't matter. There were no choices, now. I needed the maps I'd stored on my cell. I needed to move and not waste time.

I slipped the Reverend's pistol out of my waistband and into my pants pocket. Keeping my hand on the hidden gun, I turned the corner and started walking toward the Stratus. A beaten old Ford pickup rumbled down the street, its fan belt whining. I kept my eyes on the cop shop and didn't slow down. An old man in a lawyer's blue suit walked out of the courthouse and gingerly made his way down the front steps. I scanned the windows of the sheriff's office until I found the one that belonged to Rezner's office. It was lit. I told myself he was inside. He was sitting at his neatly barren desk. He was signing papers. Going through bureaucratic motions. Not thinking about me. Not worrying about me.

I was at the Stratus. I was reaching for the handle.

The Reverend's cell phone chimed in my shirt pocket and froze me in my tracks.

I plucked it out and stared at the screen. *Rezner*, it read. I stared while it rang two more times, seized with a sudden certainty that he was calling *me*. Not the Reverend. He wasn't in his office. He'd passed me, unseen, in the forest. He'd found his dead friend in the pit. He'd found the Reverend. While I'd raced back here, he'd roared his way to the Reverend's ranch. And now he was standing over Chelsea Gullins, waiting for me to answer the phone so I could hear the hellish clap of the gunshot that would kill her.

I almost answered the phone. I was that certain things had gone exactly that terribly wrong.

The front door of the sheriff's office swung open.

Deputy Michael Rezner stalked out into the retreating light of day, his face a mask of ugly fury, his cell pressed against his ear.

# T E N

I slipped into the Stratus and pulled the driver's door softly shut.

The Reverend's cell trilled a fourth time.

The Last Watchman paced outside the sheriff's office. His free hand clenched into a fist at his side.

I stared at the cell in my hand and tried to think. It trilled a fifth time and cut short. Voice mail. It had gone to voicemail. I looked up and across the street.

Rezner shouted something into his phone, standing rigid with furious anxiety. Whatever he said, it was short, sharp, and loud. He stuffed the cell back in a pocket and paced in a tight circle. Undecided. Uncertain if he was going back inside.

The Reverend's cell vibrated and the screen told me there was a new voice mail message.

I reached over, snapped the glove box open, and yanked the Sig out. I set it in my lap. If Rezner decided to get in his cruiser and charge away to investigate what was happening in his bunker, there was only one way I could go.

I'd never particularly dreamed of executing a law enforcement officer on the streets of his home town, but life throws you the occasional curveball.

As that absurd idea formed in my mind, he cemented it by lunging off toward the rows of police cruisers. His hand went in a pocket and came out with a set of keys. He'd made his decision. He was going to the bunker.

I reached out and opened the driver's door. I had one foot out on the pavement. If I pushed off and charged across the street, I could close the distance on him in a moment. I could line him up under the Sig. Take a second to steady. Blow the lunatic right out of the world.

A strong and urgent part of me wanted nothing more than to do exactly that. Of course his brother's in blue would be on me before I could drive a mile's distance. It was certain death for him. And for me. You don't murder a cop outside his clubhouse and live more than a few moments beyond the act.

And Chelsea? Would she live? Or would another one of the Sovereign who saw Rezner as their 'Sovereign One', as Terry did, silence the child?

*Terry.*

I shut the driver's door again and pulled out the dead man's cell phone. I found 'Sovereign One' in the contact list and started typing.

*'What's up? Preacher says don't bother him. His words not mine. This guy is talking about the blonde.'*

I hit 'send' and stared at Rezner with my breath held in my chest. Waiting. He took three more steps. Held the keys out and pressed the fob. Four cruisers down from him, head lights blinked once in response.

"Come on, you son of a bitch," I hissed in the silence of the Stratus' interior.

Rezner came to a stop and produced his cell phone again. I watched. A few seconds passed. Terry's cell vibrated in my hand.

*'You're shitting me,'* he sent.

I started typing.

*'Nope. Says she's still in Ann Arbor. Says he knows where she's hiding.'*

*'Get everything from him. EXACTLY where she is. When he's done spilling, finish it. Fuck Graves. Tell him I gave the order if he starts crying about it.'*

I smiled and sent, *'Understood. See you after.'*

*'We'll both go down to get her together.'*

*'Ok.'*

*'Good work, Terry. Stand tall, brother.'*

*'Always,'* I sent back, and watched Rezner turn on his heel and casually stroll back into the sheriff's office. Calm.

194

Unworried now that he was certain I was a dead man and Savannah was ready to be plucked from hiding.

I waited. I counted silently until a full five minutes had passed. Nobody came in or out of the sheriff's office. He was satisfied. For now. For now, he was certain that I was begging futilely for my life, trading Savannah's security for my own. The loose ends were being tied up. He could wear his human mask around the office until it was time to clock out and resume his real life as a murderous, delusional thing.

For now, the Last Watchman was quelled.

I plucked the keys out of the glove box, started the Stratus, and slowly rolled away.

\*

When I hit the expressway, I went one exit past the one that lead to Home Among the Pines, choosing instead to get south of it and double back in a long, circuitous route through the disused and abandoned stretches that surrounded Two Pine. I had no real fear that I was being followed. I'd bought myself time to find and rescue Chelsea Gullins. But the two women who owned the cabin I'd rented with Savannah were innocent in all of this. If I was wrong about my anonymity, I didn't want to put the owners of Home Among the Pines at risk. So I rolled through the rural stretches south of them and watched the rearview mirror for headlights.

Rain-stained and faded 'FOR SALE' signs leaned drunkenly in the infrequent driveways. The roads were pocked with potholes, some of them showing signs of green growth where nature was reasserting itself.

Nothing else moved on the roadways. I was alone.

*

I walked through the front door of the cabin.

Savannah was coiled tight in one of the pine-frame chairs directly across from me, cloaked in the evening darkness. She was dressed in white shorts and a peach top. The little pistol she'd brought with her in her go-bag was in her hand and pointed at my chest.

"Do it," I said.

I watched her hand trembling as she held the gun. Her eyes were wide with fear and an air of emotional exhaustion clung to her. Something in the quiet of the room told me she'd been positioned like that for a long time. She'd been sitting there, waiting in dread. Waiting to see who came through the door. The light of day had drained away and she'd stayed rooted in place, not so much as reaching out to turn on a lamp.

"We don't have time," I snarled. "Pull the trigger or put it down."

"Where did you go?" she whispered.

"Maybe I made a deal," I growled. "Sold you to the Reverend and Rezner. Maybe they get you and their money and I get Chelsea. That's what you want to know, right? Did I hear the truth about you and sell you down the river? Who knows? Pull the trigger and make a run with your passport and cash. Maybe you'll make it. Or maybe I'm still going to get your niece back. Your call. Who am I, Savannah? Pull the trigger or put the gun down."

I saw myself reflected in the glass slider behind her; a looming heap of crusting blood and mud. With the black titanium cuff dangling loose and the torn ruin of my shirt hanging free, I looked like some escaped lunatic straight out of a horror movie.

That she hadn't shot me the second I opened the door was a small miracle, I realized.

Savannah's bright little teeth shone in the gloom of the room as she bit her lower lip. She closed her eyes and I heard a long sigh slip out of her. She tossed the gun on the floor. It clattered across the hardwood and spun to a rest at my feet.

"You son of a bitch," she muttered, and ran her palms over her bleak, tired face. "You son of a bitch. *Why* did you go to the cops?"

I bent down and plucked the gun off the floor. I ejected the empty magazine, walked up to her, and held it out for her to see.

"If you need to fire a gun it helps to have bullets."

That close, her scented moisturizer filled my nose. She was a pale pile of beauty, narrow legs curled under her, arms crossed over her chest. Closing down. Bolstering herself for whatever ugliness I was going to unleash.

"It wasn't for you," she said.

"I know. It was for Rezner or whatever other Sovereign walked through the door."

"Are they coming?"

"Not yet. There's still time. But not much. We have to move. Now."

Her lovely face tilted up to regard me and I could see the dried tracks of tears staining her cheeks. Her lengths of coppery hair were unkempt, wild, and I resented that none of her exhaustion or panic diminished her beauty.

"We?" she said, so softly I almost didn't hear her.

"Was Paul a hunter?"

She blinked several times, confused.

"What?"

"Paul," I demanded. "Your dead brother-in-law. Was he a hunter?"

"Yes. He hunted. Everyone hunts up here. Roarke, what--"

"Then its 'we'. Get on your feet. Change into long pants and put some shoes on. Get your damned head together and meet me outside in ten minutes."

She didn't move. She frowned and started to stammer another question, but didn't have time before I seized her by her shoulders and hauled her out of the chair. She yelped, but she didn't fight me. Not like the night before when she struggled against me to get my blood to rise, to summon the lust in me she knew was there. Now she was a rag doll in my clutches, resolved to whatever punishment I meant to dole out.

"You took their money," I said, low and slow, our faces nearly touching. Her eyes were all I could see, so close, emerald, wide open, their long, pale lashes trembling. I wanted to kiss her. I wanted to drown in her eyes, down in their cunning depths.

I pushed the want away and kept talking.

"When Jeffrey Tombs got busted in Wayne County with a truck load of the Sovereign's pot, you panicked. You emptied out the bank accounts you were managing for them. You were their launderer. Paul was their accountant. He brought you in. The Sovereign needed someone to clean their drug cash and Paul sized you up right. He knew a banker with a mercenary heart, didn't he?"

"Yes," she whispered, so close I felt the warm pulse of her breath on my mouth.

"So you went into business with those freaks. I guess it was a good game. I guess it was easy money. Until one of them got pinched and you decided your loyalty to the Sovereign didn't extend past him maybe confessing to what was going on up here. So you panicked. You panicked and you stole from a group of very dangerous men. Because of that, Paul's a dead man and your niece is going to be joining him if you don't get your head straight and do exactly what I tell you to."

Savannah drew a deep, shuddering breath and said, "I'll do anything. Order me."

"Get changed. We have a hike ahead of us."

I let her go and took a step back, watching for some sign that she was going to obey. She ran her hands up to push her hair out of her eyes. When she looked at me again, it was with a new recognition. No, I wasn't the mindless beast she could seduce and aim at the Sovereign. But I was still with her, in some fashion. At least long enough to get Chelsea free and safe.

That must have been enough for her because she nodded one time, her pretty lips set in a firm line of decision.

"I'll get changed," she agreed. Her fingertips touched my cheek, a startling, electric contact. "Ten minutes."

She whirled around and disappeared into her bedroom. I watched her vanish and resented the need to charge after her and take hold of her again. I wanted to sink down to the floor with her and forget every indignity of that day, inside her. I wanted to accuse her and forgive her in the same desperate motion.

Instead, I reminded myself that there was an innocent child held in a strange room not far away. I lumbered into the cottage's tiny kitchen, a frustrated, stinging mass, and started making coffee.

When the pot was half-full, I poured a cup and swallowed it in a rush.

In my room, I shrugged out of my ruined shirt and into a clean one. I tore off the ruined shirt's remaining sleeve and wrapped it around the dangling cuff and bolt, tying it securely so the cuff was pressed against my forearm and out of the way. I rifled around in my bag until I found the spare magazines I'd brought for the Sig.

In the bathroom I splashed hot water over my face and scalp, wincing at the pain where Rezner had bounced my head against the bunker wall. The blood and dirt ran in streaks until the basin looked like a slaughterhouse floor. I kept at it until my face was clean.

I stared in the mirror and saw her where she'd sat the night before, shaving me, toying and teasing.

*'Order me. I'll do anything.'*

Maybe it was truth. Maybe she was ready to just do the right thing and not try to manage me or provoke me. Or maybe she was still calculating, choosing her words with machined precision. Baiting the hook again.

*'Order me. I'll do anything.'*

I looked at the fist-sized hole in the wall across the room. Saw her superimposed over it, naked, as pale as milk.

Letting my mind wander in that direction wouldn't help anything, so I forced her out of my eyes and stalked back out of the room before the image of her could plunge onto the bed and pull me down with her.

In the kitchen, I drank the rest of the pot in great gulps. It burnt, but that didn't slow me down. I needed to be awake. I needed to wash out some of the weariness that was threatening to blanket me and slow me down.

"I have pills, you know."

Savannah was standing there in jeans and sneakers. She'd shrugged a white hoodie on. It was too big for her, baggy, and that fact made her look darling again, like when a woman tries on one of your shirts the morning after because she knows it will cover just barely enough.

"I don't need pills. You're ready to go?"

"Not the oxy. These are wake-you-up pills."

"Yeah? What're you doing with those?"

"I don't throw anything away, I guess."

"Uh-huh. Keep them. Let's go."

I went to walk past her to the door, but she reached out and curled her fingers into my hand. Despite myself, I curled my fingers into hers, an instant impulse to her touch. She peered up at me, unsmiling, as earnest and naked as I'd ever seen her.

"I'm sorry, Roarke."

I ground my teeth down against themselves and didn't squeeze her hand or tell her that I didn't need her to be sorry, I just needed her to keep touching me and smelling the way she smelled and looking like that in the shadow and half-light of a desperate hour. I didn't tell her any of that.

"Sure," was all I managed.

"Please. I am. I'm sorry. About all of...about everything. I'll do anything. I'll do whatever you say we have to do. We can give them the money. All of it. There's more than what I brought with me. We can get it all and give it back."

It sounded true. Her face was set, unblinking, with no sign of artifice. Just a light in the eyes that said she was clear-headed and resolved. She looked like someone who'd spent the day slowly discarding her illusions, waiting for the inevitable to barge in the door and put an end to all the lies.

"It's too late for that, Savannah."

"What does that mean?"

"It means we get Chelsea tonight or it's over. Men are dead. The money won't buy her back once Rezner sees what's happened. He'll kill her and he'll come looking to kill both of us. That's the math."

"I thought…"

"You're done thinking," I said and let go of her hand. I marched out of the cottage and she followed close behind. When we got into the Stratus, she didn't repeat her kitten-curl from the night we drove up there. She sat straight-backed and snapped the seat belt in place while I wheeled the car around and pulled away from Home Among the Pine.

"What are we doing, exactly?" she said after a little while.

"You know what we're doing."

The road was empty but for us, so I hit the brights and let the Stratus surge us into the darkness and the unknowable.

"We're grabbing her back," she whispered beside me.

"Yes. We are."

*

The road was a black winding line that rolled and dipped like a progression of waves that would never crest. Vacant, shuttered houses occasionally appeared on either side, straight-edged artifacts of a vanished society. The sky above was clear, a cascade of silver pinpoints. I sent all the windows whispering down and let the clean smell of the woods whip around the car's interior.

Savannah's drape of sun-kissed curls leapt and whipped in the sudden rush of wind. She quietly pulled her hood over her head and tied the drawstrings together. She didn't say a word as the Stratus chewed through the night.

*

I don't fetishize cars as much as some, but I harbor a love of driving that borders on an addiction. Something about the incessant progress of driving disallows brooding. The devils can try and take hold, but then you crest a rise or make a turn, and they slip away, left behind, chattering impotently in the rearview. Forward motion can be stellar therapy.

Nothing beats night driving. The solitude of the car extends out into the empty stretches of the world. You're an explorer, alone, an autonaut barreling over alien terrain. Anyone who might judge you, even yourself, is so far away they aren't real anymore. You can let the snap of wind comfort you, your mind focused on nothing but the next curve of asphalt, moving, moving, outrunning all your yesterdays.

*

"Tell me how it started," I shouted over the howl of wind.

She kept quiet for a moment. Then I saw her turn toward me out of the periphery of my vision. The asphalt swept away beneath us. The forest on either side was darker than the sky above.

Savannah started talking, matter-of-fact, with no trace of a confessional tone.

"Paul brought me in. Two years ago. He was a smart guy. Not wise, I mean, but smart. Smart with details. I didn't even have to ask him how it would work on my end, with the bank and the reporting regulations. He laid it all out, every step. So I said yes. Nothing more than that. He told me and I was in, right away. And...it worked. Just like he said. There's a federal cap on cash deposits. Once you exceed the cap, as a bank officer you have to report it. So we opened dozens of accounts. Every one of the Reverend's men has a few to their name, so it wasn't all under just one guy. And every deposit was just under the threshold."

"Smurfing," I said.

"What? How do you know that?"

"Prison. It's the slang for laundering drug cash. Lots of little cash accounts that don't get reported to the feds. Small and unnoticed. Smurfs."

"Yes."

"That's not all, though, is it? Staying under the reporting limit doesn't clean the cash. The IRS will still raise an eyebrow when those accounts hit their screens at the end of the year."

"That's Paul's end. He set up dummy businesses for each of the Sovereign. Some of them would be the sole proprietors of Laundromats or do-it-yourself car washes, that sort of thing. Two Pine has four different Sovereign-owned businesses. Well, not counting the dummy consulting firm Paul and the Reverend own. We just listed that one to Paul's home address."

"Four operating businesses…" I mused.

"Yep."

"I've seen all of Two Pine. There's nothing there."

"Sure there is," she said and offered me a sardonic grin. "We're about a half mile from one. Keep driving. It'll be on the left. Free-For-All Vending Services. Rezner owns that one, actually."

We cleared the half mile and Savannah gestured out into the gloom. I slowed down to a crawl. A two-story house appeared just past a high row of hedges. The lawn was an untended tangle. No lights shone.

"This place is dead," I said and wheeled into the driveway.

"Yeah," she said, and got out of the car. I watched her walk behind the Stratus, crossing over to the mailbox at the end of the drive. When she plopped back down in the car, she was holding a fat pile of envelopes.

"See?" she said, and started rifling through the pile. They were all addressed to 'Free-For-All Vending Services'. I took some of the envelopes from her and looked through them. Offers

207

for business-grade credit cards. Offers for advertising solutions. Junk mail. The crap that gets automatically generated and thrown at you the minute you register a business with a county or state.

I handed the mail back to her and stared at the untended lawn, the empty house. The roof was littered with dead branches from the overhanging trees. The gutters sagged with accumulated leaves.

"You're listing dummy businesses to the addresses of foreclosed homes," I said.

"Yes."

"There are more of these around Two Pine."

"Three more, yeah."

"What happens when the bank that holds title to this place gets an interested buyer and comes out here and finds out what's happening? Hell, what if they hire a lawn crew to mow all the vacant properties they own? This was never going to go undiscovered."

Savannah's grin was full of self-satisfaction.

"That was my idea, actually. Paul hadn't worked it out, but it seemed obvious to me. When the market crashed and all the sub-prime mortgages caught on fire, there were houses like this everywhere. All of them dumped onto the market overnight and nobody looking to buy them."

"You bought them through your bank," I said, finally catching on.

"Yep. I picked out four that had low balances left on their mortgages and plucked them up for next to nothing. As far as the bank is concerned it's just asset acquisition at the right time, market-wise. Nobody blinked an eye."

"And if the feds come poking around the bank looking to see the papers on these houses?"

"Roarke, I'm a Senior V.P.," she chuckled. "It isn't my name on the accounts or on the real estate purchase agreements. Paul's good with money. So am I. If it ever came tumbling down, I had a lot of wriggle room."

"Then why empty the accounts at the first sign of trouble?"

I watched her self-satisfied grin spread until she was showing me her small, bright teeth.

"Because I wanted leverage."

"You wanted the money. Not just your share. All of it."

"Sure. That, too."

She was beaming next to me, like what she'd told me was so impressive she expected a compliment.

I put the Stratus in reverse and got us back on the road.

"It's funny," I said.

"What is?"

"How you can sit there and smirk like that when Chelsea's where she is."

Her smile melted into a sour frown. But she didn't look away from me. She sat there, as close as she'd been the night I'd driven us up here, and stared at me. I goosed the Stratus into a higher gear and kept my eyes off her, on the road.

"Where is she, exactly?" she said after a while.

"The Reverend's ranch. A second floor bedroom on the northwest corner."

"If Michael Rezner is there, we'll never get to her. He has a guard dog. A police dog. He always has it with him and that dog is always on guard."

"He won't be there."

"How do you know that's where Chelsea actually is?"

"I tortured the Reverend until he told me."

Savannah mouthed the word 'oh', but no sound came out.

"Then he told me about you."

Finally, she settled back away from me and turned her eyes to her window. She folded her arms in front of her and let out a long, slow breath through her nose.

"I can't keep apologizing. It won't help us."

"I don't need an apology."

"Really? Because you sure sound like you want one."

"All I want is what I promised to do from the beginning. I want to get Chelsea free. You're going to help with that. Save your apologies for her and her mother and anyone else you've betrayed. But not me."

She bunched tighter into herself, drew her legs up until her knees touched her chin. She rested her forehead against the window and closed her eyes. When she spoke, it was a sob.

"They knew. They knew she was the only person…the only one I ever…"

"Cared about," I finished for her. "You want a tip? Don't advertise your weaknesses to people you plan on stabbing in the back."

"I never thought they'd go after Chelsea."

"Yeah? Well, they did."

"I wouldn't have done it. Not in a million years. Not if I'd known they would use her to get the money back. You have to believe that."

"It doesn't matter what I believe. All that matters is what happened. They sold Paul some story that convinced him to bring his daughter up here. He must have figured out yesterday that the story was a lie and his little girl was a hostage. He balked or he threatened them. So they sent Wade and Rezner to put him down. That's what happened, Savannah."

"If I'd known, I would have--"

"What you *would* have done doesn't mean a damn thing."

"Then what am I even *doing* here?" she snapped, raising her head up to look over at me again. Her eyes were bright with unshed tears. "Why bring me along? I can't make it right. They won't give her back. So why am I here?"

211

Paul's driveway loomed abruptly out of the darkness. I brought the Stratus to a sharp halt and killed the headlights There was no light in the world, only the pins in the sky. Through the open windows of the car, I listened. Nothing but the insect hum of evening.

I looked at the shadow of Savannah next to me.

"You're here to shoot a rifle," I answered.

"I've never fired a gun in my life."

"Tonight, you will," I said, and rolled us slowly up the dark gravel drive.

*

They'd cleaned it up.

I stared through the brand new slider door at the empty lawn outside. The door's frame hadn't been painted yet. A fresh lumber odor still hung in the air. I rifled through the kitchen's drawers, eventually finding a shiny little black Maglite. I shone it around the kitchen carefully, cupping my hand over the end.

The bullet damage to the wood counter top was still there, but the hole was filled with dried wood putty. All the rough edges had been sanded down. I paced until I found the hole in the wall where one of Rezner's shots had landed. It was now covered in a smooth skin of fresh drywall.

Anybody seeing the kitchen for the first time wouldn't think anything askance. Unfinished repairs, sure. But nothing that would hint of the violence that had exploded in the home a little more than a day ago. I checked for blood and glass on the floor, but there was nothing. I turned the flashlight off again and stood in the darkness, thinking it through.

In the darkness, Savannah pointed.

"The fridge is open."

I walked over to her. She was right. A slim line of light shone where the big stainless steel refrigerator was ajar. I pushed it shut and pointed out of the kitchen, toward the stairs that lead to the second floor.

"Come on," I said. "We need to find his guns."

The first room on the second floor was a neatly kept office. Certificates of accomplishment on the walls. Photos of Paul and Chelsea. I ran the Maglite's beam over the shelves and desk. Paused its progress when I caught sight of the framed photo perched on the desk beside the computer monitor.

Paul was smiling sheepishly into the camera, dressed in a neatly pressed blue dress shirt. Beside him, Michael Rezner's stoic mask was in place. On the other side of Paul, Reverend Graves smiled his genial smile, his eyes bright with good will. It was a posed photo of friends. Three buddies shoulder-to-shoulder in the sunlight.

"The three of them started the Sovereign," I said.

213

Savannah peered at the photo and nodded her head.

"Yeah. Well, sort of."

"What do you mean?"

"Rezner already had a dozen guys who called themselves the Sovereign North. Paul said they were all survivalists and doomsday preppers. Waiting for the race war or the New World Order or whatever would give them the excuse to grab their guns and make their own laws, you know?"

"So how did that turn into an organized marijuana operation?"

She pointed a finger at the Reverend.

"All him. Paul said the Reverend started floating the idea once his church folded. His flock moved out of town. Paul's business was sinking. They were all sort of friends already, and I think the Reverend just kept bringing the idea up over beers. The Reverend had been growing his own weed for years. Then they just…you know. Started doing it. Once the money was real, Paul called me. That was more than, jeez, four years ago?"

I walked out of the room and she followed.

We stepped into a bedroom decorated in pink and light blue. A twin-sized bed with a lacy white comforter and fluffy pink pillows. The carpet was sky blue and looked so new and untrammeled it could have been used as a showroom sample.

Chelsea's room. Paul had set it up for her sometime since moving to Two Pine. There were no posters on the walls, no clothing in the closet, just a few empty hangers. No sign that she had ever spent time in the room.

The last room on the floor was Paul's bedroom. Unlike the rest of the house, it was a cluttered mess. I stepped over mounds of discarded clothing and pulled the closet doors open. One half of the interior was all hanging shirts and suit coats. The other half was dominated by a gun rack. There were two shotguns and a single bolt-action hunting rifle.

I took the rifle down. It was a matte black Browning with a detachable, three-round magazine. I pulled the magazine. It was full, so I snapped it back in place. A box of 7mm Remingtons sat on the shelf at the bottom of the gun rack. I plucked out twelve of them.

"Put those in the right hand pocket of your hoodie," I told her.

She obeyed without question, even if her eyes were full of uncertainty.

I held the Browning out to her and she took it awkwardly in her hands.

"Roarke…"

"Accuracy won't matter for what I need from you," I said. "I'll walk you through how to fire it and how to reload the magazine once you've emptied it. You can do this."

She looked at the gun skeptically, then at me.

"Savannah."

"We're really doing this? Really? Why don't we just call your FBI friend, Mr. Reinhart? Can't we do that now and tell him the truth?"

"You should have done that before," I said. "Before you hired a guy you figured was a thug and an ex-con who'd just kill anyone who kept him from Chelsea. Someone too dim to ask questions and figure out he was being played. It's too late to rewind the tape. The feds can't get here before Rezner finds out what I did to the Reverend. He'll kill Chelsea and hide her body before they're halfway up here."

Her composure broke at the suggestion and tears sprang into her eyes.

"Don't say that. Jesus, please don't."

"We do this. It was your plan. I'm going in there and getting her out. The only thing that's changed is you don't get to bake orange cake and safely wait for me to deliver her to you like a present. So wipe your eyes and find some nerve, sweetheart. You get to do the right thing for once. Who knows? Maybe you'll like the feeling."

I left her alone up there with the rifle and walked back down to the kitchen. In the darkness, I thumbed my cell alive and started clicking through the photos I'd taken the day before. I scanned the topographical maps of forest that bordered Paul's land. I'd been doing that for about five minutes when Savannah appeared at my shoulder with the Browning slung over her shoulder. Her eyes were dry and she seemed to have tamped down her fear at what I was proposing.

"What are you doing?" she whispered.

"Finding the best route to hike over to the Reverend's."

"You found one?"

"Yeah. There's a riverbed we can follow. Come on. We need you to fire that a few times before we head out."

She shrugged the Browning back into her hands and held it across her chest. She nodded once that she was ready, her mouth pursed into a serious little line. In her too-big hoodie, she looked like an adorable little girl squaring herself up to tackle an adult job.

"You're ready?" I said.

"Sure. Ready."

"Alright."

I lead her out through the new slider door. Once we were on the deck, I had her sprawl out into a prone shooting position with the Browning pointed out past the steps that lead to the lawn. I told her to splay her left leg out for better balance and she complied. I crouched down and adjusted where she held the rifle.

"Keep the butt tight against your shoulder, like that."

"Okay."

I reached down and took her right hand in mine and worked the bolt, chambering a round.

"You see how that works?"

217

"Let me do it."

She worked the bolt until all three rounds were laying on the deck beside her. I showed her how to eject the magazine and refill it. We went through it again.

"Okay," she said. "So when I fire off three, I refill with what's in my pocket."

"That's right."

She peered up at me and scrunched her nose.

"There's an off button, right? Where's the off button?"

I almost kissed her right then.

"That's the safety," I said, my voice suddenly gruff, and pointed at the nub set into the rifle's stock. "Ignore it. Just don't touch the trigger until you're ready to fire."

"Okay. Are we doing that now? Shooting it? Won't people hear?"

"There's nobody near here. Even if there is, nobody thinks twice about rifle fire around here. Okay, get back in position."

She did. I talked to her about sighting down the length of the weapon. I talked about breathing and patience.

"You don't have to hit anything. You just have to be calm and pull the trigger. Point it. Pull the trigger. Work the bolt. Do that until you've spent three rounds. Refill. Start over. Keep doing it until there are no more bullets. Understand?"

She nodded that she did.

"Okay," I said. "Show me."

218

She did. She was calm. The rifle cracked and split the silence of the night. She worked the bolt. She fired. She did it once more. Then she removed the empty magazine and refilled it with the bullets in her pocket. Looked up at me.

"Yes?" she said. "Good?"

"Good," I agreed.

I held my hand out to help her to her feet. In the star light, I could see her cheeks were flush with excitement as she slung the weapon over her shoulder again.

"We can do this," I said.

She stared into the wall of trees where she'd sent her three bullets. Her chest rose and fell quickly. She was trembling with adrenaline.

"Kiss me," she whispered.

"Savannah…"

"Do it," she insisted and peered up at me. "Not because you want to. I know you do. But don't do it for that. Do it because we're going. Because we might not come back or ever get a chance to--"

I pulled her against me, lifted her until her toes weren't touching the ground anymore, and kissed her. I held her up like that, marveled at how light she was, and let all the ache I felt for her pour out of me.

When it was over, I pulled away and set her back on the earth. Still dizzy from the warmth and softness of her, I took her hand and lead her down to the lawn and into the dark woods.

I'd prepared as much as I could afford. I'd spent all the spare minutes we had.

It was time to take Chelsea Gullins back.

\*

The Reverend's two-story ranch was a little less than a quarter mile off the road. I left Savannah behind in the woods with her rifle and circled it slowly, letting the surrounding woods in which it hid from view serve as my own cover. There was the main house and, behind it, a pole barn. In the gravel drive, two SUVs, a black pick-up truck and a Mercedes Benz.

I back-tracked and peered across the big back yard. It was a sweep of freshly mowed wild grass that terminated at the border of the state land. That way, the way Savannah and I had come, the world went on forever—a marching army of pine and oak. Somewhere out there, miles away to the east, was the blood-drenched bunker and the Sovereign' grow fields.

I stared at the western corner of the house, at the window there. Chelsea's room, the Reverend had confessed. It was on the second floor, just below the lip of the roof and just above the sloped overhang of the wood deck that stretched across the back of the house. Getting up to that window would be no more difficult than it had been to get into Chelsea's bedroom in Plymouth.

I had seen no sentries during my slow circuit of the property. A single light shone from the windows on the eastern side of the first floor, but I saw no movement inside. The number of vehicles in the drive meant there were certainly multiple men inside. They'd have guns, but that wouldn't mean much if I was quiet enough slipping up to that window.

Absurdly, I thought about Leander Smalls.

He was freshly out of prison for his third home invasion. A slight, even meek little man answering his parole officer's questions.

"I don't know why I done it," he told me. "No, that ain't true. That ain't. I know why. It's the thrill. Like no thrill you ever had. I mean, I ain't never fooled with drink or drugs. Never done no drugs at all, not even in the joint. My thrill is getting inside a house, man. Look here, when I was thirteen I did my first one. A little one-story place out in Allen Park. Nobody home. No pets. I'm out just to be out, even though I know my Moms is going to lay into me like you don't even know once I get back. I figure the beating is gonna come anyhow, late as it is. And I just got this feeling come down into me. I'm going in that house before I even know I'm doing it. Didn't ask myself why. Didn't try to talk myself out of it.

It was…you know what it is? It's what I bet explorers would feel when they come up on some new island. It ain't *their* island, you know? They's people there already. But, shit, that ain't going to stop the boats from landing and the boots to be hitting' the beach, you know? Because there's *secrets* on that island. And there's secrets in folks' homes. Treasure, maybe. Maybe. Most likely not, though. Rich folk got alarms, and I don't never mess with that sort of house. What I liked to find was just the things they wouldn't want other people to see, you know? Like if they filthy. Like if they upstanding outside with friends and co-workers, but inside the place is just a filthy wreck. Drugs, too. Find their drugs and you know you seeing something about them they never want anyone to see. That was the juice, man. Just being there and nobody know it. And you're moving' around, through the rooms, like now it is your place. You just claimed it. I dunno, mister. I know that don't go half way to explaining it way you want me to, but there's just a rush that come with it. It bit me when I was a kid, and it ain't never let me go. I'll think I left it behind, but sooner or later I'm in somebody's laundry room, walking soft, listening for sounds, and that thrill…that thrill is filling me up like a balloon."

Leander was gone now, back to the prison where he'd spent the majority of his life. The electric lure of other people's homes had tempted him almost as soon as he was on the streets again. Another conviction. Back to the cellblock. However he was getting his juice these days, it wasn't through home invasion.

I crept out onto the lawn in the moonlight. For the first time, I could relate to what Leander had said. My heart skipped up into a higher gear. Things in the periphery of my vision dimmed and went away, until there was only the window of the room where I was certain Chelsea Gullins was being held.

When I got to the deck, I slowed down and started stepping with care. I passed a large grill with an attached smoker and stopped. I took a long, calming breath. Stared into the windows that ran along the first floor. In the lighted ones on the other end of the house, nothing moved. I listened for the whine of a dog, the scuff of a boot. Nothing.

The night sky's skin was as purple as a bruise, the starscape hidden behind it. Time would not wait for me to gather my nerve. Rezner was coming off the clock. He would call the phones I'd left behind in the Stratus, if he hadn't already. He would be on the move. Panicked. Furious. His mask of sanity would fall away.

There was no more time to think.

I looked up. I could easily reach the overhang that sloped down from the second-floor window. Still, I picked up one of the black wrought-iron deck chairs and set it down just under the overhang. Plenty of things could go wrong, and there were no guarantees about who was coming down that slope. If it was just Chelsea, if I was lying dead on the floor while she scurried out, the presence of the chair might be the difference between her getting quickly away or suffering a sprained ankle on the jump down.

I used the chair for the added height and pulled myself up onto the shingled slope. The shoulder wound throbbed in protest. I ignored it. Keeping myself as flat as I could, I crawled on my belly up to the window. I pressed my forehead against the glass, peering in, desperate for any sign of what was inside. A bed to the right, against the wall. The lump of a human beneath a heavy quilt. A curl of blonde hair peeking out. A closed door to the left. Darkness beyond them both, the room in heavy shadow.

I looked over the lock screwed into the frame between the two panes of glass. Blinked several times like I was trying to get a mirage out of my eyes. Because I was.

The lock's latch was swung wide.

It was in the 'open' position.

I stared at it in disbelief. I looked at the lump beneath the blankets again. Nothing moved. The world was quiet and offered no answers.

Down below, a man's guttural laughter. An answering hoot. The Sovereign were awake and alive down in the first floor. Rezner's men, and the Reverend's. Followers, with no reason to think their hostage was at risk of rescue.

I scrutinized the lock, certain I was mistaken. They would never leave it open. Rezner was not that careless and I was not that lucky. Had never been, in all my life. Good fortune was a tall tale, something to be greeted with keen suspicion.

I tapped the window with one fingernail, three times. The lump beneath the blankets did not stir. Below, more laughter, crude and uninhibited.

There wasn't time to puzzle out an answer. There wasn't time to do anything but act. Move forward. Adapt to new variables. Move forward.

I grabbed hold of the bottom pane's frame and pushed up. The window slid up. The chilly, air-conditioned environment of the room rolled over me. It smelled like wood polish and cotton, like worn socks and humanity.

"Chelsea?" I whispered.

I leaned in and put one foot on the hardwood floor.

"Chelsea?"

A shouted denial down below. More laughter. Chair legs skidding over linoleum. I wasn't Leander Smalls, I knew. There was no thrill in this invasion, no prickly over-full balloon feeling of anticipation. Just a sick knowledge in my stomach that told me there was something I had missed. Some tiny truth, overlooked.

I stepped fully into the room and was certain the thunder of blood in my ears was so loud that it would send the men below scurrying up the stairs, ready to blow me out of the world.

I took a step toward Chelsea's bed.

The bedroom door opened. Light cascaded in.

The silhouette that followed it in held a rifle.

# ELEVEN

He was middle-aged with a thick black beard; a tall guy in jeans and work boots. His eyes flashed onto me. They grew wide in an instant as his brain made the right connections to define to him what was happening in this room.

He had time to shout "Hey!" and raise the gun barrel almost level. I pointed the Sig and shot him in the chest. His rifle discharged a thunderclap that blew a hole in the floor. He hit the floor in a sitting position with his legs splayed out in front of him. His hands fumbled dumbly at the rifle, as clumsy as a marionette with a clipped string. His watering eyes watched me with a desperate intelligence, disconnected from the stupidity of his hands.

Down below, the laughter died. Silence held reign throughout the house.

I spun and furiously swept the blanket off the bed. Stared at what I knew was there. Nothing but sheets and a pillow, all bunched up together into the approximate shape and size of the girl who was not there. Down in the basement of my mind, where I tried to keep him locked away, my father ejected a spiteful chuckle.

227

*'You tried to save the girl.'*

I choked down the urge to shout black hatred into the world. I was halfway out the window when I saw the nail on the floor. In the light from the hallway, I saw it as clearly as if it had been blown up on a projector's screen. A finishing nail, slim, with a slight bulge for a head. My eyes tracked up to the window's lock. Saw the tiny hole in the wood where the nail had been tapped into the frame. If the nail had still been there, its existence would have prevented the lock from being opened by anyone inside the room. And there, right there where the nail had once been, a slight smear of blood.

I was too late.

Chelsea was already free. She'd done it on her own. Without knowing a stranger was out in the world with nothing on his mind but rescuing her, she'd taken it upon herself to do just that. The girl had the will to work the nail out of the window frame with her own naked fingers. She'd bled to get out. She'd bled and she'd succeeded. Chelsea Gullins was free of this room.

I was not.

Foot falls on the stairs below, the creak of old wood. Further away, a man shouted a command I couldn't make out, but was easy to guess. They were on the move. Spreading out. The man on the floor behind me made terrified gasping noises. His hands managed to find the wound in his torso and press against it.

I put the girl out of my mind and climbed out the window. I crawled away from it, along the overhang, until I was between two windows. I kept the Sig steadied in front of me with my left hand cupping the bottom of the grip. More shouted exclamations. I heard the slider door bang open.

A figure appeared on the deck, moving fast. He spun, craning his neck to peer up the overhang. I saw the gun in his hand and made the decision. I took careful aim and fired the Sig. The man pitched backwards, crashed over a deck chair, and remained still.

*'Move, Roarke.'*

The shouting died around the sound of the Sig's shot. The men inside the house were moving more quietly now, fully aware there was an active shooter who'd gotten the drop on at least one of their own.

They'd be watching the deck. The dead man down there was in full view of the windows and the slider door. Whatever eyeballs weren't fixed on the deck and lawn would be heading up to get a look at Chelsea's room. I couldn't go down the way I'd come without walking into the wrong end of a shooting gallery.

Instead, I ran along the overhang, barreling toward the side of the house nearest the eastern wood-line. I'd use the side of the house as cover and pray that there were no guns readied for someone appearing that far away from the scene.

The edge of the roof sped toward me, darkness beyond. Behind me, the sound of someone scrambling out onto the overhang from Chelsea's window. I leapt into the air as a gunshot rang out. I tucked and rolled with the momentum of the fall as best I could. When I hit the ground on my left shoulder I kept pitching forward, absorbing some of the impact with my side and back. Still, I felt the air in my chest rush out in a gust and for a timeless moment I was stunned.

"He's jumped clear! Go around the side! The side, God damn it!"

I sucked a ragged gulp of air down into my chest and struggled to right myself. The world spun. Another gunshot shouted itself into the air. A plume of dirt erupted no more than a foot in front of me.

"I got him! He's over here!"

. I flipped onto my back and pointed my weapon up at the black silhouette of the ranch house. Whatever animal thing drives a man when he's cornered took hold of me. I knew I wasn't going to hit anyone. I was too disoriented. Prone. An easy target. My vision swam, and I decided I'd empty the magazine as I died.

The shooter took a step forward and was suddenly starkly visible in the light from the window beside him. He had me. I strained to get the Sig pointed in his general direction, desperate to go out of the world with a roar.

An echoing snap leapt from the tree line behind me, as sharp as a whip crack. The man ducked low as Savannah's bullet hit the wall near him. Another rifle shot from the woods. Another cracking noise as the bullet struck the house. The man brought his rifle to his shoulder and pointed it at me.

Savannah's third shot, the last in her magazine, flew true.

He made a soft noise and plunged off the roof of the Reverend's house.

"Roarke! Move it!"

I was scrambling again, struggling to get up on my feet. The world still teetered in my eyes. I sucked a desperate gulp of air, slipped, and fell back to the earth. More shouting behind. A door slammed. Heavy footfalls rang across the deck.

Another whip crack from the tree line. A man made a strangling sound. I heard his body hit the deck boards, heard another man make a mournful cry, the sound of seeing a friend or loved one cut down.

I got back up and lunged dumbly ahead, willing myself to ignore the vertigo, to just power through and put one foot in front of the other. Another rifle shot from the tree line sounded and I marked the flash of the barrel. Not far. Then another. She was firing blind, racking the rounds as fast as she could, laying cover fire for me without any real interest in hitting a target. Doing exactly as I'd told her.

It worked. I plunged headlong into the tree-line. Unseen limbs smacked at my eyes. I kept on, fear-fueled. I don't know how long I trounced forward, stumbling, falling, righting myself and hurling myself ahead.

Eventually, I was standing alone in the dry riverbed we'd followed on the march from Paul Gullins' house to the Reverend's. I blinked dumbly around. Savannah rushed out of the woods, her face distorted with a wild fear. The rifle was still in her hands.

"Where is she?" she gasped between quick, gulping breaths.

"Not there."

"What? What does that mean? What the *hell* does that mean?"

I put my hands on her shoulders and squeezed.

"No time," I said. "We have to move. They're going to follow us, Savannah."

I'd been afraid she was dipping into panic. But she heard the words and her eyes got focused again. She nodded that she understood. We both ran back down the riverbed. Off in the distance, a truck's motor rumbled to life and the anxious shouts of men still carried.

\*

"She's not here," Savannah called down from the second floor of Paul Gullins' house.

"Keep looking," I called back.

I turned over all the furniture in the living room. My boots left behind dark smears of dirt as I rushed from room to room. I threw open all the cupboard doors in the kitchen. I checked the dryer in the laundry room, the garage. I peeked everywhere that a slight, terrified girl might think to hide. The idea had seemed to strike me and Savannah at the same time, as we rushed up the back lawn of Paul's home: Chelsea might have run straight here when she escaped her room. If she knew the way, she might be hiding inside her father's house. Might have been there the whole time Savannah and I had been searching for a rifle.

While Savannah thumped around upstairs, I raced around the exterior of the house again, searching for any sign of Chelsea's passage.

On the second circuit, I ran into Savannah in the driveway, her rifle slung over one shoulder, her face etched with anxiety. She had it under control, but she had that trembling, jumpy-eyed look like it would only take a little nudge to send her over the edge into a panic. I couldn't afford that.

"We have to go," I said.

"No. Not without her."

"Any second, they can come right up that driveway or out of the trees. We have to go."

I took hold of her arm to lead her to where I'd parked the Stratus, but she jerked away and shot me a murderous glare.

233

"Get your fucking hand *off* me."

"Savannah, listen to me."

"Where *is* she? Where the fuck *is* she?"

Her voice broke into a high whine. The desperation in her eyes told me she'd reached the point I'd feared. She wasn't thinking. She was prepared to stand out on this lawn, in the light of day, and just pray that Chelsea materialized before the Reverend's men appeared. That was no plan. It was surrender.

I grabbed her by both arms, pinning them against her sides, and heaved her up into the air like a bag of sand. She started kicking around as soon as I did it. I got her on my left shoulder and marched us over to the Stratus.

"You son of a bitch!"

I got the passenger door open with my right hand and heard her rifle clatter against the gravel. Her fists rained down over my back and the toes of her boots thumped against my thigh. I leaned down and dumped her in the seat. She came right back at me, swinging her fists like a man. I batted them aside and grabbed her by the back of the head. I brought our faces together until our noses were nearly touching.

"Stop," I said.

"Get out of my way!"

"Stop, Savannah. We're going to find her. But not here. We're going to go find her. Both of us. I need you to stop this."

Her face crumpled and she began to cry. She hunched over in the seat and covered her face with her hands, a ragged sob working out past them.

I picked her rifle up off the driveway, tossed it in the backseat, and got behind the wheel. For the second time, I raced in reverse away from Paul Gullins' home.

Once I had us moving forward again, aimed back toward Home Among the Pines, Savannah cut her sobbing short. One moment she sounded utterly lost, and the next she'd shut it all down like a switch had been flipped. She wiped the moisture off her face and stared bleakly out at the road. For the first time she looked less than lovely. All her youthful vibrancy had been depleted over the last hour, leaving her looking washed out and frayed.

"Jesus," she whispered. "Jesus, what are we doing?"

"We'll find her."

"I killed people back there. Human beings. Didn't I?"

"Maybe."

"What does that mean?"

"You can take a bullet and live. It doesn't matter. You saved my life is what you did. That's how you think of it."

She didn't answer, and that was fine: a single headlight had appeared in my rearview mirror. It was an ember smoldering on the black horizon. I goosed the accelerator and we lurched ahead.

The road curved and dipped. The headlight disappeared from view.

"Roarke, she could be at the house now," she said. "She could be hiding inside and we're driving *away*."

"We're not leaving her. We'll find her."

I fumbled around and got my cell phone into my hand. The road curved steep to the left. I kept the accelerator down. Savannah smacked a flat palm onto the dash to keep herself from colliding against her door. I felt the Stratus threaten to let go of its grip on the road. The wood line loomed in the glare of the headlights.

"Roarke!"

We whipped through the turn. Gravel spat out under us. We were through it, back on a straightaway. Savannah didn't let go of the dash, her breathing coming quick and shallow. I thumbed down through the phone's contacts and made the call I knew I had to make.

It rang seven times before Jack Reinhart picked up.

"Yeah?" His voice was thick with sleep, irritable.

"Reinhart," I said. "Chelsea Gullins is missing."

"What? Roarke?"

"It was a kidnapping. The militia I had you look into. They had her. One of them is a cop from the Sheriff's office up here so I can't go to them. I tried that already. Men are dead."

Silence on the other end.

"Reinhart, you need to get men up here."

"Hold on. Hold on. Let me get a pen. What do you mean, 'men are dead'?"

I stared into the rearview. The headlight reappeared, larger now. Closer. Bearing down on us. I urged the Stratus ahead. We were rocketing, a bullet. It was faster. I knew what it was. I'd known since the first moment I spotted it in the distance.

When the red and blue light bar atop its roof leapt to life, it left no doubt.

The Last Watchman was riding us down.

"Damn it," I hissed.

"What? What is it?" Reinhart said in my ear.

"It's Rezner."

"Who the hell--"

"I have to go. Get some men up to Crawford County."

"Wait," he urged. "What the hell's going on?"

The blue and red strobe filled the interior of the Stratus. Beside me, Savannah stared at me with wide, unblinking eyes. Searching for some sign that I had a plan, that I knew what to do. I saw the ember of the headlight growing, swelling in the rearview. Yeah, I knew what I had to do. Had known it ever since Rezner dropped his mask of sanity and showed me the furious madness that dwelled behind it.

"Roarke? Answer me. What the hell is going on?"

"Just get up here," I growled and ended the call.

The cruiser's siren leapt like a banshee's wail into the air.

The crossroad that would have taken us back toward Home Among the Pines appeared. I shot straight past it. I couldn't afford to slow down. I pressed the accelerator to the floor. The Stratus was vibrating, shuddering like a living thing.

"Shoot him," I yelled.

Savannah started to turn toward me, but the road abruptly dipped down and we became airborne for a split second. She braced one palm flat against the roof, the other still pinned against the dashboard. We hit the asphalt with a squeal. I felt the undercarriage slap against the ground. We both rose up out of our seats. A metallic scream in the belly of the beast. It reared like a panicked steed, lurching hard to the left. I kept the wheel steady, saw the wall of trees rushing at us. Savannah screamed.

We fishtailed across the shoulder, throwing a storm of gravel and dust in our wake. The tires took hold, yanked us ahead. I strained at the wheel and tasted the copper flavor of blood in my mouth. The Stratus groaned, bucked, and straightened out again.

We leapt back up onto the road and I kept the accelerator down while the world came back into focus. I'd bitten down on my tongue. I spit the blood out of my mouth and looked at the rear view just in time to see Rezner's cruiser arc over the dip in the road. It was heavier than the Stratus, built for suicidal pursuit, and it cleared the jump easily. When it crashed back to earth, it didn't weave or buck. It just kept on. Closer. Closing the gap.

238

Surging at us with a black metal push bumper bolted across the cruiser's maw like the face-guard of a gladiator's helmet.

"Shoot him" I growled. "Get your rifle and shoot him through the back window, Savannah. Do it or he'll pit us off the road and kill us both."

Savannah leaned through the space between our seats. Out of the corner of my eye I saw her take up her hunting rifle and brace it against the top of the passenger seat.

"We're shaking too much," she muttered.

"Just shoot."

She did. The rifle cracked and I glanced in the rearview. The back window had a fat bullet hole through it, its edges flared like a stylized sun. Rezner was still there, a single car-length separating us.

Savannah worked the bolt and I felt the spent casing plink off my shoulder.

She fired again.

"Shit," she hissed, and worked the bolt a third time.

She fired. I heard the back window explode. In the rearview, glass swirled and fell. Rezner's cruiser lurched away to the right, disappearing from view. Savannah shouted in triumph and relief.

"I think I did," she yelled over the howl of wind that was leaping through the shattered window. "Did you see it? He went right into the trees. Roarke, did you see it?"

"Hold on."

239

I brought us down slowly until the marching pine trees were no longer a blur, until we were rolling slowly enough to do a U-turn across the empty road. Steam roiled from under the hood of the Stratus. A cooked chemical stink insinuated its way through the dash vents. Savannah sat back down in her seat with the hunting rifle laid across her lap. She blinked around in sudden confusion.

"We're *not* going back there," she protested.

"What if he found her first? What if she's in the back seat of that car?"

I didn't believe it, but it was enough to silence any more objections from her. No, he didn't have Chelsea Gullins. But I needed to see if he was dead. I needed to know.

The Stratus' headlights swam across the wood line, finally coming to rest on the scene. Rezner's cruiser had died against the tree line. I came to a stop fifteen feet from where it had crashed headlong against a massive old elm tree. The front of the cruiser was a crushed ruin of collapsing metal. The driver's side wheel was thrust up into the destroyed mess of the engine compartment, cocked out at a ninety-degree angle.

"Stay here," I said and stepped out onto the asphalt. I held the Sig out in front of me, training it on the cruiser as I slowly walked toward it. I could smell antifreeze and pine needles mingling on the wind. Exhausted ticking sounds echoed up out of the Stratus' belly as I cleared it.

240

Savannah's window whispered down.

"She's not there, Roarke."

I ignored her and closed the distance to the cruiser. The light bar was dead and the siren silenced. The cruiser had collided with the old elm with such force that everything had died instantly. The dash was pushed up a good foot into the cabin.

Rezner wasn't there. I stared at the sagging, spent airbags. Beyond them, the passenger door yawned open. I paced around the back of the car, keeping the Sig leveled out ahead of me, half-certain that he was lurking on the other side, waiting to shoot me as I came around.

He wasn't. I was alone. The forest stretched away from the road into deepening shadow. I stared into it, straining to spot any sign of him. Nothing. The world was quiet and he was gone.

I stood there a while, still breathing heavy from the chaos of his pursuit, my head full of disquiet and frustration. I thought over the madness of that night, running everything through my mind. Had I missed something? Had Chelsea been hiding in her father's house? Had I made mistakes that would prove irreparable?

"Roarke?"

I shook off the gloom of having failed to stop Rezner and left the mangled old Two Pine cruiser behind. I spared a final glance back over my shoulder at the spray painted legend, still legible across the flanks of the dead beast.

*The Last Watchman Still Rides.*

'Not anymore,' I thought, but it was a meager satisfaction.

The Stratus gave no complaint as I put it in gear and pulled down the road, but there was still a burnt odor hanging throughout the interior.

"So?"

"He's gone," I said.

We drove in silence for half a mile. The rifle was still lying across her lap.

"You did good, Savannah."

"I feel..." she started, then stopped. She was clenching and unclenching her hands, like she was trying to get the feeling back into them. "I feel insane. You know? Like I walked through a fun house mirror or something. Like the world doesn't make sense right now."

"You've been through a lot. Adrenaline and fear and seeing men shot--that's a lot to process. It'll pass. Maybe it doesn't feel that way right now, but it'll pass."

She sighed and stopped flexing her hands, letting them lie there on her lap with the rifle. She gave me a wry grin. A grin was good. A grin meant she was present and not giving in to the urge to let her mind distance itself from the realities of what she was involved in.

"I saved you, huh?" she quipped. "That's what you said."

I rolled my eyes and her grin grew with my discomfort.

I cracked both our windows. The cool night air rushed in and straight out the back.

"Tell me about Chelsea. What she knew up here. What she did when Paul would bring her up," I said.

"He'd drop off Chelsea at the girl's camp. When it was done, he'd pick her up. She talked about the camp a lot. The counselors. She wanted to see if she could start working with them when she was older. Really, that was why she came up here in the summers, as far as I could tell."

"Did she ever stay with them? At their homes?"

"I doubt it. I don't know. The camp was two weeks long. She'd do her two weeks and then I'd see her after and she'd just be…I don't know. Glowing. Happy. Like she'd found something that made sense. Something better than that wreck of a house Donna keeps."

I kept us moving at a moderate speed, not certain yet where we were going.

I remembered walking through Paul's house, not more than an hour ago.

"The refrigerator," I said. "And the empty hangers."

"What?"

"She was there. She escaped the room they held her in and ran to her father's house. She was hungry or thirsty or both. Nobody overfeeds a hostage. She went to the fridge and took whatever she could. Then she took the clothes that were hanging in that

243

closet. She *was* there, Savannah. But she left. She left and she went somewhere else. Somewhere that felt safer than her father's house."

Savannah shot me a look, her eyes growing wide as she came around to what I was thinking.

"The camp," she said in a rush. "If she didn't feel safe at Paul's, the only other place she knows is the camp."

"Yeah. Which way?"

"The next left," she said, jabbing a finger at the windshield. "Take the next left and we'll double back. God, she'd *better* be there."

\*

We rolled slowly up the gravel drive, past the five-foot-tall section of an oak's trunk that had been set on its side. Its heavily lacquered face read *Voluspa Camp for Girls*.

"Sounds like a reform school," I said.

Savannah nodded in agreement. "I know. Paul told me the widow who left all her money to build the place was named Voluspa and she insisted her name be on it. It was that or no endowment. Hold on, I can get this."

A length of steel tube mounted on a swivel was blocking the way into the camp. Savannah jogged up to it. Bent down and peered at the end of the gate. I stared at her in the stark shine of the headlights. She was still the enticing vision I'd thought about incessantly since we first met, but now there was something new. An honesty of intent. A willingness to action. She'd killed men in order to try and save her niece. To save me.

I tried to push the sentiment away. It should be too late, I knew. Too late to roll the clock back past the greed and deception that had lead us to this moment. She stole from bad men. When they took the one person they knew she loved, she found herself a monster for hire. She lied. Her seductions were just that; just more lies to keep me aimed at the Sovereign.

I didn't want to want her. I didn't want to be a fool for her.

Savannah turned away from the gate and shrugged in frustration.

"There's a chain and padlock," she called out.

I popped the trunk and got out of the Stratus. Pulled out the tire iron and walked into the shine of the headlights. Savannah's eyes lit up.

"You really think so?" she said. "It's a real chain."

I wedged the end of the tire iron down between the chain and the base of the gate.

"Why don't we just park here and walk in?" she said.

"Because someone might be looking for us and they might spot my car."

"Right. But you're in bad shape. You shouldn't--"

245

I heaved down on the iron. Felt the blood pounding through the gunshot wound. I steadied myself and heaved harder. Heard a grunt slip past my teeth.

"Roarke, we can do something else."

Pinpricks of light danced in front of my eyes and I pressed on. The chain groaned. A metallic yelp. The 'U'-shaped clasp of the padlock sprang free. I hunched over. The tire iron clattered onto the gravel drive and I sucked in an ocean of air while my vision slowly returned.

Savannah's fingertips on the back of my neck. An electric ice-chill at her touch. I blinked and she was right in front of me. Her other hand on my face, in my hair, caressing. Soothing.

"Are you okay?"

"I'm fine."

"You don't have to do this anymore. She's not being held anymore. You're...you're so hurt." Her eyes ran the length of me, taking in all the injury. "Roarke, you can stop now. I don't want--"

"We keep on."

"You don't have to."

"Until she's safe, we keep on."

I picked up the tire iron and lumbered back to the trunk while she stared at me with a mixture of confusion and worry. I drove the Stratus ahead past the gate, far enough for Savannah to swing it back shut. She climbed into the car beside me quietly.

"Well...thank you," she whispered, looking away, uncomfortable.

I almost told her to forget it, that I wasn't doing any of this for her. Only Chelsea mattered, and Savannah could walk away and disappear off the face of the earth for all I cared. But she'd fired that rifle and she'd held steady throughout all the madness of that night. That was enough to earn her the right not to be lied to, so I bit the words off before they could form and drove us forward.

The gravel drive wound through the woods a couple hundred feet before I spied the first building. It was a little pine cabin back in the trees, big enough for maybe two people.

"Staff cabin," she said when she saw me peering at it.

We took a bend and the drive widened out into a parking area. A sign at the entrance to the lot read,

"Welcome to Voluspa Camp for Girls.

Campers and Family,

Please check in at the Front Office.

Visitors require a Visitor's Pass.

All pets must be leashed."

There were no other cars in the lot. I parked the Stratus and we both got out of the wounded thing, leaving it to its inscrutable clicking and whining. I blinked around in the sunlight. Savannah pointed and I walked with her down a short path strewn with cedar chips until we came to the front office. It was a cabin identical to the first I'd seen, only the window was a service counter with a sliding pane.

It wasn't locked, so Savannah pushed the door open and disappeared inside. I stood in the silence of the little clearing, feeling abruptly useless and far from home. I'd never been to any sort of camp in my life. The closest thing to a vacation in my childhood had been those times when my drunken mother went on a big enough binge that she didn't notice my absence for days on end. Sometimes I'd slink back on my own, but not often. Usually, she'd sober up long enough to find me at a neighbor's house, or sleeping in a park, or cooling my heels in the juvie hall on St. Anthony Street with the other dead-eyed boys who were in no hurry to get back to whatever storm of dysfunction they were supposed to call 'home'.

"Roarke?"

I looked at her and pulled back into myself. The noise and clatter of the St. Anthony hall whooshed away, and I was present again. She'd closed the door to the office and was peering at me with a question in her eyes.

"Yeah," I said.

"Still alright?"

"I'm fine."

"According to the map on the wall inside, there are six cabins down this path, and another five if you go north up that path we passed. How about you take north and I'll check the other. We'll meet back here." She hesitated for a second, then added, "Is that how we should?"

It was entirely for my benefit, I realized. She recognized that something had come over me. Even if she couldn't know the source of my sudden disquiet, she'd diagnosed its cure straightaway: let the man know he's needed. Ask him what should be done, like you're relying on him.

"Yeah," I said. "That'll do fine. If you see anyone else, come get me first. I'll do the same."

Savannah's eyes lingered on me a moment more, as if checking to see if I was really all the way back in the here and now. She seemed to make up her mind, because she gave me a nod and a slight, hopeful smile before turning away and jogging down the path.

*

I always wound up in the Saint Anthony facility for fighting. Countless times for fighting. Three times they went the whole way and hit me with assault charges as a juvenile. What did I care? Detroit was predatory and I was a child alone on its streets. You could become a predator yourself and face the occasional interest of the law or you could let the sprawling ruins swallow you whole.

I fought. While my mother slept off her hangover in whatever miserable corner she was occupying that week, I waged a war of survival outside.

At twelve I stole food and fractured a shopkeeper's jaw.

Juvenile probation and a month in Saint Anthony.

At thirteen, the same age Chelsea now was, a freak from the suburbs rolled up in a shiny new Lincoln sedan and tried to pull me into his car. He ground my face down into a layer of plastic sheeting before the adrenaline storm thundered up inside me and told me what to do.

No charges for that, even if he would never regain hearing in his left ear or chew his food without false teeth. Instead they hit me with a psych commitment. Three months in Saint Anthony.

At fourteen, mother was in the ground and I was learning what foster care in the city was like. The first family I got placed with put me to work straight away selling bogus magazine subscriptions to unsuspecting shoppers in Dearborn's Fairlane Town Center mall. When I didn't hit the quota the man of the house hit me—with a pipe wrench

The cops took me away the next day, after an ambulance took him.

No probation. Incorrigible. Dim outlook. One year in Saint Anthony.

My memories of Saint Anthony were all framed in fear. The dynamics of the juvie home are no different than the dynamics of prison. The weak get bullied. The small and the slight are prey. Those who have honest human emotions learn to get rid of them. They cry them away at night when the lights are down, weeping it out of themselves. I'd seen kids like that. They'd wake up the next morning with a blank, exhausted stare. They'd be dangerous in the new day, with their hopes mashed way down where nobody could get at them, ready to lash out hard on whoever wanted to test them again. Sometimes that was enough to get them through, but mostly not. Mostly they got more of the same.

I didn't have those problems. Even as a kid, I'd been head-and-shoulders above the next biggest guy in the room. I was free to remain quiet and alone, watching the ugly spectacle play out from a distance.

I walked along the cedar chip path and thought of Chelsea Gullins. Her father was dead. Her mother was a pill-popping disaster. Her aunt was likely facing all sorts of criminal charges once the FBI started looking into everything that had happened up here.

Was there anyone left in the world who could care for Chelsea?

I didn't want to picture her in the system, in a place like Saint Anthony or in the clutches of some foster scam. I didn't want to imagine her crying in the night while she waited to stop feeling the things a human being is meant to feel.

The five cabins were situated in a rough circle, with a flat clearing in the center. A large camp fire pit was sunk into the middle of the clearing. A wooden plaque was nailed to a tree trunk at the edge of the clearing where the path ended. It read, "Camp Resilience". A white and gray wolf's head was painted beneath the words.

I pushed open the door on the first cabin and peered inside. Two metal bunk-beds filled most of the room, their mattresses rolled up tight and resting at their feet.

One by one I searched the other cabins. Nothing. Just metal-frame bunk beds and smartly rolled mattresses. I stopped at the sunken campfire ring. No ashes or half-burnt logs inside it. Cleaned properly. The whole camp had the feel of a tightly run operation, a place where discipline and order were the watchwords.

Good, I thought. Good that she had something like this in her life. I'd had chaos and uncertainty until the day I let the Marines take over control of me. As soon as I'd cycled out, it was back to old habits. Freddie Esposito happened. Prison brought a new kind of order, the locked-down and shut-down variety. I'd done alright inside. I'd colored within the lines and kept out of trouble.

Since getting out, I'd flailed around at a purpose. Tried the respectable act of parole officer. Burned that down straight away when I lost my cool and treated a child rapist the only way a sane man could.

Now I was standing in the wilderness at night with a pile of dead men behind me and a little girl I'd failed to help in any real way. Doubt and self-loathing washed over me like an oily second skin. The world grew indistinct at its edges and I felt as trapped as a sunken ship beneath the weight of the ocean. I lurched forward on suddenly weak knees, caught myself before I could tip into the fire pit.

Up through the canopy of trees.

A single light hanging there, harsh and yellow.

The rifleman atop his tower, a silhouette.

Puckett's stinking cigarette smoke in my nose.

And in the darkness, father waiting.

# T W E L V E

"I don't understand what this is."

When I said it, the world of the prison yard was hung in the weak half-light of predawn, that mysterious span of scant moments when everything seems suspended in a primordial haze. That's the time, I think, when the day you've just lived becomes yesterday. The world begins anew in the hush and anticipation of those moments before the sun pokes its first finger into the air.

The escaping darkness slipped away from the mass of my father as quickly as it left everything else. The deep lines of age, the creases of hardship, these things were gradually revealed across his face, like an invisible sculptor was finally etching in the touches of character upon his work. His shock of hair was gray. As he thought about what to say, he didn't seem aware that the retreating night had robbed him of some of his mythic size.

I was sitting in front of a man, not a myth, for the first time since being taken out of my cell by Officer Puckett. A huge man, with a seething cauldron of malice behind his one good eye, but a man just the same.

"This place will kill you," he said finally.

"I'll make it."

"Not prison," he snapped. "The world. Outside. It'll tear you down. It'll do it a little bit at a time. Bit by bit. You won't notice it at first. Until you're already weak. Until you're some weak, dying nobody. It's other people, Roarke. That's what does it. Other people will kill you slow if you let them."

I felt myself sneering. Sick of his malignant philosophy.

His face didn't change. We weren't having a conversation, I realized. He had gotten around to what he wanted to say. This was why I was here. To listen to this speech.

"This is what weakness gets you," he said and pointed a finger at his dead, sewn-shut eye. The scar above and below it was as straight as a spear's shaft. "Three years after they put me inside here they housed me with a man named Fenton Rirson. He was a killer out of Georgia. Stick ups and strong arm robberies mostly. Crazy, impulsive shit. Whispers followed him in, saying that when the cops busted in on him this last time he was in the middle of eating a man he'd taken hostage. Eating his guts, the way an animal does. I didn't know about that, one way or the other. You never know what to believe. He was quiet and he kept himself clean. Didn't ask me about my life before being in here. Three months we just kept the peace, see?"

"Sure," I said, thinking about the little bald Aryan I'd had to choke until he saw the lay of the land.

255

"Well, turns out the reason Fenton didn't ever talk much was because he was too busy planning things out. After three months he used his bed sheets to strangle me. Did it all real quiet and slow. Quiet enough that I didn't know what he was doing until I woke up with him pulling on the sheets with all his weight. He was under the bed. He'd looped the rope he made out of the sheet over my throat, slid under there, and pulled down with everything he had. I don't know how long that went on. It felt like days. But I knew something. Learned it, while he was choking the life out of me. I was sputtering and fucking dying there, and this one perfect truth grew in my head. You know what it was, that truth?"

"Go ahead," I answered.

"Weakness is what you give away to other people."

"Yeah? Okay."

He didn't snarl or threaten me like he had the first time I'd grown a sarcastic tone with him. There was a point to be made, apparently, so he just kept on in his low, rumbling voice.

"You killed that spic had the knife. And he gutted you up. But that ain't what put you here and it ain't what's eating you away bit by bit. That pretty girl, the one you saved, she's whose killing you, son. You said she looked over the whole bar and she picked *you*. Looked right at you, didn't she? Just as beautiful as could be. Yeah, I can see it. And she pegged you straight away. Roped you in with her big pretty eyes. And here you are. A fucking convict with a belly full of scars and years to sit around thinking things over and over again. Because you let another person rope you in. That's what *they* do. Other people take you apart and use you up if you let them in. I learned that so close to death, the world was nothing but black and soundless. I knew then I should have killed Fenton the first night he was in the cell with me. Not because he was bad or maybe ate another man. But I gave him a chance, like a fucking fool. I gave him room to live, and that was my *weakness*. And I was paying for it by getting choked to death."

"But you didn't," I said. "What happened to Fenton?"

Father grew a stony grin that had no mirth in it, only cold satisfaction.

"Shit. I thundered up out of that bed," he said. "Got mad as hell and got free. He had a knife he made out of a toothbrush down there with him. When I yanked him out from under the bed, he took my eye out with it. So I went to work on him something fierce. I was riled up. Somewhere in the middle of all that bloody business, I figured if he liked to eat people like the rumors said he did, I'd give him a last meal. I reached down and scooped up the eye he'd taken out of me and made him swallow it whole. Stopped breaking him long enough for him to sit there and cry while he gulped it down. And when he was done, I went back to work...disassembling him. That's what the report I signed says I did. I 'disassembled' Fenton. Which is just a pussy

257

way of saying I slopped him from the floor the ceiling. They found me the next morning with what was left of Fenton. First guard who saw it screamed like a woman and ran. Never saw him again. That's why I've been in solitary ever since. They'll never let me out, not after that."

His gaze slid off me, over my shoulder. I heard Puckett's footfalls come to a stop just behind me.

"That's it," Puckett hissed. "Kiss your kid goodbye, or whatever the hell you need to do, because we're getting back inside now."

I understood the urgency in his voice. It was near shift change. Very soon, a new set of men would be waiting to relieve Puckett and the rifleman up in the tower. They needed to get us inside, back in our cells, before anyone might notice we'd spent the night out in the glow of the moon.

"Don't ever give them anything," my father said to me, ignoring Puckett and his order. "Inside here or out in the world. Don't give them *anything*. That's all I've got for you, boy. Don't you ever be fucking weak for someone else. Now get on the ground."

He was up on his feet. Quicker than I would have guessed. He towered over the yard, over me, and I heard the words repeating in my head. *Get on the ground.* Part of me understood, before my mind did. I was lunging down and away from the table when he planted one foot on its top and pushed forward with a scream of utter undying hatred.

He soared over me, arms outstretched, hands aimed like claws at Puckett's confused, sputtering face. The same survival impulse that forced me to the ground had me scrambling away, onto my belly and to the other side of the table.

Behind and above me, Puckett screamed. I heard them both collide and hit the ground. Snarling, exultant laughter choked its way out of my father.

When the tower guard's rifle cracked, that gale of triumphant laughter died. A second rifle shot. Then nothing but Puckett's mewling whimper keening through the yard.

I spent an unknowable length of time huddled behind the cement table, certain that the rifleman was straining to get a clean shot on me. Alarms whipped themselves into a frenzy. Boots thudded out into the yard. Rough hands hauled me up to my feet.

The guard in the tower got my father in the head on the first shot. The interior of his skull was a red exclamation point in the dirt. The second shot, to his back, was just unnecessary insurance. His single eye stared up at the morning sky. Radiating outward from that eye were wrinkles of insane exertion and purpose. His death mask was contorted with spite.

Later, days after the questions stopped getting put to me and I was allowed to come up out of administrative segregation and return to my cell, I started getting little slivers of what had gone down. Eventually, I heard enough to piece the truth of things together.

My father was a terminal cancer case. Some guys said it was lung. Another inmate who worked in the infirmary swore he heard it was pancreatic. Either way, he was on the way out soon, no matter where the disease originated.

What everyone agreed on, though, was that Puckett had wanted an inmate named Cletus Wainright dead, and he'd tried to enlist my father to do the killing. An old timer named Lamont Seward, a man who'd been inside the walls longer than I'd been alive, explained it to me in detail a month after my father was gunned down.

"Man, Cletus fucked up," Lamont said. "He went off the meds, you know. Can't do that if you're schizophrenic, man. Anyway, he calls Puckett over to his door, right? This was last year, just before you come in. Puckett gets up and walks up there and sees Cletus got a razor he pulled out of a disposable. Just the thin blade in his hand, and his shirt sleeves rolled up all the way. And Puckett says, 'Where the fuck you get that razor blade, Cletus?' But Cletus, he just smiled and says, 'Hey Puckett, watch this'. And he starts cutting. Goes in at the wrist, and pulls straight up his arm to the elbow. Puckett? He just stares, man. Cold as hell. Doesn't do *nothing*, with the crazy fool committing suicide right in front of him. So Cletus, he does the same thing to

260

the other arm. All the way to the elbow. And he's bleeding *out*, man. Like a river. And Puckett don't even blink. He's staring at Cletus like he's watching something boring on T.V. Cletus is going white. And he's a dark brother, man. But he's gushing blood. He goes down on his knees. Puckett still standing there like a robot. And Cletus finally says, 'Hey, you gotta go get help. You gotta go get the nurse.' I guess the crazy in his head kind of died down enough for him to recognize he was dying.

So, he's begging for his life, 'You gotta get the nurse, Puckett'. Puckett shakes his head real slow, back and forth. And he says, 'All I have to do is stand here and watch you die.' Straight as a heart attack, that's what he tells the dude. Cletus begs some more, but he's weak as hell now from all the blood loss. Puckett doesn't say anything else. He just keeps staring like a freak until Cletus' eyes roll up in his head and he passes out.

That's when Puckett goes and gets the nurse. You know, only after he knows Cletus blacked out, his last thought being that he's a dead man. Anyway, he pulls through. Nurses tourniquet that shit off and rush his ass away. They sewed him up and a few weeks later he's back in his old cell. Only, now he's shaky and weak. Like, permanently, from the damage he done to himself. Stutters like a skipping song. Can't hardly hold a spoon in his hands. Nerve damage, I figure.

Few months after that, it gets around that Cletus has a lawsuit against Puckett. Maybe Puckett figured nobody's going to believe a schitzo. But somebody's believing it, because word is Puckett went to your old man about killing that crazy motherfucker after a judge refused to throw the suit out. They're getting ready to pick a jury, so Puckett's got to get rid of the man before anything ever gets on the record, right? So he goes to see your old man. Dangles the chance to see his son before the cancer gets him if he'll agree to croak old Cletus. Look, I ain't the one to speak against someone's blood...but that was *not* the man to make a deal with, feel me? Everybody knows your old man doesn't do deals. Not for *nothing*. Hardest man I ever seen. Inside or out. A fucking stone island is what he was."

When I asked Lamont if my father was friends with Cletus and if that was why he went after Puckett in the yard, I got derisive laughter in return. No, my father had no friends. He'd gotten his meeting with me, sure enough. And once he'd gotten what he wanted, he'd guaranteed that the cancer wouldn't slowly eat him down to nothing.

Plunging his thumbs into Puckett's eyes and blinding the guard for life was nothing personal. It was just a way to make certain his own death came quickly and on his own terms.

For two years, until I was set free, I puzzled over what he'd been trying to tell me out there in the darkness of the yard. The first few months I adopted his message. I went ice cold and clung to it as the only bit of wisdom my father had imparted to me: *let nothing in and give nothing to others*. But it didn't stick. How could it? How could I hold onto the sentiments of a man who had executed innocent people, who abandoned me to be raised by a drunken, heedless woman among a blasted and forsaken city?

By the time I got out of prison, my intention was firmly set. I left him behind. I left his poisonous screed about pure autonomy back there with him.

Somehow, in some way, I would be of use to the world he despised and rejected.

\*

"Roarke."

Father was gone. Clapped back into the past, frozen in that moment when he forced the rifleman to gun him down and spray the yard with the malicious interior of his skull.

"Roarke?"

Savannah. Standing stock-still on the other side of the fire pit. Her face was etched with alarm. I blinked the visions of prison out my eyes and pulled back into myself. I was on my knees in the dirt beside the fire pit. The ground was dark around me, as if my shadow had seeped down into the earth.

"Did…" I started to speak, and stopped. My voice was a weak croak.

"Oh my God," she whispered and rushed over to me.

"Did we find her?" I managed.

She didn't say anything. Moving quick, she tugged out of her oversized hoodie. The shirt she wore beneath it was purple, thin, and tight across her breasts. She smelled like flowered cream. Even after all we'd done, she smelled like that.

"Jesus," I mumbled. "You're unreal, you know that?"

"Hush. Just stay still."

She wrapped the hoodie around my arm. I stared down at my shadow in the dirt and that's when I saw it wasn't a shadow and knew why she was so alarmed. It was blood. My blood. The wound had reopened. I looked at the arm. It was as slick and saturated as if I had been performing a reckless and incompetent heart transplant.

Savannah tied the sleeves of the hoodie in a knot and wrenched them tight. I let out a moan at the reawakened agony of the wound and fell sideways.

"No, no," she stammered. She pulled at me. "Not yet. We have to get you to the car. I can't drag you, Roarke. You have to get on your feet. Roarke? Can you get up? You have to get up."

The pain of the knot pressing hard against my injury was enough to bring me around. Enough to get me on my feet again. I was shaking and weak, but the signals I sent to my legs were received. I put one foot in front of the other while she held onto me and guided us back down the path.

"She's not here?" I said.

"We'll find her," she answered. "But you have to get to a hospital."

I stopped walking. She peered up at me in consternation.

"Not until we find her."

"Roarke, are you utterly out of your mind?"

"Not until we find her. If I go in the hospital, I won't be coming out until the feds have decided if I'm getting charged for the bodies or not. We can't do that to her."

"*You* don't have to do this anymore."

"Yes, I do."

"Why? You've been through--"

"If I stop I'm just a killer, Savannah. If I stop now, I'm just some...some damned rabid dog."

Her eyes filled with understanding. Not the particulars. I'd never shared those with her, with anyone. But still, she looked like she'd heard the truth of what I'd said. She looked like she was seeing me for the first time. That realization made me wonder what she really thought of the chewed up and stomped on brute she was propping up.

Savannah stood on tiptoe and kissed me very lightly.

"Just keep walking," she said, voice thick with emotion. "We'll go back to the cabin and figure this out."

Her mouth on mine was enough of an elixir to get me moving again.

When we were back to the Stratus, she eased me down into the passenger seat and buckled me in. She guided the wheezing and tired beast out of the camp and onto the empty roads of Two Pine. I stared at her delicate profile, lit by the dashboard's glow.

"You're so damned beautiful," I said.

Softly, Savannah began to cry.

*

She poured me into one of the chairs on the cabin's deck and slipped away after telling me that she would find Rhonda and get the woman to come and tend to my wound again. I made some weak protestations, but she was gone without a backward glance.

I sat there in the darkness and quickly fell away.

When my cell phone chimed and snapped me back awake, I was still alone. I had the sense that not very much time had passed. The cell chimed a second time. I had to strain my left hand over to my right pocket to clumsily fish it out. I put it to my ear.

"Are you safe?" Reinhart. Sounding more awake than before. Focused and harried.

"I'm alright," I said. "Are you here?"

"Hell no," he said, his voice edged with exasperation. "The Agent in Charge down here is throwing static. He's been on the phone with the Crawford Sheriff. Nobody seems to know anything. There aren't any reported killings or kidnappings. No reports of you or anyone coming into the department to make a statement or get help. The Sheriff says he thinks we've been pranked and my boss is pretty damn sure he's right. I need more details if I'm going to get the go ahead to come up."

Raised voices reached me from outside, down the way Savannah had gone. A door slammed.

"Like what?" I said. "I told you a minor girl was kidnapped. Now she's missing. Five of her kidnappers are dead. Maybe six. What the hell else do I need to tell you, Reinhart?"

"*Maybe* six?" he shot back. "What's maybe about it? You killed six human beings? Is- holy shit –is that what you're telling me? Where are you? Where are you, *exactly*?"

I heard the front door of the cabin open and immediately slam shut. Stalking footfalls across the hardwood flooring.

"A preacher named Wayland Graves," I said to Reinhart. "He owns a big spread in Two Pine. Look it up. That's where you'll find some of the bodies. But don't go in by yourself. If there's anyone still in the house when you get there, they'll be armed."

He was insisting something when I ended the call and thumbed the phone off. I looked down at the numb length of my dangling right arm. Blood was still trickling out despite Savannah's impromptu tourniquet. A small puddle was forming on the deck boards.

When the slider door whisked along its track and thumped against the frame, it wasn't Savannah who stepped out into view, it was Sharon. The hard-faced and athletic woman saw me, set her feet in a wide and imperious stance and stabbed a finger in my direction.

"You need to get the hell off my property," she growled.

"Sit down."

"Screw you. I told the blonde and I'm telling you now: pack your shit and get moving. It's that or it's the cops."

She balled her hands into fists and put them on her hips, daring me to deny her. That's when I saw the gun. Some sort of pistol was wedged into the waistband of her khaki hiking shorts. She saw me looking at it and her eyes narrowed.

"Yeah," she said. "It's like that."

"You don't need it."

"I'm not discussing it with you. I told you to go."

"Lady, I couldn't make it to the porch on my own steam. You go on and call the cops if you want. They'll take me out in a squad car or an ambulance. Probably a body bag, though, all things considered. I can't stop you. But it's a mistake."

"Yeah? How?"

"There's a little girl in real danger, that's how."

She opened her mouth but nothing came out. Her gunslinger's squint slackened and for the only time since our talk in the kitchen that morning, she looked less than certain of herself.

She started to say something when the front door slammed shut again. Hurried footfalls followed. Savannah appeared on the deck, followed by the short and stocky Rhonda.

All three women stared at one another in an uncertain silence. Rhonda held a cardboard box in her hands and gave Sharon an expectant, pleading look.

"We have to help," the short, round-faced woman said.

"We can't," Sharon hissed.

"There's..." Rhonda started, and stopped as if she'd caught herself about to blurt out something unwise. She shot me a sidelong look and continued more deliberately, "There's a girl involved. I believe them. That they're trying to help a lost girl, Sharon."

I watched the flinty woman wrestle with what to say. Her face flushed red as she and her partner stared at one another. Just when I thought she was about to shout some sort of condemnation, she abruptly turned and stalked back inside the cabin. She reappeared immediately and shot her accusing finger at me again.

"She'll patch you up. In the morning, you're both gone. For good. That's the end of this. You stay here and you don't go outside and you don't come asking us for anything else. And when the sun rises, you get the hell out of our lives."

And she was gone again. The door slammed a third time in her wake. Silence descended over the three of us. Rhonda was the first to break it. She hustled over to me and set the cardboard box on the table. She peered down at me and pursed her lips with concern.

"You up for this?" she said.

"I think so."

"You're falling asleep."

"I'm good."

Rhonda was re-sewing my wound with a curved needle and Savannah was gripping my other hand, staring into my eyes, when I gave in to the fatigue and hurt. I closed my eyes. Heard Rhonda say, "It's okay. Let him. I'm almost done."

When Savannah woke me up, Rhonda and her box of medical supplies were gone. It was still dark. The earlier cloud cover had blown off east, leaving the two of us beneath a brilliant, crystalline expanse of starlight. There are no skies like that in Detroit. I lost myself in it for a moment, a tickle of vertigo in my stomach, as if it was a physical possibility that I could fall up and tumble into eternity.

"You need this," Savannah said, and touched the lip of a bottled water to my mouth. I sipped as she tilted it. The first touch of water in my throat made my thirst suddenly real, suddenly furious. I drank the bottle in great gulps. Savannah went inside the cabin. When she returned, the bottle was refilled. She curled up on my lap and I drank again. When the bottle was drained, she set it on the table and leaned in to me, her nose against my neck.

"Go back to sleep," she whispered.

I didn't want to. I wanted to talk with her. I wanted to be alone under a beautiful night sky with her, whole and untroubled, at ease. But the day had been too long and far too taxing. I let the smell of her and the warmth of her carry me back down to rest.

*

In that moment of trembling half-light, that same moment of the new day when my father was whisked forever out of the world, Savannah silently shed her clothing. She stepped out of the pile they made on the deck and stared serenely at me, a gossamer-crowned Faerie childe, pale and elemental.

"I've made up my mind," she told me.

"I don't understand."

"That's alright."

She came to me on silent footsteps. Stared into my eyes as she unfastened my belt. She pressed her mouth against mine and drew the ache and arthritic weakness out of me. When I stirred to her, she slid down until we were as joined as any man and woman can be.

She rocked slowly, haltingly. It was nothing like before. She moved over me with a tenderness that I hadn't known was a part

271

of her nature. Her breathing quickened in short little gasps of mounting tension. I gave in to her intent. She was healing me. Showing me the truth of who I was to her. Her hands cupped my face and she moaned "I'm sorry" into my lips, again and again, until the cresting of her orgasm made speech impossible.

I wrapped my arms around her and there was no pain in the act. I was whole, at least in that moment. As whole and unburdened as I had ever been. I crushed her against me and pulled her down, rooting her while the spasming release took me over. We shuddered. Her tears, mingling between our lips.

"I'm sorry."

"I know."

She helped me up and led me to the bathroom. I stripped slowly while she turned the knobs on the bath and got the shower jetting hot. We stood together inside the tub, under the spray. She used a soaped sponge to scrub the blood and dirt off me while I held my bandaged wound outside the curtain. When she was done and I was clean, I repaid her with my good arm, running the sponge the length of her.

We lingered a while longer in the steam, flesh sticking to flesh.

"Eat?" she murmured. "Or sleep?"

"Sleep."

We curled together onto the bed, pink and drowsy from the heat. Her hair was wrapped in a towel atop her head. I kissed her ear, the nape of her neck. Stroked the curve of her hip softly until my eyes closed.

*

Jack Reinhart pounded on the bedroom door's frame until I snapped awake. My hand reached out to the empty spot where Savannah had been.

"Get your clothes on," Reinhart ordered in that too-loud voice cops use as a substitute for natural authority. "You've got one minute to get up and get out here."

He lingered there in the doorway for just a second, staring at me with a disquieting mixture of outrage and sympathy. His left hand was holding a clear plastic evidence bag. My Sig Sauer was inside it.

"Where is she?" I said.

It wasn't what he expected, because his eyes narrowed and he shook his head.

"Jesus, Roarke," he muttered and walked away. I heard the slider door open, followed by the clumping of his shoes on the deck.

I dressed quickly. The smell of coffee drew me to the kitchen. A full pot was steaming under the machine. I poured two cups and stared out the window at the line of black SUVs parked in the long drive. I counted seven FBI agents. Two of them were

273

speaking with Rhonda down on the front office's porch. Others walked in and out of the various cabins. I didn't see Savannah anywhere among them.

Reinhart took the cup I offered him and gave me a curt nod of his head. He took a sip, winced at the heat, and set it on the deck's rail. The sun was suspended in the noon hour above the pine.

"Who tried to put those on you?" he said, pointing at the dangling handcuff.

"A local deputy. One of the leaders of the Sovereign."

"Still alive?" he said and pulled his ring of keys from a pocket. He thumbed out a handcuff key and made an impatient motion at me. I held my wrist out and he inserted the key. The black titanium set of cuffs clattered against the deck boards.

"For now," I answered.

He looked me up and down and shook his head, scowling.

"You look like hammered shit, Roarke. You need a hospital."

"Maybe later. After we find Chelsea Gullins."

He made a sweeping motion that encompassed all of the pine forest that surrounded the deck.

"This is what everyone raves about, huh?" he said. "Getting away to the Great Outdoors? Personally, I don't see it. They got a Starbucks up here?"

"Not that I've seen," I said.

"Savages."

"How'd you find me?"

"Savannah Kline called us four hours ago," he said, watching me to gauge my reaction.

"Where is she?"

"In custody. Same as you."

"Chelsea Gullins needs to be found, Reinhart."

"I know that very well," he shot back and took another tentative sip of the coffee. "The Kline woman filled in a lot. My guys swarmed Wayland Graves' house an hour ago. We've got three of the Sovereign in custody. From what I hear, two of them are fighting to see who can confess the quickest. One."

"What?"

"One," he repeated. "That's how many dead bodies we found at the Reverend's. Three more men have bullets inside them. One of them is in bad shape but the other two will make it fine. How many more bodies are we going to find, Roarke?"

And there it was. Jack Reinhart was as much of a friend to me as I would allow anyone to be. We'd watched some boxing matches and sipped beers. Traded stories over a meal now and again. But in the end, he was cop.

The smart thing would have been to ask for a lawyer and screw my mouth shut. There's no profit in spilling your secrets to the law and hoping they feel sympathy for your point of view. People think they can reason with cops. They think they can

275

explain themselves. They think they can lie their way out. It never works.

"Are you looking for Chelsea?" I said.

"Yes. But there isn't much to go on. There are a lot of unanswered questions, Roarke. Savannah left a lot out of her story trying to protect you.'

I understood. He had two investigations to contend with. Chelsea was one. The deaths that occurred up here was the other. As long as he was juggling both, his resources and his attention were divided. This was why he hadn't slapped his own cuffs on me and thrown me directly into a cell. He was letting me share coffee with him in private in order to give me the chance to do the right thing, to free him and his men up to devote their energies to finding a missing innocent.

"How many people can you get to look for her?" I said.

"I have nine up here now," he answered. "Seven more are driving up. We'll rope in the local sheriff's office. We'll organize volunteers. I won't drop the ball on that end of things."

He looked me square in the eyes as he said it, unblinking; letting me know that he understood this was the only real issue that animated me.

So I told him. Everything. I talked and he listened while we slowly drained our coffee mugs. I told him about finding the murdered body of Paul Gullins and shooting Wade when the fool tried to pin me down inside Rezner's rifle scope. When I told him about Rezner and the blood-soaked bunker in the woods, he held up a silencing hand and talked into his radio's shoulder mic. Nobody was to contact the sheriff's office until he gave the go ahead. Deputy Michael Rezner was a wanted suspect to be treated as armed and extremely dangerous.

I kept on, laying it all out. My escape from the bunker. Savannah's cover fire and the Sovereign who died trying to hold onto a hostage they didn't know had already escaped on her own.

When I was done, he'd written several pages of notes in a little spiral-bound pad.

"This preacher," he said.

"Yeah?"

"He's dead?"

"He was breathing when I left him."

Reinhart was still and silent for a long while. He pretended to stare out at the panorama of nature beyond the deck, but I knew he was trying to sort it all out in his head. I'd laid down a smorgasbord of killings for him to chew over. As keenly as I'd ever felt it, in that long silence I was back in the 'criminal' box he and his kind categorized me as.

"I can't let you just walk out of here," he said finally.

"They all had it coming."

"Yeah? Is that a legal statement or a moral one?"

"Both."

"Maybe you were justified in all of it," he continued, as if I hadn't spoken. "Maybe you weren't. I'm not a judge. We'll get you to a hospital first. I'll call you a lawyer myself. What happens after that is out of my hands."

I drained my cup and set it beside his on the rail.

"Find Chelsea Gullins, Reinhart. The rest of it is just process. I've been through it before. Find the girl."

None of the trouble went out of his eyes. He frowned and shook his head in bleak resignation.

"If you go down on this, so do I."

He didn't have to elaborate. He'd steered Savannah to me. Recommended me. He'd asked around about the Sovereign on my behalf. Taken my call the night before. It wasn't just his career on the line if the judicial system decided I was a criminal again. It was his freedom. My misadventures in the wilds of the north could tie themselves back to him so securely that some creative prosecutor up here might feel inclined to hang the word 'accessory' around Reinhart's neck.

"I won't mention you," I said. "Neither will Savannah. This was me. Just me."

"I'm not asking for that," he muttered.

"I know. But I'm still offering it." I stuck my hands back out between us and said, "Put the cuffs on, Jack, and stop wasting time. This is your show now."

He scowled and pushed my hands away.

"I'm not putting the bracelets on you," he said. "If that comes later, fine. For now, I'll get you transported to the hospital. No, don't look at me like that. We'll get you looked at and admitted for the gunshot. That'll give me time to find a lawyer to come stand at your shoulder for whatever comes next."

Reinhart walked me out of the cabin and past the other agents outside. Rhonda was sitting on the steps of the front office. The squat, round woman saw me and her face lit with worry. Without the sturdy and certain presence of Sharon at her side, Rhonda looked like she was brimming with anxiety. I looked into the windows of their front office, but didn't see any sign of her flinty, pistol-toting partner. Rhonda's eyes darted over the agents that were occupying her land, then back to me.

"Thank you," I said without slowing.

She nodded reflexively and opened her mouth, but Reinhart led me past her before she could get any words out.

Reinhart came to a stop at the rear passenger side door of the last black SUV parked in the lane. The windows were tinted opaque.

"We'll do what we can to find that girl."

"I know you will, Jack."

"You're done, then? I don't have to worry about your stubborn ass trying to get back into this mess?"

"I'm done."

He left me there without another word, so I opened the back door of the SUV and climbed in.

The agent behind the wheel craned his head around and scowled through the metal grate that separated us. He stared at my hands and shook his head.

"I don't know how I feel about that," he said.

"You want to cuff me, I don't mind."

He looked out the windshield at Reinhart, who was conversing on the porch with Rhonda.

"I guess Reinhart knows you," he mused, uncertain.

"I can sit on my hands if you want."

"Cute."

"I'm Roarke."

"Fairchild."

"If I start chewing my way through the bars, just shoot me and I'll sit back."

That got a genuine chuckle from him and he looked at me again.

"Not worried about me, buddy," Fairchild said. "But I'm responsible for this one, too."

I looked at Savannah seated beside me. Sometime between my falling asleep and her meeting with the feds she'd called in, she had changed into a knee-length white skirt and a loose cotton blouse the sunny color of dandelions. Her wrists were cuffed in front of her and her seatbelt was clasped in place.

Savannah watched silently, inscrutable. She looked like she was holding back a tempest of emotions and explanations behind her eyes.

"We know each other," I said. "It'll be fine."

If my assurance meant anything to Fairchild, he didn't acknowledge it. Reinhart was waving him over impatiently. He gave a frustrated sigh and got out of the SUV. His door shut with a heavy sound and I was alone in silence with Savannah. I reached out and took one of her hands. It curled into mine, squeezing hard. The links of her handcuffs rattled and she let out a sob that she quickly choked back down. She was trembling with anxiety, brimming with it.

But when we looked at one another, there was a resolute strength in her gaze.

'*I've made up my mind,*' she'd told me as she stood naked in the night.

I hadn't understood then but I did now. While I dozed out there on the deck, Savannah had performed a cold calculation. The two of us were not suited to finding her niece. We had no resources beyond our intent. We were just two people. The FBI had numbers. They had authority and tools. If Chelsea was to be found soon, if there was to be any hope of that, the child needed more than her aunt and a beat-to-hell hired hand. Savannah had weighed her own self-interest against Chelsea's and made the only decision a decent human being could.

All the while that we'd made love and showered and fallen into bed together, she'd known what she needed to do. She'd called the feds and offered up enough detail about her conspiracy with the Sovereign to get them to race straight out here.

"I wouldn't have forced you to do this," I said.

"I'm glad you said that. Keep holding my hand, okay?"

"Okay."

She forced a smile and for a moment she looked like the Savannah I thought I knew. I leaned in and kissed her. "We'll get through this together," I whispered. "You aren't alone."

The driver's door lurched open. Fairchild climbed back into the driver's seat. He started the engine and craned his head around to look at us both. He was a young guy, with a soft round face and a hairline already in full retreat.

"We're going?" I said.

"Boss says it's the hospital for you," he said, then looked at Savannah. "I'm to take you back down to Detroit, ma'am."

"I understand," Savannah agreed.

Fairchild afforded her a brief, sympathetic grimace before turning back around. He put the SUV in reverse and started rolling backwards down the drive. He whipped the SUV out onto the road and put it in drive. Gravel kicked out of its treads as we surged smoothly ahead.

"Just sit back and enjoy the ride," he drawled.

We zipped back along the county road Savannah and I had first traveled over only a couple of days before. It seemed longer ago than that.

"You'll need a lawyer," I said in soft tones, still holding her hand in mine. "I can get one for you. Don't make any more decisions until you've seen him, alright?"

"Roarke?"

"They'll find her. After that, we'll get through whatever they throw up at us--"

She squeezed down on my hand to shut me up. Tears were welling up in her eyes, fear seeming to have abruptly won over in her struggle to keep herself poised and contained.

"Roarke…there's more," she whispered. "I want to tell you the rest of it but I don't want you to hate me."

I leaned into her with my mouth against her ear and closed my eyes.

"Tell me."

"There's someone else in all of this," she said, so halting and soft I could barely hear the words. "And he has the money."

My eyes were still shut and I was breathing in the intoxicating smell of her when Fairchild died at the wheel.

# T W E L V E

Blood sprayed across the driver's cabin in a high-velocity mist.

Savannah screamed.

Wind from the agent's shattered window clamored over us.

The world didn't make sense in that first instance. I blinked and tried to come fully aware, to instantly comprehend what was happening. Far away, a rifle cracked.

"The *wheel*," Savannah gasped.

We both watched in silent horror as Fairchild slid to his right, down and out of view. Both watched his hands slip limply off the wheel as he sank away. Ahead, the road steadily sloped upward and I could see the green signs of the highway overpass.

My fingers curled into the metal grate that separated us from the driver's cabin. I peered down, my nose pressed against it. Fairchild's head was a shattered mess. He was slumped on his side, his service pistol beneath him. His right boot was cocked at an angle, wedged down against the accelerator. I looked at the digital speedometer, watched it tick up from forty-five to fifty in rapid order. It kept climbing.

"Shit," I hissed.

"Roarke--"

"It's okay."

I yanked at the grate. It was no use. I yanked again and shouted something obscene when it didn't buckle.

"It's him, isn't it?" Savannah gasped. "It's Rezner."

I heaved on the handle to my door, then reached over and did the same to Savannah's. Nothing. It was a vehicle designed for prisoner transport. The doors wouldn't open and the windows didn't even have buttons.

Outside the windshield, the SUV was still running parallel with the course of the road. We were up the slope and nearing the expressway cloverleaf. If the alignment on the vehicle held us true we'd arc over the bridge and down again. I didn't see any vehicles ahead of us on the bridge. I looked at the speedometer. Seventy-two.

I got on my back, shoving my shoulders against Savannah. She cried out as I pinned her against the door. Using her as a brace, I brought my feet up, knees against my belly. I took a deep breath and kicked out at the window as hard as I could. It made a tremendous noise, but the glass held. I repeated the kick, shouting a curse through my clenched teeth. The window shattered against the heels of my boots. Outside, the tree line was a rushing blur. At that speed, if we went out the window the asphalt and gravel would chew us like so much meat in a thresher. Mangle and break us. In my mind's eye I saw

Savannah's slight, pale body tumbling in a red line over the roadway. I blinked the nightmare out of my eyes.

"Roarke!"

I bolted upright and stared through the grate again. We rushed past the northbound entrance. Ahead, three-foot high metal guardrails lined the overpass bridge. The SUV was vibrating now. I looked at the speedometer. We'd peaked over eighty.

However we stopped, it was going to be violently abrupt. If we made it over the arc of the bridge, it would be an oncoming car or a tree that brought us to a stand-still. I pressed my back against the seat and groped for the belt. I tugged it out and slapped the clasp into the lock.

I was reaching for Savannah's hand when a third rifle shot leapt up into the air.

I heard the rear passenger-side tire explode and felt a wild fear thrash itself alive inside me as the SUV abruptly jerked left, then roared right. The road disappeared. We thundered through the guardrail with a metal scream. We shot out into the air, nothing but sky in the windshield. The engine continued to hum along, ignorant of the fact that we were plunging through space, that the only road it would find was twenty feet below.

Savannah's hand found mine, clamped down.

The world turned upside down.

The expressway appeared, rushing up at us. The roof of a tractor-trailer zipped by. Fairchild rolled up against the grate, abruptly free of gravity's pull. One dead eye lolled at me in its socket like he was trying to get my attention and maybe warn me about the obvious.

We hit the expressway pavement nose-first. All the remaining glass in the vehicle exploded. The impact tore the seat belt free of its lock and I crashed against the metal grate.

A split second of black nothingness as the world turned off.

When my brain reset, my eyes opened. I was staring up at the backseat. The seat belts dangled like jungle vines just above my nose. We were upside down. I was sprawled in a heap on the roof of the smashed vehicle, covered in a patina of safety glass fragments. Something was pressing against my legs, heavy and immobile. I blinked around. Savannah was sprawled in a pile across me. The green globes of her eyes stared vacantly at nothing, still wide with the terror of our descent. I shoved at her but she didn't move. I felt as weak as a child. Blood ran into my eyes, stinging. I didn't know if it was mine or hers. A scream overcame the ringing in my ears and it took me a second to realize that it wasn't a person—it was the SUV's horn, stuck on permanent wail, the plaintive cry of a dying animal.

"Savannah?" My voice was a strangled croak.

So close it drowned out the horn, the squeal of brake-locked tires burning themselves across the pavement.

I craned my head around and stared out at the silver car fishtailing toward me across the expressway. I saw the driver's panicked expression as she held the wheel with locked, rigid arms-- a pretty woman, with shoulder-length curls and bulging, horrified eyes. Her blouse was purple and unbuttoned far enough that the tanned slopes of her breasts were visible.

The last thought that went through my head before she careened straight into us was that she should have buttoned one more button, for modesty's sake.

The paramedics were going to get an eyeful.

\*

Strong hands seize me under my arms. They heave me from inside the scattered puzzle that used to be Fairchild's vehicle. The whoop of sirens and my heels dragging lines through broken glass.

Somebody is asking questions. Shouting them.

The sky is an awful gray shroud and I know Savannah Kline is dead.

\*

Lights and questions and too-effective air conditioning. Wheels clattering over linoleum. A line of fluorescence leads me to a squatting machine-coffin. I am fed in. Not a coffin. A vibrating, living thing. The smooth-stomached beast clacks and thrums like a metallic insect. Somewhere, its attendants are muttering and laughing amongst themselves.

*

Darkness.

A spot of flame, down in the earth. Growing. Flaring and revealing.

The Old Soldier's ancient, gnarled limbs wind ever upwards, past the wall that encloses my house, spiraling beyond the wind-scoured stone towers of this necropolis that is home, up and up and into the night sky until the stars are baubles suspended within its canopy.

"I never had a love in me, Roarke."

Father is caged in the roots of the tree. Their knotty lengths are woven into him, through him, until neither has a beginning or end. He is a moldering mass, half swallowed in soft, erupting earth. His craggy, stone-etched face slowly turns to regard me. His one eye is a furious ember lighting the darkness around us, burning with orange wrath and ill will.

"I know that," I tell him.

"Then why are you weak? I gave you the wisdom I earned through suffering. I told you truths in the night. Why are you weak?"

"I'm alive."

289

The smear of his mouth splits and becomes a vicious sneer of teeth and gum; as near a smile as he can summon.

"What did you forget?" he moans.

"I don't know."

The ember flares bright and furious and the thing among the roots cackles with contempt.

"No truce for your enemy!" he bellows. "Find him where he cowers! Find him in his corner!"

The binding roots constrict and heave him up out of his barrow. Thick clots of earth fly away as he rises. He looms over me in shadow, stinking of rich soil and florid decay. His mouth is an echoing cavern.

"No truce for your enemy!"

He grows and surpasses the wall, surpasses the slow-motion apocalypse unfolding beyond it. Swelling, he is darkness, eclipsing the stars, swallowing me in his frigid depths. The hate-light of his single eye winks out.

Darkness reigns.

\*

When I woke, a woman hovered nearby.

Her name was Catherine Eir and she was a thick-hipped, strong-eyed woman in a white coat who told me she was my doctor.

"You don't remember being admitted?" she said.

"Some. It's kind of in and out."

"Do you remember being taken for a CT scan?"

"I think so, yeah. I signed a lot of papers and they wheeled me down to the machine. You weren't there, though."

She smiled faintly and jotted something on a clipboard.

"No. This is the first time we've met. Do you feel nauseous?"

"I don't think so."

"Good."

She poured water from a white plastic pitcher into a Styrofoam cup. Held it patiently while I sipped through a straw. An I.V. was running out of the hollow of my left arm. A saline bag dripped above me.

"Give me the rundown on the damage, Doc."

"How do you feel?" she asked. "How is your breathing?"

"Like my chest is full of glass," I answered. "Every time I inhale. Ribs, right? How many are broken?"

"Two. The CT scans were encouraging. You don't have any serious head trauma."

"So, a concussion."

"Yes. Think of it as a bruise on the brain. The best advice is that you need to rest. No strenuous activity. No sports. Take some time off work and just be as relaxed as you can for a few days. That will help with the ribs, too. There isn't any sign of injury to your internal organs, so rest is the best advice for that as well. You'll need to keep taking antibiotics for the wound to your right arm. We've cleaned it and re-sewn it, but there was already an infection when you were admitted. I've written a prescription to help with the pain."

"No more pain killers," I said.

She came alert at that, and looked at me like she was searching for something, some flaw in the design.

"You've had addiction issues?" she ventured.

"No. Bad dreams."

"I don't understand."

I saw my father again in the fever dream, a shadow as big as the world. Heard him cackling, spouting madness. I didn't want any more dreams. The bleak terrain of my yesterdays belonged where I'd always kept it, locked down tight in the basement of my mind.

"No more opiates, alright? I don't need them. I'll take Tylenol and whatever antibiotics you have for the infection. But you can keep the hard stuff. It doesn't agree with me."

Doctor Patel wrote some more on her clipboard. She looked like she was struggling to keep her annoyance off her face. And failing.

"The fractured ribs will be quite painful."

"I'll sip my air."

"Well, that's the problem. We need you to breathe normally or there's a risk of developing pneumonia. Proper pain

292

medication will allow you to breathe normally. We have alternatives to morphine-based pain relievers."

"I'll tough it out."

It went on like that for a while. She ran down the potential consequences of my acting like what she increasingly seemed to view as a bull-headed moron, and I continued to say things that assured her that she was right. When she exhausted all of her warnings and recommendations, she left the room in a tense march.

Once she was gone, I swung my legs over the side of the bed and sat upright. The pain that flared through my chest was like a giant fist squeezing me. I sucked shallow breaths and remained still until the fist loosened its grip.

I stood. When I was confident I had my feet under me, I clutched the wheeled I.V. pole and made my way over to the hospital room's little lavatory. Stared in the mirror at the heavy black crescents of bruised skin hanging beneath eyes that were so shot-through with broken red capillaries I wouldn't have been surprised to see blood welling up out of my tear ducts. The man in the mirror was a stranger. He was haggard and pale, a slack unshaven ghoul.

"Did either of them live?"

Reinhart had appeared in the mirror behind me. His reflection was silent and I saw my own exhaustion twinned across his handsome face. I turned and shuffled back out of the lavatory.

Reinhart shook his head.

"Savannah's dead," he answered. "On impact. You want the details?"

"No. What about the driver? The woman who ran into us?"

"Fractured collarbone, face full of airbag, and a crazy story to tell her friends."

There were two chairs near the window. I eased down into one. It was late in the day. Long shadows preyed across the hospital's parking lot.

"How long have I been here?"

"Just today. You were admitted around twelve-thirty. It's eight-thirty now. I talked to your doctor the first time I came around. She said they couldn't let you sleep with the concussion. Said they'd bring you around chemically if they had to. That's why I came back, to see if you were still out."

"It feels longer than that," I admitted.

"Sure."

"Have you found Chelsea, Jack?"

His expression darkened and his eyes got cold with impatience.

"We've had a lot going on, Roarke."

"So the answer is no."

"You think I answer to you?" he shot back. "Not in a million years. Count your blessings you aren't cuffed to that bed. Chelsea Gullins isn't your concern anymore. None of this is. I

294

came to tell you you're done. What happened out on the expressway doesn't change that. You're done."

"But not under arrest."

"Like I said, the Sovereign we have in custody are spilling everything. Your version of things is checking out. So rest up and let the nurses spoon you your applesauce. I have to go."

"The local Sheriff? Where does he stand on all this?"

Reinhart snorted and grew a satisfied, ugly grin.

"One of his deputies was running a drug ring, kidnapped a little girl, kidnapped the man sent to help her, and is the number one suspect in the murder of an FBI Agent. If he ever gets around to you, it'll be to try and pin a medal on your chest before you have a chance to sue his department into bankruptcy. Don't worry about the Sheriff."

"I'm sorry about Fairchild."

Schultz's grin vanished and he stared past me.

"Sure," he muttered in a dead, inflectionless voice. "I know you are."

"You have the Reverend yet?"

Reinhart waved his hand like he could swat the question away and snapped, "Your only job is to lounge around in that bed and answer any more questions we might throw at you."

"It was Rezner who snipered us. You said so yourself. Nobody knows where to find him?"

295

His patience was spent. Reinhart stared at me, unblinking, the muscles in his jaw clenched into tight balls.

"So no to Chelsea, no to the preacher, and no to Rezner," I said. "Thanks for coming by, Jack."

We stared across the room at one another while the silence thickened around us. He looked exhausted and wound tighter than I'd ever seen him. None of the easy grace that'd earned him the nickname 'Golden Boy' was anywhere to be seen. I wondered if maybe our friendship had reached its breaking point. One of his men was dead. Bodies were strewn across the county. A minor child was unaccounted for. It wouldn't take too many mental gymnastics for the FBI agent to lay all of those things at my feet and decide I was really nothing more than an ex-con he didn't want to know anymore.

If that was how he saw things, he didn't put voice to it. Reinhart just scowled, turned on his heel, and walked out of the room on stiff legs.

I'd been wrong to handle him that way. I knew it as soon as he was gone. I'd roped him into a hydra-headed calamity, one of his own men was dead, and I'd thrown his lack of progress in his face.

But Chelsea Gullins was still missing. Rezner was alive and free.

I could apologize to Reinhart later, after those two facts were corrected.

I sat there with the piles of broken glass shifting around in my chest every time I inhaled. A black, brooding melancholy descended, filling the void Reinhart left behind. I had won nothing. Proven nothing, to myself or anyone else.

In the midst of that cloud of bitterness, I allowed Savannah to come to me. Let her curl cat-like into my lap. I hunched miserably around her and filled my lungs with the smell of her flowered moisturizer until I was gagging on the memory.

I wallowed like that while the shadows in the lot outside lengthened and spread into a blanket over the world.

The day was dead and only night remained.

*

I cut the self-pity short. I let Savannah recede and got to my feet. Pushed the call button beside the bed and set about doing what I knew needed done.

When the duty nurse appeared in the doorway, I was dressed in my filthy, blood-stained slacks and shoes. Teeth clenched against the grind of injury, I eased into my shirt while the nurse tried to make sense of what she was seeing.

"Sir? You…you need to get back in bed…"

Her uncertain gaze shifted there, to the I.V. needle and hose discarded on top of the sheets.

297

Before she could think about calling for help or blabbering reflexive advice at me, I reached into my wallet and plucked out a credit card.

I held it out to her and said, "Be a sweetheart and tell Doctor Eir I decided she was right. I'll take the strongest stuff she's got- - to go."

*

Crawford wasn't big enough to support a real taxi service but the tech behind the hospital's pharmacy counter used an app on his smartphone to find a local man who used his own vehicle as an unlicensed, off-the-books cab.

"He calls it Johnny Cab," the middle-aged tech said with a smirk. When I didn't say anything he arched a brow and continued. "Total Recall? The robot? You never saw it?"

I shrugged indifferently and he passed over my bag of prescriptions without further comment.

Outside in the parking lot, darkness hadn't dispelled the July warmth. Crickets in the ditches clacked on in their endless way and the halogen bulbs atop the security poles were swamped with orbiting fleets of gnats and fat black moths.

I swallowed a handful of pills and waited.

Twenty minutes crawled by before I spied headlights pulling into the lot. The rumble and belch of an unhealthy engine grew loud as the headlights approached. When the car pulled up in front of me it revealed itself to be an old foreign hatchback, equal parts sun-bleached blue paint and scabby brown rust. I reached for the rear door handle but the passenger window whispered down and the man inside shouted over the burping clamor of the car's motor, "You can sit up front, fella. Don't bother me none."

I opened the passenger door and made a long, awkward show of easing myself down into the bucket seat. With the interior bulb lighting us up, the driver and his mess of discarded fast food wrappers were on full view.

The owner and operator of Johnny Cab was a fat twenty-something sporting a lumberjack's wild beard. He was wearing thick cotton pajamas with the face of a cartoon character printed all over them. His bare feet were mashing the brake and clutch down. Dirty, too-long toe nails. A cigarette was burning in his left hand. As I settled into the seat, he ashed the cigarette out his window and stared at me.

I managed to get the door pulled shut, wincing at the sharp agonies blooming throughout my chest. The interior bulb winked out. The driver stayed silent and made no move to put the rattling old contraption in gear.

"I guess I got you out of bed," I said.

Nothing.

The interior of the car smelled like hamburgers, smoke, and mildew.

"Third exit south of town," I said.

He sucked down on the cigarette and in that moment his big round head was lit jack-o-lantern orange.

"Well shit, buddy" he whispered through a gout of exhaled smoke. "You're that damned killer, ain't you?"

# THIRTEEN

"Nope, never heard of any of the guys you went up against," Mitch Gillinwaters, owner of the illegal Johnny Cab, told me after making it clear he was more than happy to get roused out of bed to escort around a damned killer.

He flicked his cigarette carelessly and drove with only the first two fingers of his other hand touching the wheel.

"Don't bother me any. Hell, you're the closest thing to a celebrity I've had in this old beater. Sorry about the mess and all. You don't look too good, buddy. I guess you really gave those sons of bitches a lesson, didn't you? I bet you did. I'd have liked to see that."

As he talked and wheeled us away from the hospital, I quickly categorized him as a man-child; one of those harmless modern American males who happily remained frozen in the amber of their youth. He was a big, hairy, thirty-year-old who wore cartoon jammies, had a plastic super-hero symbol dangling under his rearview mirror, and who named his ratty ride after something obscure he cherished from an old sci-fi movie. I imagined his life beyond the interior of his car. I saw an expensive computer in a cluttered corner of his mother's or

301

father's house, the same house he'd been born in. He would refer to that corner as his 'command center'. He had lots of different handles on-line. Played a lot. Slept a lot. A big bear of a child, surrounded and bolstered by his nostalgic comforts, the things that soothed him and kept him from engaging the world of adults.

"Not even the militia?" I said. "Sovereign North? Never heard of them?"

"No. But if it was all Two Pine guys, I wouldn't know about them. That place is a cemetery. Hell, you know that, don't you? You've seen it, right?"

"Some of it."

The rattling old hatchback wheezed down the main drag.

"You're on the TV, too," he said and took both his hands off the wheel long enough to light another cigarette. "Did they let you watch it in the hospital?"

"I didn't see anything."

"I watched some of it on the station out of Traverse." He started to go on but caught himself and looked at me out of the corner of his eye.

"You mind me talking about all this?"

"I don't mind. Did they say anything about a missing girl? A child?"

We caught a red. Mitch brought us to a shuddering halt. A wide smile grew under his wild lumberjack's beard.

"Honest? Man, that's why I came out on this call. The guy who texted me for this ride said the man who needed a cab was beat up bad."

"He was a pharmacist."

"Who?"

"The man who texted you."

"Ok. Anyway, he actually warned me off in the text. Said maybe you were involved with what was on the news."

The light turned green and the hatchback coughed its way up through the gears until we were zipping along again.

"But you still came out."

"Hell, yes! The news says you were working to rescue that little girl. Says you're some sort of vigilante. I kind of thought it'd be wild if the same guy checking himself out of the hospital was that dude. I had a feeling, like I just knew it was you. You believe in that sort of thing? Like maybe I was supposed to be the guy to show up when you needed a ride?"

"No."

"Not even a little? I do. Stuff happens, you know?"

Ahead, the Crawford County Sheriff's office came into view and, just beyond it, the courthouse. I squinted through the gloom. The parking lot between the two buildings was teeming with activity. I spotted several of Reinhart's black SUVs packed in among a mass of other vehicles. Men and women streamed in and out of both buildings, crossing paths as they hurried back and forth, sometimes stopping to speak in little huddles.

A line of black FBI windbreakers filed out of the cop shop. The agents carried stacks of cardboard file boxes. A warm satisfaction filled me when I pictured them stripping out Rezner's meticulous little office. Bagging his plaques and certificates. Pulling his proud framed photos off the wall. Confiscating his computer and shipping it out to be scrubbed and analyzed. The lunatic's façade was getting torn down. The truth of him would be pieced together.

"Look at all that," Mitch breathed and brought us down to a chugging crawl. "I've never seen that many cops in one place. Buddy, I guess you brought some real serious trouble with you, huh?"

"The trouble was already here."

"Look at that."

I followed his pointing finger. A television news van had pulled up into the far end of the lot. It came to a stop and the driver hopped out. A well-coiffed man in a blue suit walked around from the other side and the two of them opened up the back doors of the van.

"Pull over there," I told him.

He didn't ask any questions, happy to be in the middle of whatever he thought all of this was. He guided the hatchback into the strip mall parking lot across the street and swerved us nose-first into a space so we were facing the spectacle.

My stomach churned. I put a hand on the dash and hunched over. A nauseous vertigo swam up the channels inside me, from my gut to my head. It carried an awful, shaking weakness with it.

"Hey! Hey, you alright?"

I fumbled the door open and managed to lean out far enough to bark the contents of my stomach onto the asphalt. There wasn't much. I kept heaving until it was nothing but yellow bile churning out of me.

Still shaking like a palsy-stricken old man, I straightened up and pulled the door shut again. In the silence of the car's interior my breath was a loud wheeze. I forced myself to sip my breaths until the burning hell of my chest cooled, eased to a bearable ache.

"Look, you need to go back," he said. "This has been cool, meeting you and all. But you need to get right back in the hospital, dude. You're literally green right now."

"I'm fine."

"Naw, man. You ain't."

"Relax. Just give me a second."

He craned around into the back seat and produced a half-empty bottle of water. Held it out between us.

"You think you can keep this down?"

"Yeah."

I took the bottle. Tapped another handful of pills into my mouth to replace the ones I'd just splashed across the lot. Washed them down with a swig of warm water.

"Uh, I don't think you're supposed to take that many."

"You're a doctor now?"

"That was a lot of pills, man."

"I'm fine. They aren't opiates."

"Meaning?"

"They don't put you to sleep."

"Still. I'm just saying, maybe read the instructions before you gulp half a bottle down."

The two-man news crew was walking up to the mass of milling authority figures across the street. The one in the suit had a microphone in one hand and the driver had a big camera rig on his shoulder.

"I bet they'd shit if you went over there," Mitch said around a chuckle. "That'd be funny as hell. The Two Pine Vigilante appears from the darkness. They'd freak."

"You made that up?"

"The Two Pine Vigilante? Yeah. You like it?"

"No."

"Are you going after that cop? The one who everyone's looking for?"

"No. I was hired to find a little girl. It's not my job to track down a fugitive."

"You don't sound so sure."

"Shut up a second, okay?"

I counted the people in the lot and came up with eight FBI agents, six sheriff's deputies and another half dozen officials in suits and ties. That only included the people outside. More would be inside. More than two dozen cops, lawyers, and county officials were all right there, right now.

"Those bastards," I hissed and opened the door again. When I planted one boot out on the pavement, Mitch held his palms in the air and looked dubious.

"I was *joking*, man. Are you nuts? You can't go over there. What if they arrest you?"

"They won't."

"Okay, but how do you know?"

"They let me walk out of the hospital. How much do I owe you?"

He grimaced and said, "Let me take you back to the hospital. Seriously. No charge. Come on and shut that door now, alright?"

"Thanks for the ride," I said and stood up outside. I pulled two twenties out of my wallet and held them out to him. He hesitated, ready to keep cajoling me back to the sick bed. I let the bills fall on the passenger seat and craned my head down so we were looking eye-to-eye.

"I have a promise to keep."

The big kid relented. He smiled sheepishly and swiped the bills up into his hand.

"Nobody's going to believe I gave you a ride, man. The vigilante in my cab. Crazy night, right?"

"Keep an eye out," I told him, letting the vigilante bit go without comment. He'd refer to me however he wanted once I was gone.

"Keep an eye out for what?"

"The missing girl is thirteen. She's got curly blonde hair and she's thin as a rail. A track athlete. Her name's Chelsea and if you see her out on the roads, she'll be frightened. Understand?"

Mitch's face hardened with sudden interest. I could see it in his eyes: the vigilante had just given him a mission. I watched the wild notion solidify behind his eyes. He cleared his throat and nodded his head once.

"Understood. If I see her…should I call the cops? Or…?"

I told him my cell number and he plugged it into his smart phone.

"Call the cops first. Call me after."

"Will do. Jesus, I'm not going to sleep tonight. No way."

"Just keep an eye peeled on your way home. That's all you need to do."

"Yeah, *right*," he drawled and backed out when I shut the door. The hatchback stuttered up to speed as he pulled out and turned south. Not north toward the hospital or home. South. I watched the taillights of his car dwindle away and realized the big, strange cabbie was officially 'on the case' with the vigilante he imagined me to be.

He was heading for the empty stretches of Two Pine, looking for the girl on the news.

In that moment, I felt bad about the mental image I'd painted of Mitch. Maybe he was a big kid permanently stuck in his juvenile years. So what? All it had taken was the suggestion that he might be of use to a lost kid and the wild-bearded, pajama-clad cabbie was off like a shot to go spend the night looking for her.

I turned and looked at the mob of officials across the street. Right there were all the resources Chelsea really needed-- the vehicles, radios, men and women, the training and the know-how --all of it uselessly piled up outside their clubhouse while the hour grew late.

Brimming with outrage, I started walking across the street. I would march over there and present myself to the news crew. I would stare into the camera and talk about Chelsea Gullins. I would condemn the milling mass of authority. Demand they get out into the surrounding neighborhoods and do the only thing that mattered: search for the girl. All of them. From the county administrator down to the courthouse janitor. Get out and start looking. Stop worrying about damage control and law suits. Get up. Spread out. Find the girl.

I made it to the middle of the road before one of the bodies in the lot swiftly separated itself from the others and headed right at me.

Jack Reinhart's face was a mixture of incredulity and wrath. Behind him, faces turned. The cameraman looked in our direction.

"Keep walking, you dumb son of a bitch," Jack hissed under his breath as he reached me. He took me by the elbow in a vise grip and steered us toward the sheriff's office. The milling mass in the lot started whispering amongst themselves.

"You gave me your word, Jack," I said, loud. Loud enough for everyone to hear.

"Shut up and get inside. Jesus, man. What the *hell* are you thinking?"

He marched us up the stairs and into the lobby of the cop shop. As the door swung shut behind us I heard someone call out my name. A man. The news reporter, I knew. Jack was moving us toward the secure door that lead into the heart of the department. He waved a hand at one of the three agents behind the reception window and I heard the buzz of the door's lock being retracted.

I stopped walking. Jack yanked at my arm and shot me a constipated scowl.

"You gave me your word," I repeated. "You'd do everything to find her. Remember that? I do."

A mix of emotions played over Reinhart's face that I couldn't decipher. He seemed to be abruptly uncertain of himself, transmitting conflicting signals in an attempt to settle on an expression that would get me through the door.

"You're all holed up in here," I said. "All you brave little badges sitting on your thumbs waiting for the county attorneys to map out how this wasn't the fault of anybody with an official title. Right? Is that the size of things, Jack? Everybody plays cover-your-ass while that little girl is still alone in the wilderness?"

"Roarke..."

"Get your hand off me, Jack."

"God damn it, stop. Stop and listen to me."

"I won't tell you again."

Reinhart let go of my elbow and took a step back. His conflicting expressions settled into an unblinking resignation. He inclined his head toward the agent behind the glass again. This time, when the electric buzz sounded, Reinhart pulled the steel door open and held it.

"You want in?" he said. "Is that what this is? You think you should be inside this?"

"I want her found."

"And you'll throw us under the bus with a TV news crew. That's what this little stunt is about."

"If that's what it takes to get everyone moving."

"You really think I wouldn't move heaven and earth to find her, Roarke?"

"I only know what I see, Jack."

Reinhart nodded like he was confirming something to himself. His eyes were heavy, his chin bristling with a day's growth. He looked exhausted. At the end of whatever internal resolve was keeping him from fraying into pieces.

"Alright. You're in. Come on with me and let's see if you like what that gets you."

*

Reinhart lead me through the building. I saw a handful of FBI and only two county deputies. We passed Rezner's office. The walls were bare, the desktop empty.

When we came to a stop at the end of the hall, Reinhart told me to wait and disappeared inside the last door. He closed it softly behind him and I saw that the plaque affixed to the center of the door read, 'Sheriff J. Bruckey'.

I waited.

When Reinhart opened the door again, his face was a blank. He motioned me in as he stepped back out into the hallway. He touched my arm as I started to walk past him.

"Remember," he said softly, "I tried to send your ass home."

I walked into the Sheriff's wood-paneled office wondering at the sympathy that had tinged his voice. He pulled the door shut behind me and I heard his boot-falls recede down the hall.

Across the office, a middle aged black man wasn't bothering to get up from behind the desk. He had a round face and pinched little eyes that watched me with no sign of concern. His suit was blue, his tie was red, and I guessed that if he stood up he might have an inch or even two on me. His big hands were tented over the flat plane of his stomach, the long fingers decorated with a fat gold university ring.

"What now?" I said.

"Agent Reinhart says you're Roarke."

"That's right."

"You want to sit down, Roarke?"

I eased down into one of the two over-stuffed leather chairs on the other side of the desk from him. Behind him, rows of commendations and awards were fixed behind glass.

"You're moving slow," he said. "I assumed you'd be in the hospital overnight. The report I read says you got pretty banged up."

"I'm fine."

"You think I'm the Sheriff?"

"Nope."

"What gave it away? Black man in the great white north?"

"Your suit's too expensive."

313

"That's it? A Sheriff can't maintain a wardrobe?"

"Well, it doesn't help that you don't look like the old white guy in the photos behind you."

His wide mouth broadened into a grin that never touched his eyes.

"Roarke, my name is Edgar Slopes. I'm an Assistant United States Attorney for the Eastern District of Michigan. Do you know what that means?"

"I think so."

"Tell me."

"The kidnapping is federal. Murdering an FBI Agent is federal. Probably the conspiracy charges for drug running are federal, too."

"They surely are."

"Then I guess you're the man in charge. That's why you're sitting in that big chair while the Sheriff is off finding someone eloquent to draft his resignation letter for him."

Edgar Slopes pursed his lips and gave a little sigh.

"He'll make it through, actually. This kind of town gets real tribal when someone like Sheriff Bruckey can point a finger and say 'outsiders'. He's a cagey old buzzard from what I've seen. It won't take long for him to paint all this horrible shit as nothing more than the big bad federals poking their nose in where it doesn't belong."

"That won't wash away the fact that one of his deputies is a murdering lunatic."

"Reinhart said you were about to go put your face on television."

"Yeah. I was."

"So now I need to worry about you, too. Is that it? I don't have enough to try and tackle? I have to put my thumb on you?"

His voice dropped into a lower register as he said the last bit. I saw the truth in his small, unblinking eyes. He'd find a way to lock me down if that was what he decided was prudent. He'd hold me in a cell until he was satisfied I couldn't do anything to thwart him.

"Chelsea Gullins should be your priority," I said. "That's all I care about. We all need to be out looking for her. I'm not your enemy."

Again, the wide and confident grin that didn't touch his eyes.

"You're whatever I say you are," he chuckled. "You see that, right? If I decide you're a public menace, that's the story of you. I write up charges, I get on the phone with news outlets to prime the pump, and then I run a neat and tidy little grand jury on you. After that you're on the fast track to a federal prison cell. That's me, Roarke. I'm the guy who gets to say what you are."

His naked threat dispelled the mystery of Reinhart's sympathetic last words to me. I'd pushed my friend to the point where he had no choice but to deliver me up to a man who would view incarcerating me as just another day on the job.

It didn't change anything. I'd promised to help a girl I'd never met when my knuckles were still raw from beating Buster Long. I'd wanted something to prove. About me. About my nature. She was still lost and my promise was unfulfilled. I stared at Edgar Slopes and knew his threat meant nothing to me in that moment.

"When she's safe, I go back home," I said.

"See, I don't think that's true. I think when you see that little girl, you'll just switch gears and decide you're the man who has to chase down Deputy Rezner. Agent Reinhart thinks so, too. That's why I sent him to the hospital to get you to go home. That would have been enough for me. I would have forgotten about you. But you didn't go home. You came straight here and tried to blow me up on a TV camera. You see why I'm concerned?"

I didn't have anything to answer him. He had my number. He'd had it before I ever stepped into this room. Edgar Slopes had come on the scene and gotten briefed about everything going down. While I was down in the fever dream with father, Slopes had puzzled me out. Sized me up. Attempted to move me off the game board by having Reinhart send me back home to Detroit.

"Deputy Rezner is your business," I said and hoped it sounded like less of a lie than it was. "My only job was to get the girl safe. There's no profit for me in Rezner. He killed one of yours. You worry about him."

Edgar Slopes smirked and leaned forward in the chair. He folded his big arms over each other on the desk.

"He killed one of yours, too."

"Savannah Kline was a client. A client who already cut me my check."

"Oh. So you're just in if for your fee. That's the story?"

"I'm in it to do what I said. We need to find that girl tonight. Not tomorrow. Not later. Now."

The big man stood abruptly. He smoothed his tie down straight and walked around the desk until he was at the door.

"You know what?" he said. "Maybe you're not full of shit. Let's go find out. Come on with me."

\*

We crowded into a small elevator on the other end of the first floor, both of us big enough that we were shoulder to shoulder inside.

"I've had a little experience with militias," Edgar Slopes said and pushed the button for the basement. The doors clanged shut.

"Sovereign North isn't a militia," I said.

"That's looking to be true," he agreed. "Pot barons, more like. Which shows you what a bunch of dumb hayseeds these boys were. Marijuana isn't the future if you're looking to get into that sort of game. Sooner or later this whole country will legalize it.

317

If they'd had a brain between them, they'd have gotten into meth. You can set up a meth lab anywhere. Still, maybe they were never real militia but this Deputy Rezner was real enough about it."

"Michael Rezner is insane," I said. "I saw his real face."

"Yeah? What did it look like?"

"Miles of outrage."

The doors opened again and Slopes lead me down a short concrete hall lit with overhead fluorescents. We stopped at a door that had a 10-digit combination pad set into the wall beside it. Slopes reached into his suit coat and came out with a little slip of paper. He read it and tapped six buttons on the pad before stuffing the paper back in his pocket.

"Let's get a look at the real Mr. Rezner," he said and opened the door.

The room on the other side was small and lined with metal shelves. The shelves were stacked full of brown cardboard boxes, all of them labeled with case numbers and dates. An evidence room.

Edgar Slopes brought us to a stop in the center of the room. There was a table there. Sitting on the table were two cardboard boxes identical to the those on the shelves. I scanned their labels. They bore the same case number and today's date.

"We searched Rezner's house a little after Agent Fairchild was murdered," Slopes said. "He wasn't there, of course. There's no telling where he's hiding. Not yet. But nobody hides forever. And his face is getting plastered everywhere."

"How'd Rezner know where we'd be?"

He looked puzzled.

"Fairchild. Me and Savannah. How'd he know where to position himself to take his shots at us?"

Edgar Slopes shrugged his shoulders and said, "No answer, yet. But if you want a wild-ass guess, I'd say he spotted the FBI vehicles on the roadways and knew you'd called in the cavalry. So he did the smart thing and set himself up where he could shoot anyone coming or going close to the expressway exit. It's the only real artery into Grayling. He's a cop and an ex-Marine. He probably knew you and the Kline woman would get transported that way sooner or later."

"Sure," I said, even if I didn't believe it.

Slopes reached over to one of the shelves and plucked a small, rectangular cardboard box down. He flipped its lid open and produced a pair of blue latex gloves. He handed them to me. While I pulled them over my hands, he produced a second pair from the box and wiggled his long fingers into them.

"The preacher you savaged," he said, casually. Like we were talking about a shared acquaintance.

"What about him?"

"He made it out of that hole in the woods. No small feat, mind you. Not after what you did to him. We've got him under guard at the hospital. As beat-ass and broken as that old man is, he still likes to talk. I guess that goes hand in hand with the sermon business."

"Sure."

"He's selling us the line that it was *all* Rezner. Grabbing the Gullins girl. Grabbing you. Swears to God he was just looking to grow a little weed on the side since the economy hit the shitter but Deputy Rezner took over and started making crazy decisions. His exact words were 'Mister Slopes, sir, I was as much a hostage of that madman as poor little Chelsea Gullins.' What do you think of that?"

"I think either the Reverend was going to kill me or let Rezner do it."

Slopes lifted the lid off the first evidence box on the table. Inside were several indistinguishable objects stacked inside clear plastic bags.

"I think he'd have left it to Rezner," he agreed. "Probably, Wayland Graves isn't a killer. He doesn't have that cold kind of dead spot in his eyes. Not like you."

"What's that mean? You want to charge me on him and the other one I left down there? You didn't have to bring me here for that."

Slopes grew a wide grin. His teeth were perfectly even and so white that I was sure he'd paid for them.

320

"Maybe I changed my mind," he said. "It's been known to happen on rare occasions. Maybe I got a look at you, run down as you are, and made a slight course correction. Here, have a look at this."

He reached down into the box and pulled out one of the bagged objects. He held it out and I took it in my gloved hands. I smoothed the plastic to get a clear look at what I was holding.

It was an old hard-bound copy of *Mein Kampf.*

"You're kidding me."

Slopes' derisive laughter told me he wasn't.

"Original German, even. A collector's item for freaks. Deputy Rezner had all kinds of shit like that stashed away in his house," he said. "White Supremacy newsletters. The *Turner Diaries.* Dozens of survivalist screeds and how-to primers on facing the collapse of the republic."

Slopes waved a hand across the room to encompass all of the dozens of stacked boxes.

"It's all here. The entirety of one severely paranoid son of a bitch, packed and sealed and labeled."

He took the book from me and came out with a second bagged object.

"Personal journals. Quite a bit of poetry, believe it or not. *Bad* poetry. Really rigid rhyme schemes. All of it about him standing tall, the last free man waging a one-man war against the tide of minority rule. Refers to himself as the Last Watchman in almost all of them."

Another bag came out.

"U.S Marine Corps Scout and Sniper Training Manual. Dog-eared and covered in his own handwritten notes on how to improve the practices."

He offered it over to me but I shook my head and said, "I've read it before."

"I bet you have. I just bet you have."

Still another bag came out.

"This is my favorite," he sneered. "A painstakingly graphed detail of the state capitol. As far as we can tell, it maps out the routes and methodology for laying siege to the legislature in Lansing. You know, just in case the number of brown people in this country hits the magic number that demands real Americans burn the whole party down."

I watched him as he pulled out more evidence of Michael Rezner's insanity. He kept talking as he held the bags up and set them back down. Going on in a mocking litany. I could see him in the courtroom, a giant in a fine suit whose physical presence demanded attention and whose easy scorn could torpedo a defendant's fate with casual precision. He wasn't talking to me, not really. He was making his lawyer's case against Fairchild's murderer, driving Rezner's character so far down into the dirt that no sober person could feel sympathy for him.

"Enough," I said.

Slopes cut his show short and cocked his head, peering across the table at me like I was a curiosity. Gauging to see if his display had created the desired effect in me.

"I don't need to see any of this," I said. "Why bother? I already know what he is, Slopes. I've seen it firsthand."

He touched a finger to his chin and nodded in feigned realization.

"Oh, that's right. I forgot. You only care about the girl."

"This is getting us nowhere."

"And you'll leave Savannah Kline's killer all to us."

"Why wouldn't I?"

Edgar Slopes' expression turned pensive. He carefully plucked each bag of evidence off the table and set them back in the box. He was silent and didn't look at me. When the lid was back on the box, he tapped it a couple times with his fingertips to make certain it was snuggly in place. He pursed his lips and sighed.

"Because you haven't looked in the other box," he said very softly. "Go ahead. Open it. Then we can see what's what and who's who."

"I don't care what--"

"Open it."

I felt myself growing impatient enough that the urge to just turn heel and walk out was very real. But I didn't. Something in

Slopes' expectant silence wouldn't allow it. This was why he had brought me down here. The second box. Everything else had been preamble.

I watched as my hands reached out and took the lid of the second box by the corners.

Watched as they lifted the lid away, revealing the contents beneath.

Heard my father's feverish command from within his nightmare barrow.

*'No truce for your enemy!'*

Chelsea Gullins was inside the box.

# FOURTEEN

They were the same pair of jeans she'd worn in the framed photo I'd noticed in her bedroom. The ones with the worn away knee. The way it happens when a kid is active. Sliding into bases or falling off a bike. Eventually the knee wears out. But the jeans get more and more comfortable with wear. And the kid doesn't care about the knee, not really. Probably she likes the jeans *more*. The missing knee looks cool. It reflects something about her nature.

Inside the gallon-sized evidence bag, those jeans were soaked in blood.

A second bag contained the torn remains of a pink cotton top. A cartoon bunny was printed on the front. Blood throughout. Clinging in thick globules to the inside of the bag. Staining the shredded shirt a deep purple.

Mixed in, caught in the stains and frozen in place, were several strands of curly blonde hair.

That was what remained of Chelsea Gullins. Hair and blood and torn fabric.

Slopes was speaking again, his deep baritone managing to scale the wall of horror ringing my mind.

"They were in Rezner's garage. Inside a garbage bag. He used a four-inch serrated blade on her. Tried to clean it off. But blood gets down under the handle a lot of times. We found it in a drawer with his tools. Nothing's certain, but we think he killed her last night. Three hours or so after you and Savannah Kline ran him off the road and into a tree."

Once over the wall, his words wound their inevitable course and I made the connection: I'd sent Rezner into the woods. He'd escaped the wreckage of his Two Pine cruiser and fled into the trees. I hadn't pursued. I'd driven away with Savannah and settled on searching the girls' camp for Chelsea, to no avail.

Rezner found her.

She'd been lost in the wilderness since making her escape from the Reverend's home. Out in the deep end, the ancient ocean of pine and elm. She should have been as anonymous and alone as any human can ever be. But the unrelenting cruelty that serves as the real engine of this world had seen to it that Rezner found her. Not me. Not some late night hiker or passerby. Rezner. The single living thing in all the world that actively wanted her dead and hidden from sight.

"Hey. Don't do that."

I was squeezing down on the bag of her remains like I could compress it out of existence. I saw the veins in my arms bulging

326

out like high-tension cables, felt myself vibrating with an unyielding strain. Slopes was at my side abruptly, reaching out with his big hands to try and unclench my fists. I was stone. I was steel. I was locked down and gone.

"That's *evidence*."

The words were an adamantine spike in my brain. Evidence. That was the sum total of Chelsea Gullins, now. There was no resourceful athletic girl in the world anymore, who had spelled her hope out on her closet mirror and willed herself out of a locked room. There was only evidence in a process. A case number scrawled across a label. Two bags full of a dead child's clothes.

I let go of them. Mechanically, I opened my hands and took one measured step backwards. I felt like an automaton. I knew I had to get out of that room. I knew there was a direct course of action to be set. I knew there was no truce for my enemy. But I wasn't in control. She was a black acid cloud hanging in my head, saturating the machinery of me so thoroughly that I could only manage to signal a command for that one footstep backwards. I could only remain on my feet, upright, frozen and full of all the rotten things a man can feel about himself.

Slopes picked the bags up off the floor and set them back in the box. I stared at his back as he reset the lid and peeled off his set of latex gloves. He leaned forward with his palms on the table, letting his arms hold his weight. An exhausted posture.

The stance of a man with a great load of worries strapped to his back. He remained like that for a long time while I stared through him, through the boxes, and at the awful truth of what I'd failed to do.

"You can go, Roarke. Get out of here."

He didn't turn to look at me. Just remained rooted where he was. His voice was thick with an unknowable emotion.

"Why did you do this?" I heard myself say.

"Get out of here. Go home."

"I'm not going home."

*

Reinhart called after me when I rushed out of the sheriff's department.

"Roarke, hey, hold up!"

I'd been a fool, so I could not stop for my friend.

I'd been a fool. I'd bought into Savannah's machinations. Let her line me up and fire me into this madness. I'd been a fool, thinking I was the sort of man who could help Chelsea Gullins. I'd been a fool and let Savannah inside, let her charms and seductions draw the weakness of the world into me. I'd been a damned fool, feeling somehow healed, somehow whole, when Savannah slid over me that final time on the deck.

While Chelsea was getting butchered, I was indulging my own weakness.

"Roarke!"

The savaged shirt in a blood-smeared bag.

The discolored jeans.

I lunged into the night and silently begged the darkness to blanket every other thought and image from my mind. I marched until a swell of green vertigo sent me vomiting across the curb. Hauled myself upright, wheezing. Shaking, I blundered ahead.

Grayling receded, taking Reinhart with it. The last set of street lights came and went. I was alone on the edge of town. I didn't slow. Home Among the Pine was only a few scant miles south. The Stratus was there.

Far down the road, headlights swam up the expressway ramp. I tensed, an image of Rezner roaring out of the night blooming in my head. It wasn't him. Wouldn't be him. He was a maniac, certainly. A child-killer. But he was not suicidal. He wouldn't race straight up into the hands of the men bent on catching him.

When the headlights were close enough that I could hear the clattering noise of the engine, I knew it wasn't Rezner. I stopped my march and allowed a whisper-thin bit of relief to wash into me. I'd been prepared to stagger and even drag my shattered body all the way to Home Among the Pine. Now I knew I wouldn't have to.

Mitch Gillinwaters guided his beaten old Johnny Cab to a stop beside me. The window came down. From behind a thin curtain of cigarette smoke, he smiled up at me and scratched his bearded cheek.

"Hey, man. I was swooping in for a pit stop and some more coffee before heading out there again. What are you doing? Do you want to search for her together? You shouldn't be walking around, man. Seriously, get in. Come on, we'll grab some caffeine and map out where to look."

I got into the passenger seat.

"Chelsea Gullins is dead," I told him and shut the door.

Mitch's face sank. He stared dumbly ahead. I watched the energy drain out of his eyes while all his fantasies of finding and helping the little girl evaporated away.

"Don't tell anyone until the feds put it on the TV. Her mother hasn't been notified yet."

"Jesus. That's so horrible."

"Yes."

"How…how did she die?"

"A man named Michael Rezner butchered her with a knife. Turn us around. I need to head south."

That seemed to shake him out of his fog. The bushy, barefoot cabbie looked at me with an expectant light in his eyes.

"You're still in this, aren't you? Right?"

"I need to get to my car."

"Do they know where this guy is?"

"No," I said. "I need to get out of here."

Mitch Gillinwaters didn't ask any more questions. He just put the old wreck in gear and did a rumbling U-turn across the road. He wedged a knee up against the wheel to free his hands up for lighting another cigarette. A practiced maneuver.

"Can I ask you what will sound like a weird question?" he asked once we were on the expressway and barreling south.

"Alright."

"Was she a happy kid? Did...did she get to be happy?"

"I never met her. Let me see your phone."

"Huh?"

"You have internet on it?"

"Uh, yeah. Who doesn't?"

"Me. Let me see it."

Mitch passed his smartphone over. I bent over the glow of its face and started tapping the virtual keyboard.

"This is all just such a damned shame," he said, and kept on like that. Shaking his head and smoking and maybe realizing his romantic fantasy about the Two Pine Vigilante blowing into town and saving the day was something a kid would hold on to. Maybe it took another kid's death to push Mitch Gillinwaters a little further into adulthood, because when we pulled into the drive at Home Among the Pine, he'd been silent for some time. He looked closed off, brooding on the ugliness of things.

331

"Thanks for helping," I said.

"I didn't do anything," he groused.

"You wanted to. Means something."

"Who would do that to a kid?"

"Plenty. Too many. I don't know, Mitch. I don't have any answers. I have to go now."

I pushed myself out of the car. Sitting still, even for the short trip from Grayling to Home Among the Pine, had stiffened me up again. Doctor Eir had assured me the morphine-alternative pain killers were the real deal. As I straightened in the warm night air, I decided maybe Doctor Eir was a world class liar.

I handed the smart phone back to Mitch and reached for my wallet.

"Did you find what you needed?" he said.

"I think so."

"Well, I guess it's a good time for you to get out of here. The radio was saying there's a severe weather warning for tomorrow. My mom's already talking about having me drive her up to her sister's place in Traverse to ride it out. They need to let the search volunteers know she's dead before that storm hits."

"I'm sure they will. Don't worry about it anymore."

I tossed another group of twenties on the passenger seat. Mitch didn't look at them. He peered up at me with his mouth set in a stern line.

"Get that son of a bitch."

I watched him turn the cab around and roll on out, back to his life.

*

I didn't climb into the Stratus right away. I stood in the darkness outside the cabin Savannah and I had rented. Down the winding drive, no lights shone. Rhonda and Sharon had no other renters and it looked like the two of them were either gone or asleep.

I was the most alone I'd been since escaping the Reverend's bunker.

*'Get that son of a bitch.'*

Mitch's parting words. They'd sounded silly to me, coming from him. Easy bravado from a guy who didn't understand violence unless it was the virtual sort played out on a computer monitor. Tough talk. Talk is easy.

I swallowed some more of Doctor Eir's ineffective pain pills and winced against the scrape of broken ribs.

Still, tough talk or not, Mitch had just stated explicitly what Reinhart and Slopes couldn't. Taking me down to the evidence room. horrifying me with what they'd found, and letting me walk back out was Slopes' way of saying 'Get that son of a bitch'. Or, it was his way of fooling me into rushing out and *finding* Rezner.

333

Why not? I'd blundered into Rezner's madness on my own before. Thwarted his plans and exposed him as a lunatic. Ruined him and turned him into a fugitive. Why not bring me down to the evidence room and fill me full of madness before turning me out and maybe seeing if I would cross paths with Rezner again?

Sure. There were no downsides. Maybe I'd kill the monster, and that would be that. Maybe he'd kill me and I would just be another body they could throw on his shoulders when they hauled him in front of a grand jury.

Or maybe they'd just follow me.

Maybe they'd use me to find him and swoop in before either of us could do the only thing that made a damned bit of sense: eradicate the other.

Alone in the darkness and silence of the night, I knew that was Slopes' real plan. I was to be his unwitting tracking hound. He'd rubbed the bloody clothes in my nose, filled me up with the scent of death, and sent me ranging ahead. If I found Rezner, the FBI would do their best to be on us both before either of us had a chance at satisfaction.

I pulled my cell phone out of my pocket. Saw Reinhart giving it back to me in the hospital room. They'd had it for hours. Plenty of time to rig it into a signaling device. I slipped the cover off the battery housing. Pulled the battery. Looked it over.

There was no little chip or hidden transmitter. That didn't mean anything. Software uploaded to the phone would work just as well. And they'd had time to do it, while I was languishing in a hospital bed, father's ember-eyed *draugr* screaming the truth at me loud enough to get the signal through from wherever he was now.

I reassembled the phone and went to work searching my car. I emptied everything out of the trunk and the glove box and slowly examined it all. I painstakingly patted down every inch of the interior cabin. Pulled the console and dash panels. Searched the fuse box and double checked the owner's manual to make certain there wasn't a new, unnecessary fuse wedged surreptitiously inside the box. I used a black Maglite from the trunk to look over the engine. I unscrewed the Maglite, poured out its batteries, and poured them back in. I got under the car. Let out several grunts of pain as I wiggled around the undercarriage. I kept on. Time burned away but I had to be certain. Tires came off. Tires went back on. I used an Allen wrench to pull the headlight and taillight shrouds.

When I was finally done and the Stratus was reassembled, I had three different tracking devices in the palm of my hand. One from under the bumper, one from behind a dashboard panel, and the third wedged into the passenger seat by way of a half-inch incision in the leather.

In the hospital room, Reinhart had lied to me about Chelsea Gullins and begged me to go home.

Now I understood why. Slopes. Reinhart had known what the federal prosecutor had planned for me, and he'd done his best to point me in another direction.

I still had the plastic bag that had contained my keys and cell phone when Reinhart handed them back to me. I turned the cell phone off. Then I put it and the three tracking devices inside the bag.

I felt myself grow a fierce smile as I stared at Slopes' handiwork. I would meet him halfway. I'd find Rezner, for certain. But what happened after that would not be for Slopes or anyone else to say.

That was the only thing in my mind as I drove the Stratus slowly back down the lane. Headlights abruptly appeared, swimming up from the road. I heard an engine loudly rev and the headlights shot toward me. They jounced over a dip in the ground and veered to my left. A boxy black Jeep with a red canvas top came to a sharp halt between me and the front office building. Rhonda's round face was visible through the driver-side window.

Her eyes teemed with a vivid fear.

I rolled my window down as the short, plump woman climbed down out of the Jeep.

"I'm leaving," I said. "I'm sorry for bringing all of this to your door. I won't come back, Rhonda. You don't have to be afraid of that."

It must have been within hailing distance of what she needed to hear, because her face softened from 'panic-stricken' to 'nervous as a cat'.

"You're...going home?" she said as she hurried around to the back of the Jeep, her eyes shying away from mine.

"Eventually. Thanks for patching me up."

I watched her fumble around at the rear of the Jeep until three canvas shopping bags spilled out onto the ground at her feet. Rhonda moaned in despair and hunched down over the mess. I got out of the Stratus reflexively and got down beside her to scoop up the scattered groceries.

"You don't have to."

"It's alright."

I stuffed a few cans of corn into a bag. Frozen chicken breasts. A brown box I had to glance at twice before I understood it was cereal made from flax. Last was a box of gauze wrap. I straightened up and held the bandages out.

"I guess I should probably pay you back for having to replace these."

Rhonda shook her head in a stern line and took the box from me.

"I didn't ask for money when I did it," she said.

"I know."

She took all three bags in her hands and hefted them up.

337

"Okay, thanks," she said in a rush and turned toward the front office steps. "Have a safe trip, okay?"

I watched her disappear inside before I eased back down into the Stratus and drove away from Home Among the Pine. By the time I was southbound on the expressway again, I'd pushed Rhonda and Sharon and their idyllic oasis out of my mind. That was all behind me.

Rezner was not.

*

Seventeen miles south of Grayling, I exited the expressway and rolled into a 24-hour gas station with a trucker's diner attached to it. Big rigs squatted on one side of the lot, shadowy behemoths that rumbled and sighed depending on whether their owners were priming them to leave or settling them down for a few hours of shut eye. A handful of their drivers were sitting around inside the diner with white carafes of coffee in front of their eggs and hash browns. Midnight breakfast, gulping caffeine and heavy calories before getting back to the job of chewing the miles down.

I topped off the Stratus' tank and plucked bits of the shattered rear window out of the crevice where the interior met the trunk. I was alone at the lines of pumps. When the tank was full, I hung the nozzle back up and took my time washing the windshield with one of the t-shaped squeegees that hung in buckets beside each pump. Found some more glass bits to toss in the trash. Couldn't think of any other time wasters, so I went inside and pretended to use the restroom. Bought some gum from the bored attendant. Watched the lot outside while he made change.

Only when I was walking out of the station did another vehicle pull up to the pumps. A blue Ford Ranger pickup. A husky and balding man dressed in sweatpants and a hoodie hopped out into the jaundiced glow of the lot's halogen lights. He gave me a curt nod of the head as we crossed paths, then disappeared inside the gas station.

The bed of the pickup was a rectangular gulf of shadow. The halogens lit a slim section of the bed's interior, near the driver's cabin. I could see several pieces of luggage bungee strapped in place.

I made a quick series of steps over to the pickup and pulled the baggie that contained my cell and the tracking devices out of my pants pocket. Feeling around the hard-shell suitcases, I wedged the baggie down between two of them. Got back behind the wheel of the Stratus. Scanned the length of the gas station and diner. No eyes on me. Trucker's sipped their coffees. The attendant loitered behind his register, slack, disinterested.

When the husky traveler returned, he sipped an energy drink in a little blue can and put a few gallons in the Ranger. I watched him get back in the truck, start it up, and peel away into the night.

It didn't matter what direction he went. Or how far he drove. I didn't need much time, not really.

I knew exactly where I was going.

*'There's someone else in all of this,'* Savannah had whispered, before Fairchild died at the wheel. *'And he has the money.'*

I drove away from the gas station-diner, back into the night. I didn't push Savannah away. I let her nestle down in the passenger seat, like she had on our drive north. I breathed the memory of her in and shot straight south. She kept me awake. And if she wasn't enough, if I began to flag, I would summon the bloody remains of the girl I'd never met, sealed away in evidence bags in the basement of a lousy little cop shop.

That would be enough, I knew, to keep me flying, stoked with hatred, a bullet aimed at the man who could lead me straight to Michael Rezner.

# FIFTEEN

It was a winding, scenic road that ran along the southern bank of the Huron River north west of downtown Ann Arbor. Across the river, tremendous mansions squatted among the trees overlooking the water. I passed private roads with names like *Secretariat Drive* and *Centennial Way*. Ann Arbor, at least the little bit I'd seen of it, was well-to-do. But this expanse of water-fronting neighborhood was where the *truly* wealthy lived, the families who likely ran the city and who owned the land that supported the thriving storefronts of Downtown.

A wooden bridge appeared ahead of me, its slender length spanning the river. I slowed the car down and looked for a street sign. *Colonial Drive.* I pulled onto the bridge. The nest of mansions swung into view, growing larger and more distinct as I advanced across the wide, brown width of the river these people most likely thought of as a moat.

The Stratus' tires made stuttering noises over the wooden planks of the bridge as I crossed. The first light of dawn was still a few hours away. Few lights shone in the mansions stacked above the river's bank. Soft, wealthy souls, sleeping untroubled sleep inside their sprawling, tended estates.

Not all, though. At least one soul residing on Colonial Drive could not possibly be resting easy. And that was the only soul I'd come to see.

Once over the bridge, the road was a smooth, unmarred black ribbon. I followed the ornamental hedge rows, winding up, past sweeping lengths of lawn and wrought iron gates.

The address I was looking for appeared at the very end of the drive, where the road widened out into a circle turn-around. A four-foot brick wall fronted the road, split in the middle by a wrought iron gate that's thin bars were fashioned to look like swirling branches with little delicate leaves stretching out of them.

Beyond the gate, the driveway disappeared into the darkness. I could see the silhouette of a three-peaked house. Further on was woods, the bruised night sky, and a pale scythe's edge of moon.

I left the Stratus idling and stood up outside. I'd stiffened into wood on the drive down, so I took a moment to stretch as much as my ribs would allow. All along the battered length of me, my joints made little firecracker pops, the only sound in the world besides the unhealthy wheeze of the Stratus.

I thumbed a few more of Doctor Eir's ineffective pills into my yap and walked up to the rectangular intercom that was sunk into the wall next to the gate. There was one button on the face, so I pushed it in and held it down for a count of five.

I waited in the glare of the headlights. I didn't wait long.

"Yes?" the intercom answered in an uncertain male voice. "Who...who's there?"

"There's a camera in the intercom," I said. "You can see me, Richard. You know who I am. Open the gate."

"I have no idea who you are. It's very late. You'll have to go."

"I'm coming in. And you're letting me in."

"I...why on earth would you say that?"

"Because you and Savannah Kline hired me, Richard. I did what I was asked. Now I'm here to get paid what you owe me. Open the gate. If I have to drive through it with my car, your alarm will go off. Neighbors will start looking out their windows. Cops will come. You don't need cops. Open the gate."

"Sir, if you don't leave I will absolutely call the authorities."

He managed to get it out without stuttering, but the fear in that voice was unmistakable.

I turned around and walked back to my car. I nudged the hi-beams on and put the Stratus in gear. Touched the accelerator and crept slowly ahead. There was about ten feet between the nose of the car and the gate. I kept my foot steady, giving the Stratus just enough gas to keep rolling steadily, slowly.

Five feet.

He shouted something through the intercom that had the shrill tone of a plea, but I couldn't make it out.

Two feet.

A green light flashed once on the intercom's face and the gate's halves swung smoothly inward. I nudged the accelerator down and drove up to the expansive home of Richard Eastman, President of First Ann Arbor Bank and Trust.

*

I tried the heavy brass handle on one of the double oak doors that fronted the mansion's marble-slab porch. It turned smoothly and I pushed the door open. The foyer was all white walls, marble floor, and a high, vaulted ceiling with a glass chandelier throwing sparkling polygons of light around the place.

Richard Eastman stood near the intercom and alarm control panel just inside the door, his eyes bulging comically, like a kid caught in the act. He was a guy of middle-height and middle age, with mousy, guileless eyes and a narrow line of a mouth. He had the standard businessman's conservative haircut, and looked healthy in a treadmill and sensible eating sort of way.

What looked like lemonade sloshed out of a glass in his hand. I shut the door behind me and pointed down the hallway behind him.

"Let's go."

He had his puffing up moment then, straightening himself and pulling his shoulders back. I guess the way he set his jaw in a hard line and squinted at me was supposed to be his tough face

344

but there was nothing real behind it so he just wound up looking like he was getting ready to lecture a subordinate.

"Mister, I've been more than accommodating with this nonsense. I don't think we should carry it on any more. I will call the authorities. That's not some bluff, I assure you. Now, please leave and don't come back."

To drive his point home, he raised the glass of lemonade up and used it to gesture at the alarm panel beside him.

I walked right up to him until we were an inch away from each other. I stared down at him.

"Keep listening to the voice that told you to open the gate, Richard."

"Please...please leave."

"This other voice you're trying to put on for me, it's not going to work. Let's go sit down and get this done."

All it took was my putting my hand lightly on his shoulder for Richard Eastman to comply. His moment of bravura evaporated and he looked away. Walking like that, with him just in front of me, I guided the man through the first floor of his own him. There were a lot of rooms.

"Big spread for a bachelor," I mused as we peeked into a kitchen large and resplendent enough to belong in one of those magazines that advertise to the rest of us how the lucky few of the world live. A jug of pre-mixed margarita sitting next to a tray of ice on the counter told me it wasn't lemonade in his hand.

Richard Eastman had been sleepless and drinking alone in the wee hours.

"I'm divorced," he stammered. "She...we split up. She has the children today."

I kept piloting him around with my hand, softly. In the back of the house we found a home office with a big bay window looking out on the emerald carpet of his back yard. All the furnishings were mahogany or leather. Certificates and awards I didn't bother to read cluttered the walls. An antique ship's wheel hung on one wall. Beneath it, a miniature three mast galleon with clean canvas sails was perched atop a mahogany display stand.

"I have three children," he whispered.

"I'm not going to hurt you, Richard," I said. "I told you, I came to talk. Why don't you go sit down behind your big desk over there and try to pull yourself together? Nobody's getting hurt tonight."

He did like I said. I meandered around the room while he watched me like I was a venomous snake someone had just tossed onto the carpet. A wooden, hand-painted globe of the world stood in one corner. I tested it with a finger and it spun nicely on its perch. Bookcases neatly filled with rows of titles I didn't recognize. No framed photos of an ex-wife or of any children. He'd lied about their existence, I realized. I wondered how many times he was going to lie to me before I started getting what I wanted.

346

I sat down in the straight back leather chair across the desk from him and folded one leg over the other.

"Where's my money, Richard?"

"How would I know that?" he protested.

"Tell me who I am," I said. "Let's start there."

"I have no earthly idea who you are."

"Really. That's funny. Because I remember you. I got a good look at the bottom of your face, Richard. You tried to disguise yourself with a baseball cap and some silly camouflage outfit. But I have a thing about faces. I remember them. And I remember yours from when you shot my tire out and tried to sound like you were one of the Sovereign Nation. I thought I heard someone else in your truck, just before you hightailed it out of there, but I never gave it much thought until a few hours ago."

As I talked, Richard's mask of befuddled innocence started to cave in on itself. He swallowed with a dry clicking sound in his throat and his eyes stayed out of mine.

"I didn't ask myself why one of the Sovereign would try and scare me off when he could have just followed Savannah out of the restaurant. I didn't know about the money then. By the time I did, I didn't care. I just wanted to get Chelsea Gullins back from what you got her into. Whose idea was it to dress you up like a redneck and threaten me after the lunch meeting?"

347

His eyes stopped darting around the room, like he'd found something to seize onto. Some sort of lifeline. He cleared his throat and took a small sip of his margarita.

"Hers," he said flatly. "Everything was her idea. She thought threatening you would make sure you would go with her to see about getting that girl back."

"She was right. Pulling the money out of the accounts?"

"Like I said, all her."

"Not paying the Sovereign when they grabbed Chelsea? That was her, too?"

"As unlikely as it sounds, yes. You...you met her. You know how persuasive she is. Did she tell you to come here and do this? Is that how you found me? She's cut me out? That's why she won't answer her phone?"

"I found you online. You put your face on your bank's website. Like I said, I remember faces."

Some small relief seemed to settle in behind his eyes. Savannah hadn't sent me. Savannah hadn't 'cut him out'. He talked about her like she was still alive and I realized he wasn't sleepless and drinking alone because he'd seen the news of what had gone down up in Two Pine. Richard Eastman was just worried that his partner had turned on him. She wasn't answering his calls. And now a bloodied-up brute was calling on him in the dark of night.

"You two are lovers," I said.

"What? Oh. I suppose the word is apt. Where is she? Will you tell me that?"

"What's the plan, Richard? Get Chelsea back and then what? Run off with the Nation's money and sip Pina Coladas for the rest of your lives?"

He snorted at the suggestion and a faint, disparaging smile touched his lips.

"Heavens, no. There isn't that much. No, Savannah just wanted to be safe. When she heard some young man with the Sovereign Nation had been arrested, she insisted we pull the accounts and begin getting everything in order in case the authorities came around. We were cutting ties with the Nation, not planning a retirement to Bermuda. Everything after that...well, it just sort of went hinky on us, didn't it? We made rash decisions, I can see that now. Still, you're here expecting payment, so I suppose things have sorted themselves out, yes?"

"I'm here for the money," I said.

Richard pursed his lips and his nervousness seemed assuaged. He was on familiar footing. Dispensing insubstantial payment to a hired hand.

"How much did she agree to pay you? We never discussed that point, to be honest."

I told him and he made a slight waving gesture with his fingers to signal how insignificant the sum was. I watched him reach for a pen. A checkbook appeared from out of a small box on the desk.

"All of the money, Richard."

"What's that?"

"Savannah sent me for all of it. I guess I lied to you. I wanted to know who else was employing me. The truth is, they won't give Chelsea back. We tried, but it didn't work out. Savannah's decided to pay them. I think it's the smart thing, too. You need to give me the money so I can take it to them and get that little girl back home."

Richard leaned back in his chair and stared at me, uncomprehending.

"I...I thought you said you just wanted to be paid."

"That was to get in the door. Savannah said you wouldn't agree to pay the Nation back. I needed to get past the gate so I lied. But it sounds like you've been taking orders from her the whole time anyway, so I think she's probably wrong. Let's get the money and take it to them. You can come with me if you're nervous about handing it over. We can drive up there, get Chelsea and Savannah both, and just put this whole thing to rest. How's that sound, Richard?"

I watched him closely, watched the dozens of different calculations going on in his eyes. This was his moment, even if he didn't know it. The chain of events he'd triggered by betraying the Sovereign Nation had gotten men killed, mostly by my hand. Then Savannah and an FBI agent. Then a little girl. And now I was sitting here, giving him a final chance.

All throughout the drive down that night, I'd filled myself up with outrage. While the mile markers vanished behind me, I dwelled on Chelsea Gullins. Drove myself mad with the loss of her, with the ugly, stupid and savage way she'd died. I'd driven myself crazy with the thought of it until I was brimming with it and primed to lash out.

Talking my way into Richard's home instead of battering the gate down had taken an effort of will. Keeping my voice calm and modulated, keeping the death urge out of my eyes while he sputtered and blathered out half truths about his involvement, looking at the privileged man surrounded by his wealth, all of it had taken a supreme effort.

Now it would go one way or the other. He would hand me the money because he knew finally that, yes, a little girl's life was more important, more sacred. If he had that much humanity, I could let Reinhart and his men catch up with him and lock him in a cage for the rest of his life. I could live with that.

Or he wouldn't agree. He'd chose the money over the girl again. He'd prove that this bloody horror show had all been his doing, a manifestation of his own inhumanity. And I would release the pressure valve inside me that had kept me from killing him on first sight.

Richard sighed and ran his palms over his face. He slouched and fidgeted and didn't say anything for a while. I watched him. Three times, his eyes strayed down and to his right. He chewed his lip. I remembered Wade, his face a mess. His eyes had darted that same way while he sat across from me and worked himself up to a decision.

"Richard," I said.

He jumped in his seat and stared at me.

"If there's a gun in that desk, Richard, it had better stay in that desk."

"What?"

"You don't look like a man who's made a habit of pulling guns on people," I said. "I'm not the guy you try it out on. If a gun comes out, this turns into something awful for you."

"Don't be absurd," he huffed.

"Are you going to hand over the money? We need to do this quickly."

Richard Eastman cleared his throat, looked directly at me, and said, "I'm afraid that's out of the question. If you've failed to get that girl back, well, no offense but that's *your* failure. Savannah wanted to make the effort, and I agreed. As far as that goes. But the money stays where it is. Everything's cleared up on my end of things. They can threaten to go to the authorities, but I promise you there is no paper trail to be followed to me or Savannah. No, you and Savannah and me are quite safe. When

352

they get tired of puffing their chests out and they see the reality of their situation, that girl will be sent back home and this entire comedy will be put to bed. Tell Savannah that, and tell her to start answering my damned calls for Pete's sake."

"You're making a mistake," I said.

He grew a patronizing smile and shook his head at me.

"Look, friend, that isn't for you to decide. Like you said, I agreed to bring you into this when Savannah couldn't let the issue drop. She seemed to think a hired investigator could get things sorted away. I didn't necessarily agree, and now that you're telling me you haven't got the girl and you want to go ahead and hand over all the money to those ridiculous hillbillies...well, I'm inclined to say I was right all along."

"I'm not an investigator, Richard. Not really."

"No? Then what are you, exactly?"

"Choose the girl. Choose her over the money. I won't ask again."

Richard looked away from me and started moving papers around on his desk. It had a practiced feel to it. His silent way of letting a subordinate know the meeting was concluded. A dismissal.

"I can't help you. When you see Savannah, have her settle your bill and tell her to call me, won't you? I need to be kept apprised."

I closed my eyes.

I was back in the evidence room. My hands were twisting the plastic bags of bloody clothing. A single curl of blonde hair was stuck to the skin of the bag. I was vibrating with tension, seized with horror.

"Was there something else?" Richard said, impatient and peevish.

I opened my eyes.

*

Killing Richard only took a few seconds.

I bounded up and around the desk. He started to pedal away in his office chair and made a panicky noise. I pulled open the drawer he'd been eying. Yanked out a black Beretta pistol.

"Hey! Don't!"

His hands came up. I swatted them away. In one quick motion I leaned in, pressed the barrel of the gun into the soft flesh under his chin, and pulled the trigger. I went deaf under the crack of the shot reverberating through the room. Richard's skull managed to hold, but his eyes dimmed dead in an instant and the skin around them began to darken from the explosive pressure that detonated behind them.

Viscera oozed out of the corpse's ears. A line of blood wound down out of its left nostril. It slumped awkwardly in the chair when I let it go. Its head lolled off to one side and its mouth slackened open, revealing perfect white teeth.

I put the pistol in its right hand, the one Richard had used to hold the pen when he thought he'd be writing me a check. I aimed that hand up at the ceiling and pulled the trigger again. A first, hesitating shot, they'd guess. Maybe he flinched away that first time, had himself another drink, and found the nerve with his second shot. The residue test on its hands would show he'd fired the gun himself.

I leaned over the corpse and opened the web browser on Richard's computer. Found a news story detailing the deaths in Two Pine. Scrolled down until it mentioned Savannah and her involvement in some sort of as-yet poorly understood conspiracy. I left it there.

Calm, feeling centered and sane for the first time since opening the second box in the evidence room, I paced out of the den, down the hall, and opened the front door. Mild night air washed over me. I looked for lights in the windows of his distant neighbors. Gradually, my hearing returned and I listened for sounds of human beings stirred to wakefulness.

I stood like that for several minutes.

When I was satisfied that the other pampered souls of the community were still sleeping their untroubled sleep, I went back inside and started methodically searching each room in the house for the money Richard had prized more than a girl's life.

*

In the basement, which had been fully furnished into a swank private bar and lounge on one end, and a fully equipped gym on the other, I found a black duffel bag wedged up above the drop ceiling tiles.

When I dragged it down, set it on the bar and unzipped it, I was staring at a mass of crisp new hundred-dollar bills. I poured the bag out and started counting. There was eight-hundred and forty thousand dollars on the bar. I put it all back in the bag and felt my calm shatter.

Less than a million. The Sovereign had been running their grow operation for maybe six years. A dozen men involved. Dead men. A dead woman and a butchered child and lives ruined. All for less than a million. Divided out among all those shattered people, it was no fortune. Split up, it was what any one of them could have made for themselves in a dull, daily nine-to-five job.

I sat heavily on one of the bar stools.

All of it, from beginning to end, had been a calamity of stupid, near-sighted choices. The Reverend and his gaggle of followers had managed to put together an illicit drug operation, dealing a product that was getting legalized in one form or another all across the nation. It was the business model of

356

schmucks and wannabes, happily playing pretend until their resident psychopath couldn't deal with being betrayed.

I supposed nobody had recognized it in him. They didn't know what he was, behind the mask. So everyone kept playing pretend, making decisions like they were in a movie. Grab the girl. Make some hard threats to the lady banker so she'll see we aren't a bunch of yahoos to be stepped on. Right? She'll turn the money over and we can get back to taking it easy. No problemo.

Stupidity. Nothing but stupidity.

I sat there and yearned to be clapped back behind my gate, back in the Detroit cell I'd bought and re-fashioned to my needs. My father had been right. I'd ventured out into the world of civilians, the world of others, and I'd let them get inside me. I'd let the idea of a scrappy, determined little girl make me weak. I'd let her aunt's seductions make me weaker still.

All I was left with was a sick, gnawing sense of loss and bitter ideas of what might have been if I'd made different decisions along the way.

I wanted to lock myself back behind my wall.

I would, I knew. Alone, I could heal and let time erode the black disappointment that was swamping me. But there was one person I still had to answer to first.

\*

With the Stratus' headlights switched off, I stared in the rearview and watched the gate to Richard Eastman's mansion silently swing shut again. I'd used a thick terrycloth rag to wipe away every sign of my passage, working backwards from the basement to account for all the places my fingertips had touched. In a hallway closet I found the hardware for the gate's intercom and video camera. There was no recorder.

I rolled slowly out of the neighborhood, only turning on the headlights once I was back on the bridge spanning the black length of the Huron River. In the east, the first tentative tips of sunlight were trembling into the slaughterhouse for another shift.

*

I'd never met Donna Gullins, though I'd formed a decidedly bleak opinion of her and the filthy, chaotic environment she'd been subjecting Chelsea to.

Standing over her drowned body, I didn't have enough left in the tank to spare her any sympathy.

She was a bloated, discolored mass in the upstairs bathtub. When I pulled the plastic curtain aside, a cloud of tiny flies scattered around the room, then gradually settled back over her distended abdomen.

I remembered the sour stench that had permeated the house and the few flies darting around the kitchen mess the first time I'd come calling on Donna Gullins,

She'd been here this whole time.

While I had paced through her house and made the decision to go find her child, Donna had been a fresh corpse in the tub. The odor of the house had been strong enough then to mask any stink of decay she'd thrown off. But now the smell of her presence was like a physical force filling the house, soaking into the walls and carpets.

I bent down and lifted an orange prescription bottle off the floor. The cap was nowhere to be seen and several pills were spilled over the tile floor. I read the label. Hydrocodone. More bottles and baggies scattered throughout the house had yielded stashes of Xanax, Zoloft, Percocet, and a half dozen others with no labels or markings to identify them.

I didn't know if I could add the death of a junkie falling asleep and drowning in her own bath to the red ledgers belonging to Richard, Savannah and the Sovereign. Maybe her missing child had pushed her intake up and her OD was assignable to all of them. Or maybe it was just dumb coincidence and she'd have slipped sleepily out of the world like this sooner or later anyway. Junkies die. That's what they do.

I left her and went back downstairs.

The black duffel bag was sitting on the carpet in the middle of the living room. I'd intended to break the news of Chelsea's death to her and to explain my own involvement in trying to find the girl. I would offer her the money and hope the pill head's eyes didn't light up so bright at the prospect that any sign of mourning her child vanished.

I shouldered the duffel bag and walked into the kitchen. Climbing through the upstairs window again hadn't been an option in the light of morning with pedestrians and work commuters out in the world. I'd used the wedge end of the Stratus' tire iron to pry open the back door connected to the kitchen after knocking earned me no response.

I didn't know where I was going next, though I had a vague idea of going home, leaving the front gate open, the front door unlocked, sitting down and just waiting to see if Rezner would come hunting for me once he learned that Eastman was dead and his money was forever lost. I was the last of the people who had thwarted and defied him. His making a house call and trying to blow me out of the world wasn't some unlikely fantasy. He'd come for me. If the feds didn't find him and put him down first, Rezner would take his shot at me. Slopes had been certain of it and I was, too.

At the back door, I stopped.

A tingling and mystifying sensation washed over me, through me, like a whisper-thin web of electricity just beneath the skin.

I turned and looked back across the kitchen, at what I had only seen in the periphery of my vision. It had taken a second for that half-glimpsed thing to seize me and force me to turn around and confront its existence.

I stared. I don't know how long. Comprehension wound its way into my mind, brushing away the acid fog of defeat, filling me with a bright and shining certainty.

Chelsea Gullins was not dead.

# SIXTEEN

Hours north of Detroit, the sky opened, thickened to a dark iron hue and poured down. I watched the road grow slick beyond the slapping wiper blades and goosed the accelerator down anyway. Ahead, lighting sang and arced. When the answering thunder clap arrived, I felt it climb in through the shattered rear window, felt it reverberating along the dash, up through the body of the tired car and into me.

On the radio, a mild and professional voice stopped talking about the severe weather warning and announced that federal authorities were calling off the search for Chelsea Gullins. Her death was being added to the crimes for which fugitive Deputy Michael Rezner was wanted. The announcer kept on but I stabbed the radio off.

I didn't need to hear more.

The FBI and Slopes had just unwittingly broadcast to the world that Rezner was being framed for a murder that had not actually occurred. Fugitives keep their ears and eyes tuned in to news broadcasts. Rezner was smart enough to add things up and reach the same conclusion I had. That meant we were aimed in the same direction. We were both looking for Chelsea Gullins again.

I ground the pedal into the floorboard and ranged deeper into the storm.

*

By the time I killed the engine and climbed out of the Stratus, the world was threatening to wash away. Great gouts of rainwater overran the gutters of the little cabin Savannah and I had rented. The waters surged over the porch and out. The gravel drive was a rushing slurry of brown flow.

I lurched away from the steaming and ticking hood of the car. My breath came in short, sharp bursts of renewed pain but I didn't slow. I splashed down the lane until I was back at the front office building of Home Among the Pine.

Sharon was there.

The sturdy woman with the spiky blonde hair who'd threatened me with eviction and possible violence in our previous encounters was standing in the shadows of the porch with a shotgun pointed at my chest. She had the butt of the gun wedged against her shoulder and her right eye was trained down its length.

"That's the second time you've brandished a gun at me."

"Won't be a third," she snarled.

"Put it down. I know you have Chelsea. I think Michael Rezner knows it, too. You aren't safe."

"Buddy, you can go straight to hell."

"I'm going inside. So are you."

I walked toward her. Saw her tense up. I mounted the stairs and brushed the barrel of the shotgun out of my way. Sharon hissed an obscenity as I shouldered past her, into the front office building.

I held the door open and said, "Come on out of the rain, Sharon. We need to talk about keeping Chelsea safe and how to keep you and Rhonda out of prison."

Her eyes stayed cold and accusatory but she shouldered the shotgun and walked wordlessly into the office. I watched her as she moved behind the reception desk. She laid the weapon across its top and folded her arms across her chest.

"I'm not saying anything to you," she snapped. "Rhonda thinks you're a good sort. I don't. I think you're a bag of muscles with marbles upstairs."

"Yeah, something like that."

"So get back in your car and go on."

"Where's Chelsea?"

Sharon squinted and it looked like an effort to keep the lie out of her eyes as she said, "Dead according to the FBI."

"Yeah, they think so. So did I. I killed a man because I believed it. But then I went to see Chelsea's mother and try to be some sort of comfort to her. And do you know what I saw there?"

Uncertainty crept into her stare and she just shook her head.

I took a step forward and snatched the shotgun off the counter before she could get her fingers back around it. She charged around toward me and I met her with a shove. Sharon stumbled backwards and shouted something obscene. Her hands balled into fists. I grabbed her upper arm with my free hand and wheeled us both ahead, through the door that separated the front office from the attached store she and Rhonda ran.

"You son of a bitch!"

She managed to land some blows with her free arm but it didn't slow us down. I scanned the shelves in the little room. They were stocked with condiments and junk food, plastic cutlery and bug repellent, instant coffee and sparklers. I didn't see what I was looking for, so I kept propelling us ahead while Sharon swore and swung. We plunged through another door, into a kitchen on the back of the building, a little dining nook attached.

Around the half-sized dining table stood three chairs. Two of them matched the table. The third was a metal folding chair.

"Breakfast for three?" I said.

"Fuck you!"

I pushed her ahead, letting her go at the same time. She stumbled a couple steps, came to a stop, and whirled around with her fists still ready to keep swinging.

"I'm going to kill you if you don't get out of here!"

I ignored her and reached up to the top of the kitchen's refrigerator. I plucked down the box of flax-based cereal from the row of breakfast cereals lined up beside one another. *Golden Bounty*, the box read. *All-natural flax flakes for healthy living.* It was the box I'd picked up and put back in its bag after Rhonda had spilled her groceries the night before.

I tossed it on the floor between us.

"Who the hell eats that?" I said. "Not too many people. Not Donna Gullins. Junkies don't care what goes in their mouths. But a conscientious little track athlete probably does. Some smart kid trying to look after herself, she might pick out that kind of cereal. Might have it stocked on a kitchen shelf at home."

Sharon's rage dimmed slightly, battling with the need to keep denying the truth of what I was laying out.

"That sounds insane, you know that?"

"By itself, maybe," I agreed. "But then I got to thinking. Where did Chelsea go when she escaped the Reverend's house? Savannah figured it would be the girls camp Chelsea was so devoted to. But she didn't go there. Why would she? She knew it was closed right now. Nobody would be there to help her. So she did the smart thing because she's a smart kid with a lot more guts than most. She went to where the camp counselors live. She came here. She came here and you've been hiding her ever since."

Sharon wasn't a natural liar. I could see the truth of things in her face as I talked. She looked down and away from me when she said, "You're wrong. You're just wrong and that's crazy."

I shrugged and said, "Fine. I don't have a computer. But you've got one out in the office. Why don't we go look up the camp website together? We can both take a look and see what kind of outdoorsy, independent-minded women run the Voluspa Camp for Girls. Maybe you're not a liar and it won't be you and Rhonda staring back at us on the screen. Maybe an abandoned town in the middle of nowhere has more than two liberated gay women who know how to sew wounds and hunt."

She was silent, looking away, out the window at the sheets of whipping storm. I followed her eyes and saw wind-battered tree tops straining under the ruptured sky. Lightning flared and when the thunder came it rattled the jars of canned fruit preserves on the shelf beside us.

"I won't let anyone hurt her," Sharon whispered, still defiant. "She's been through too much already."

"Where is she?"

"Jesus, can't you just go for good? Can't you just leave it alone?"

"Not until she's safe, no."

Sharon pounded a fist down on the counter and shouted, "She is safe! Here! With us!"

"Rezner's at large, Sharon. By now he's heard the news. He's being framed for her death. And it was no accident that he knew where to position himself to try and sniper Savannah and me on the highway."

That shook some of her resolve. Sharon crossed her arms, a defensive gesture.

"What do you mean? He knows about us?"

"He was friends with Chelsea's father once upon a time, wasn't he? And he's a local cop. If he knew from Paul that Chelsea was in love with the girls camp, he'd know where she might run. He'd know who the local women were who ran the camp. I think he was coming for all of us that morning but he saw the FBI vehicles on the roads. So he took a position near the expressway and waited. Luckily, it was me and Savannah who got transported out. If it had been Chelsea, she'd be the one getting cleaned off the asphalt instead of her aunt."

Sharon shook her head like she could wave the image out of her mind.

"He's got no reason to do that. He's running. He isn't even in Michigan anymore. If I was him I'd be in Canada by now."

"Maybe."

"But you don't think so."

"I think Michael Rezner is a paranoid freak that'll lash out against anyone he thinks has done him wrong. I'm on that list. You and Rhonda are on that list now and so is Chelsea. He's dangerous and he has nothing left in this world but his sense of outrage. The Last Watchman isn't a runner. If he knows he's going down, he'll want to make a final stand. That's who he is."

All the bravado had drained out of her. Sharon hugged herself and stared anxiously out the window. I didn't need her to fold. I needed her to keep her head on straight and take me to Chelsea.

I held the shotgun out between us.

"Take it," I said. "I'm not your enemy."

Sharon looked at the weapon, then at me. She shook her head and barked a rueful laugh.

"Jesus. Who *are* you?"

Standing there with my clothes plastered to me like a second skin, a pool of water spreading at my feet, I didn't have a satisfying answer. She took the shotgun back and propped it against the counter.

"I really thought we'd covered all our bases," she sighed. "I thought this was all over."

"Not yet. Whose blood did you use to frame Rezner? They'll test it, you know. They'll know it isn't hers."

More bursts of lightning strobed through the window. More thunder. Outside, the world was chaos.

"I'm not an idiot," Sharon drawled. "I know they test blood. Its hers. Rhonda ran an I.V. and drew about a pint. I took her old clothes and slashed them up with a serrated hunting knife. Mixed in a bit of her hair."

"When?"

"The last time I saw you. When I tried to get you to leave? Savannah told us enough. Told us about Rezner and how he had killed Paul Gullins. She didn't know Chelsea had shown up on our doorstep an hour before you two came back. So once Rhonda patched you up again, we explained to Chelsea what we wanted to do to make sure Rezner never bothered her again and she agreed. I took the bloody clothes and the knife and put them in a garbage bag in that bastard's garage. The plan was to fake a call to the cops and get them looking through his place. I wasn't sure how we'd do it but then he went and murdered that FBI guy and I didn't have to worry about making any calls."

She fell silent. She looked exhausted, a woman who'd been trying to do too much in too short a time. Making rushed decisions. Dangerous choices.

"That's what I thought," I said.

Her eyes searched mine and she said, "What do you mean? Thought what?"

"You and Rhonda. You aren't just hiding her until Rezner's out of the picture. You staged her *death*, Sharon. You can't just give her back to her mother after that. But that was never the plan, was it? You and Rhonda, you plan on keeping her, don't you?"

The lightning show outside illuminated her in stark detail. Her face got hard again but whatever she was going to say in answer died in her throat when the thunder rolled immediately in.

We both moved, leaning out over the counter and peering into the obscured, frenzied expanse of land outside. I could only just make out the nearest cabin, maybe a hundred feet away, a murky shadow behind the sheets of storm rain and bending trees.

"There was something else..." she whispered.

"Yes."

I'd heard it, too. Another sound, riding piggy-back on the thunder. Hiding inside it.

We stood shoulder to shoulder and stared at the scene outside. The world seemed to be in the process of disintegrating. It was afternoon, but the storm had extinguished the light of day and cast us all down into an unnatural dusk.

Another charge of lightning, throwing everything into a photo negative.

Thunder clambering with a giant's feet, everywhere at once.

And the other sound. I knew it for what it was.

"That's a rifle," I said. "It's him. He's timing the shots to the lightning. Where are they, Sharon? Where are Rhonda and Chelsea?"

And as I said it, I saw them. Two figures burst out of the distant cabin. Smears of flesh tone in a dark impressionist painting. Rhonda and Chelsea, holding hands and running. The rifle sounded again, no longer concerned about the cover of thunder. His prey was out in the open and moving.

They were gone. The storm surged, washed over the space between us, and when I could see through it again the two of them had vanished into the black expanse of woods behind the cabin.

Sharon saw them, too. A tortured sound that was hardly human wrenched out of her. She hefted the shotgun in one hand and plunged out of the room. I listened to her boot falls ringing heavily, then the door slamming wide. She was gone, charging into the storm after Rhonda and Chelsea.

I didn't move to follow her, not right away.

Instead I reached across the counter and pulled a large kitchen knife out of a standing rack. Slipped it down in the waistband at the small of my back.

Rezner was positioned to the south, I knew. His last shot hadn't enjoyed the baffling cover of the thunder claps. He was somewhere between the road and the edge of the southern wood line. Rhonda and Chelsea had burst out of the cabin and run roughly north, instinctively bolting in the opposite direction of the gunshots.

I peeled off my sodden shirt and began to lash it around my left forearm.

Rezner would not come straight down on them. To do that, he'd have to step out into the open of the yard that separated the front office from the cabin they had fled. No, he'd be methodical. He would circle east through the woods before cutting north and bearing down on them, always staying in the shelter of the trees.

I yanked tight on the knot I'd tied in the shirt and headed out of the building.

The heavens washed over me and scoured me with taloned fingertips. I hunched forward against the wind and set a pace that I thought I could maintain without vomiting or collapsing from the fire in my sides.

Sharon had gone north. I aimed myself midway between where I imagined she had gone and where I guessed Rezner would be. I would intercept. He would never see any of those women again. I would intercept him, cut him off and run him down.

I would put an end to it all.

*

At the wood line, the reality of my condition reasserted itself.

I slipped into the darkness beneath the pines and vomited a spray of bile. My stomach contracted and I choked against the agony flaring in my sides. The storm shouted on, unrelenting.

Shaking, I resumed the same loping pace and dared the dumb, protesting points of pain to rise up again.

The land rose and sank. I scurried up a slope and half-jogged, half-slid down into the muck and rushing water below. Only the earth and the trees moved, swirling at my ankles and whipping above. No living animal remained in the broken world. The things that lived here were hiding, burrowed away in dark places. There was the storm and there was me.

And somewhere, there was the man I would kill.

I kept on.

*

I heard the beast before I saw him.

A growl from deep in his breast, full of an anticipation for blood.

I wheeled toward that sound and Wagner bounded out of the shadows. The German Shepherd propelled itself into the air, a wild length of teeth with eyes gone black under the killing drive.

Instinct sent me lurching backwards. I got my left arm up, ducking my head down behind it. Wagner's jaws clamped down on the sodden shirt I'd lashed to my forearm. It was no real armor. The beast's teeth sank through it and seized tight. Immediately, he planted himself in the swirling muck and began to viciously shake his head back and forth, trying to shred my arm down to the bone.

I heard myself scream out. I flailed for the knife I'd wedged at the small of my back, but it was no use. I was pinned on my back under Wagner, sliding around in the mud as he yanked and heaved on the arm.

Rezner had taken a hound and weaponized it. Its eyes swam in their sockets, unfocused, drunk on the bloody business and driven wild with the calamity raging around us. Those eyes filled my vision, swelling large until I could see myself reflected perfectly in their void- a small, pink-skinned thing he would chew and grind down until the offending scent of life was gone.

I lashed out. Wagner ignored the blow and swept up onto me. His hind paws found purchase across my stomach and they began to buck, clawing furrows in the field Freddie Esposito had already disfigured.

A burst of light bleached the world. The fear shot away with it. Wagner was heedless to the change in me. He didn't hear the roll of thunder. It wasn't out in the world with him. It was inside me, blasting the panic and pain away in a single, clean clap of murderous fury.

The adrenal storm, the madness of my father's blood, had returned.

I stopped flailing. In one deliberate motion, I reached out and seized hold of Wagner's snout. I closed my hand and kept closing it as gouts of my blood ruptured out around his teeth. A sudden whimper. I tore him off of my ruined arm. Rolled, propelled with urgency, faster than he could account for. The dog was under me now, kicking and squirming at the unyielding grip I had on his maw.

I would drown him in the mud. I would drive my knees into him and shatter the length of him. I would tear him as he meant to tear me, as devoid of thought or conscience. Wagner howled in despair and recognition of what was happening.

Beside us, pine bark flew away in an explosion. A gunshot.

The adrenal storm would not relent. It did not allow for any sane impulse or instinct of self-preservation. I didn't duck away or scurry for cover. I spun in the muck and charged in the direction of the gunshot. Another sounded. A flash from the gun barrel. Some dull touch creasing my side.

Rezner. A silhouette stalking forward. Becoming real. His face a contorted mask of fury as I hurled myself into him.

We both tumbled backwards. Sprawled through the roiling wash. A moment of dizzy weightlessness. Falling, we collided again at the bottom of an over-run basin, a hollow in the earth that the storm had filled until it was a swamp.

We both found our feet. His hands were empty, the rifle lost somewhere in our fall. He regarded me with the same unbridled hate that must have radiated off of me. It was a last moment of recognition. There was only a single final solution to the question of the other.

Rezner lunged.

I buried the length of the kitchen knife in his navel until his momentum snapped the handle. He made a sound I couldn't hear over the thrum of blood in my ears. I watched my hands seize him as his eyes bulged.

Down. I pulled him down into the storm water. My fingers crawled over him until they were around his throat. I pushed with everything I had left inside me. Watched his face disappearing beneath the water. Stared unblinkingly into his eyes until they were gone, swallowed over.

His hands shot up and clawed, desperate and wild.

I roared above him and choked him until he was limp and dead in the drowning pool.

Long minutes might have crawled by, but I wasn't aware of their passage. Eventually, the blood madness receded. The thing beneath my hands was dead, so my inner storm blew itself out, leaving me shaking and hunched in the clotted brown water.

Head bowed, I sucked acres of air and shuddered at the grinding agony in my chest, I heard a broken sob and for a moment thought it was my own. But then I saw her.

I stared.

Chelsea Gullins was poised above us, at the lip of the slope Rezner and I had plunged down. Her hiking shorts and cotton top were as soiled as everything else caught in the storm and her blonde curls were plastered to her forehead and neck. But it was her. Not an idea of her, not a picture of her to prod me on and keep looking. She was real and she was alive.

In that first blink of time, I saw the shock on her face. The horror. She had watched me kill a man. She had witnessed a bloodied, crazed maniac drown another human being.

I stared and didn't attempt to say anything to her. There were no words to make the world sane.

Rhonda appeared, Sharon a step behind.

Rhonda turned Chelsea, quickly, guiding the stiff-legged child away with a protective arm cast around her. Sharon stayed. She held the shotgun across her chest and squinted through the rain at me. Slowly, Rezner's corpse poked above the surface of his grave-- first the clammy white backs of his hands, then his death mask, a frozen and unsounded scream etched across it.

She saw him. Recognized the dead man in the depths.

Sharon dropped her shotgun to the ground and rushed down into the water. Her hands took hold of me and for the only time since I'd met her, she smiled.

"Up we go," she said. "It's all over now."

# EPILOGUE

When they weren't waking me to make me sip water or swallow pills, I slept in the bed of the cottage I'd rented and did not dream. I didn't count the days, just let them slide over me without resistance.

One day, I began to eat. Rhonda fed me applesauce and sponged the sweat off of me.

Another day, I chewed chicken Sharon cooked on the grill outside. She watched me eat with a motherly satisfaction that I found at odds with the image I had of her as a stern and withholding sort.

My arm was swollen, but sewn shut. More stitches across my side where Rezner's bullet had creased the flesh. Rhonda brought me soup another day, then coffee the next.

I ate and drank and let them tell me what was what.

"She wants to stay with us," Sharon said after she pushed a plate of cheese and bread into my hands. "And we want her to stay."

I chewed the bread and told her about Donna Gullins. I told her about the duffel bag full of money in the trunk of my car.

"You'll spend it on her," I said. "It'll take some real work. You can't put her in public school. Not unless you all move far away. If they find out who she is, the state will take her. She'll go to foster care and you two won't ever see her again. You'll need papers. Documents. Probably a lot of counseling, too. I can help with the documents when I get back home. There are people who can make them for you. Jesus, don't get weepy. It doesn't suit you."

When enough days had wandered by that I could shower and dress on my own, I knew it was time to leave. I gathered my belongings. I made the bed and cleaned the bathroom. I washed my coffee cup and breakfast plate and stepped out into the early morning half-light.

At my car, I heard a child's unguarded laughter and looked across the drive, at the deep expanse of yard. In the distance, Chelsea Gullins was sitting on the top of a picnic table, her back to me. Rhonda was seated in front of her. They were playing cards. I watched Chelsea slap a card down on the table top with exaggerated enthusiasm and heard her laugh again.

I tossed my bag of belongings into the back seat of the Stratus and saw that one of the women had duct taped a sheet of clear plastic over the shattered rear window.

When I straightened back up, Sharon was marching up the gravel drive.

At her side, Wagner obediently kept pace. His snout was muzzled and Sharon held the other end of a thick leather leash.

"Don't forget your friend," she said and came to a stop beside me. Wagner sat on his haunches and did his best not to look me directly in the eye.

"I don't know the first thing about dogs," I said. "Give him to a shelter."

Sharon nodded her head like what I was saying was perfectly acceptable. Then she guided Wagner up into the back seat of the car and shut the door behind him.

"Well, I'm glad that's settled," she said. "He'll eat cooked meat, but he prefers it raw. And he seems housebroken. Also, his commands are all in German. Chelsea's the one who finally guessed that. I guess she's a fan of opera music. Here, I wrote them down."

She held out a slip of paper. I stared at her and the dog in my car who'd come far too close to killing me the last time we'd met. He saw me watching him and slunk down until his head was hidden under the window.

"I'm just going to drop him at the first truck stop south of here," I said.

"No you won't."

"You're so sure?"

"Yeah. You're not that guy."

I sighed and took the paper from her. We shook hands and it turned into hugging. It was awkward and I realized she wasn't any better at it than I was.

Chelsea's laughter broke the moment and we both looked over. The thin little blonde girl swept the cards up into her hands and started shuffling them again. Rhonda watched her patiently, a content grin fixed to her round face.

"Do you want to go over and meet her?" Sharon said.

Chelsea's attempt at shuffling went askew and she started picking up the cards that had slipped out of her hands. She bent around to grab one and she was suddenly looking our way. She cocked her head to one side and I saw Savannah in that moment, standing outside the restaurant where we'd met, pinning all her hopes to me.

"No," I answered and gingerly maneuvered myself down behind the wheel of my car. "She doesn't need anything from me. Not anymore."

Country road yielded to highway.

The highway took me home.

Made in the USA
Monee, IL
15 May 2020